LIGHT FROM THE DARK

PROTECTING WHAT'S THEIRS

R SULLINS

Light From The Dark

PROTECTING WHAT'S THEIRS

R SULLINS

Foreword

Thank you for wanting to read LFTD. This is one of my favorite books I've written. It was also the quickest one I've ever written! The words just flew with this one.

As usual, you will find that my heroine has been through some shit and feels a little lost at the beginning. Don't think she is weak, though! Give her a chance to recover from her ordeal before you judge her.

There are some themes in this story that could be triggering to some sensitive readers. A full list can be found on my website. Without a doubt though, you can expect violence. A lot of violence. We *are* dealing with serial killers after all.

Introduction

She escaped the cage of one serial killer, only to fall right into the arms of another…

She was everything they had been waiting for.

Brent and Ethan had been in a committed relationship since high school.

They were both dominant men and enjoyed testing each other's limits,

But they each knew they longed to feel the softness of a woman.

But not any woman.

The perfect woman for *them*.

Casey had been running for so long, and so far,

she didn't even know where she was anymore.

Literally, she had no idea where her bus dropped her off.

All she knew was that she was tired, deep down in her bones.

She knew the small town seemed nice, and the owners of the diner were good people.

She also knew that the men she had caught a glimpse of made

her heart beat faster—and if the rings they wore were any indication, they were both taken.

Brent and Ethan needed to convince this frightened young woman to stay in town long enough to give them a chance.

They knew she was running from something, and to them, it didn't matter what that was. They were ready to protect her from anything.

But how would Casey feel when she found out one of her men had even more blood on his hands than the killer she was running from?

Prologue

CASEY

I DIDN'T KNOW how long I had been lying on the cold, damp basement floor. I'd been locked in a small cage that reminded me of a large metal dog kennel and only had room to sit with my knees bent. Or lay down on the freezing cement floor facing the wall, which is how I spent most of my time. Shivers wracked my body so hard it hurt and I wish I had become immune to the cold since I had been there so long. I wouldn't see anything if I stayed facing the wall. Not that I opened my eyes often. Ignorance was bliss. If only I could just as easily turn off my hearing.

I didn't know where I was, but I knew exactly who had taken me. Well, not his personal information. I just knew the name that the media had given him. I was in the basement of the infamous serial killer that had been terrorizing the ocean-side city of Castle Grove, California, for nearly six months. Unfortunately, just like many others, I walked around acting like being abducted by a serial killer could never happen to me.

The *Castle Killer* had captured everyone's attention immediately with the way he would abduct young women in their early twenties and then hold them captive for several days. Their families would be frantic, of course, but there had never been any hope of finding the women. Not until their bodies were found naked after being tortured and with only an empty cavity where their hearts had been.

I listened to the whimpers of the girl strapped to the metal table in the center of the room and tightened my arms around my legs. Then I heard what had made her start crying and begging. The door to the room opened soundlessly. Unless he made a noise, I couldn't hear when he entered. His footsteps, though. His steps were always slow and steady. They were heavy, as if he were wearing work boots instead of sneakers.

I stopped making any sounds after the first day I woke up inside my little prison. Screaming did absolutely nothing except make my throat raw and painful. I was sure, though, once it was my turn on that metal table, I would be making a lot of sounds. Just like the girl that had been strapped there since my arrival.

If I remember correctly, her name was Megan. Her face had been on the news a couple of days before I'd been taken. She was a beautiful girl, just graduated from college, engaged to be married and had looked so happy in the pictures they flashed on the news every hour of the day, along with the hotline to call if anyone had seen her or could give information. I imagine that my face is being shown on a continuous loop now, too.

He hadn't taken two women before, not so close together. I thought of my mother and her love of true crime shows. She would have told me it was an escalation. If it were Sunday night, and I was over for family dinner and it wasn't me that was here, instead of some other poor woman.

I had been either arrogant or just plain stupid. I didn't think twice about walking home alone. It wasn't late at night since the bookstore I worked at closed at eight and my apartment was only a few blocks down. Looking back, I think all it did was add to my thought that I was safe. No one would take me at eight in the evening. But here I was, proof that serial killers didn't wait until darkness fell to find a victim.

"Please, please let me go." It was the same thing Megan said every time the Castle Killer entered the basement. Her hoarse voice was raspy as she pleaded with him. I quickly covered my ears and squeezed my eyes shut as hard as I could when I heard the first scream tear from her throat.

Unable to block out her painful screams of terror, I let my tears soak the cement beneath my face. Nor could I block out the wet sounds of her blood as it dripped off the metal table and plopped onto the ground, rolling slowly towards the drain in the middle of the floor under the table.

He never spoke a word. The only time I actually looked at him was right after I had been taken. I hadn't seen much of his face. He always wore what looked like a painter's overall set to cover his clothing and hair. All that could be seen was his nose and mouth, since he always wore goggles. After that first day, I decided I couldn't watch him do what he did.

He seemed void of emotion as he walked over to a long table set against the opposite wall from me. I couldn't see what was spread out there, but I didn't need to see it to imagine all the different instruments he used in his torture methods.

As I lay there huddled into the smallest ball I could make myself. I could feel the never-ending tremors ravaging my body. It wasn't just from the cold. When Megan's cries of pain tapered off, and there was nothing but gurgling sounds coming from her, I lost any hope I had been trying to hold on to. I felt myself pee, soaking my legs and puddling around my hip. I sobbed quietly as I lay there, naked and shaking uncontrollably. I knew I had just heard a woman die. I also knew my time had come. He would be coming for me next.

I heard the door to my cage open, and I scrambled as close to the wall as I could, wiggling on my hip, which had long since gone numb. I felt him touch my dark blond hair softly, as if he were petting me, and I couldn't even bring myself to fight him. I was trapped, and I knew I was going to die. There was no fighting this monster.

After stroking my dirty hair several times, I heard something drop next to me, and then my cage door was closed and locked again. I didn't dare move or even breathe. I listened to the chains rattling on the table as he removed them from Megan's body. There were other sounds I couldn't quite place for a few minutes, and then a grunt as he lifted her. His footsteps took him to the door of the basement, and then it slammed shut behind him, leaving me in nothing but silence again. I lay there for a long time before I was finally able to bring my hands down from where they had been gripping my ears.

I felt something lying against my leg. With a whimper of pain from not moving my aching limbs for so long, I managed to twist my body enough to see what was against me. I had to blink several times to bring my bleary vision into focus. Once I realized it was a bottle of water, I struggled to sit up. I was so weak. It was the first thing he had given me since I had been tossed in the cage.

I debated for all of three seconds before I reached for the bottle with trembling fingers. I had to wrestle with the cap since I didn't have enough strength to open it without a struggle. Once I finally got it open, I put it to my lips and took large gulps, letting it soothe my raw throat. It felt heavenly, but my stomach lurched violently after several large swallows. I pressed a hand to my mouth to hold back the vomit that was threatening.

Once the worst of the nausea settled, my eyes went toward the table against my will. There was blood covering what I could see, and it was still dripping slowly down the sides. I quickly looked away, not wanting to see more.

That's when my eyes caught on the latch of the cage. The lock was in place at the top, but the latch at the bottom of the cage didn't have a lock on it like the last time I had looked days ago. I reached out and carefully pulled the latch out of the hole and gasped when it twisted enough that I could slide it back. I didn't question why he decided not to add the second lock. Maybe he thought I was too weak to escape. I didn't care.

I pressed against the wire and saw it give about an inch. The metal wire was thick, but it was just a cage. With enough force, maybe it would bend. I desperately needed it to bend. I scooted around until my feet were in front of me, and while bracing my weight on my hands, I pushed with both feet as hard as I could. It bent out several inches. There was no way I would be able to fit through that opening, though.

For several more minutes, I pushed hard, willing the metal to bend more. I spread my feet wider apart and put pressure near the edge of the hinges as well as the bent opening. I gritted my teeth and shoved with all my might. When I had stopped, panting with effort, the bottom of the door was gaping open at a sharp angle.

I slid around until I was on my belly and stuck my head through the opening. For what seemed like hours, I twisted and squirmed as I did my best to squeeze through the hole I had created. I cried out as a sharp wire dug into my back and left a burning line as I continued to pull myself through.

Fueled by nothing more than pure desperation, I fought to get out. Once, when I got to my hips, I thought I was stuck, really stuck. I wasn't a big girl; I was only five foot three, but I liked donuts with my morning coffee and had a few extra pounds around my hips and boobs. I bit my lip hard enough to bleed as I stifled my screams of frustration. Finally, with twists and yanks, I had my hips through and clawed my way forward on my hands as my legs slithered through.

I slipped, my elbow hitting the cement hard. I looked up to see I had reached Megan's blood. It was thick and viscous, having cooled, and what hadn't slid down the drain was beginning to coagulate into a puddle. Tears filled my eyes, and I immediately wiped my hand on the floor, leaving bloody fingerprints behind as I wiped as much of the blood off as I could.

I rolled over once my legs were finally free and sobbed up at the ceiling, taking shaky breaths and not quite sure I believed I had done it.

I could allow myself only a minute to be relieved, though. With my heart racing, I stood on my feet, bracing myself against the table, smearing more blood on my hands and chest. I tried to take a step toward the door, but my knees immediately buckled. Trying to catch myself on the metal table, my hands slid in the blood, making me nearly fall to the floor again before righting my body.

I tried walking again, moving slower while holding on to the table, using it as a crutch. Once I got to the end of it, I took a deep breath, inhaling the stench of blood and piss, and who knew what else. I let it out in a rush. I took one step and waited to see if my legs would hold me. I felt like a baby deer taking its first steps, but my legs carried me forward.

With my hands outstretched towards the door, I took several staggering steps until I collided with the heavy metal. Reaching for the knob, I twisted, and while I had expected it to be locked, I nearly screamed in rage and frustration when it wouldn't open. Turning my back to the door, I leaned heavily against it and looked around for another way to escape. I hadn't come this far, fighting for every inch, just to be trapped by a locked door.

I knew he was gone. He'd taken Megan's body, intending to dump it in some abandoned lot somewhere. I tried to think of where the previous victim's bodies had been found, I but couldn't think. My brain felt fuzzy, and my head pounded like I had the worst hangover of my life. I tried thinking of how long I would have until he returned. I didn't even know how long I had wrestled with the cage. It could have been hours for all I knew. I was on borrowed time.

My eyes darted around the basement frantically, until my gaze landed on his table of torture implements. There, amongst the various sharp and bloody tools, including blades, shears, and even pliers, was a solid, heavy-looking hammer. I didn't even try to imagine what he used it for. I staggered over and picked it up. It was heavier than it looked. Either that or the days I had spent here had stolen all my strength. I could barely lift it.

I carried it back over to the door and eyed the doorknob. The door was made out of heavy metal, but the knob, though sturdy, was just a regular doorknob with a keyhole. There was no deadbolt in the door. I worried there could be a latch with a padlock on the other side. Regardless, I was desperate enough to try breaking through the fucking thing.

I raised the hammer over my head and brought it down hard on the doorknob. It made a harsh sound that hurt my ears, and the vibration from the impact made my arms ache, but I didn't care about anything but getting the fuck out. I swung again and again and again. It took several swings before it bent at an odd angle. I adjusted my hold, widened my stance, and swung at it from the side like I was swinging a bat at a ball.

Over and over, I swung the hammer. My arms were aching and felt like jelly. I wasn't confident in how much force I was actually able to put into my swings, but I couldn't stop. I didn't stop. Not until I heard the knob fall to the floor with a metallic crash and roll in an awkward wobble for several feet. I stared at the doorknob, bent and dented all to hell, in disbelief.

When I tore my eyes from the knob, I dropped my hand to my side; the weight of the hammer wrenching at my shoulder. I pushed at the door with my free hand. It didn't move. Dropping the hammer, I threw my whole body at the door in desperation. I didn't realize I was screaming and crying as I repeatedly flung my entire body, bruising my shoulder and hip, until I heard a clunk, and the door swung open. I fell onto the floor in a heap, landing hard on my hands and knees. Then I lifted my head and stared at the wooden stairs in front of me.

I began to crawl up the stairs as tears blurred my vision. I didn't notice the scrapes, the bruises, or the new splinters digging into my fingers. All I saw was the ordinary, everyday door that was in every house I had ever been in. I pulled myself up once I got to the top, twisted the knob to the simple wooden door, and then pushed.

I shielded my eyes from the bright light, blinking rapidly as I took in the modern kitchen. This looked like the home of a family of four who enjoyed spending time together at the kitchen table. It didn't look like the home of a serial killer.

I stumbled across the room, leaving a bloody trail behind me, and through the living room, past a lovely leather couch and big screen TV hanging on the wall. I walked to the front door, turned the lock, and swung it open to see a row of similar houses lining the neighborhood.

I stumbled out the door and down the steps, breathing in the fresh air and listening to the birds chirping while a dog barked somewhere nearby.

When a woman driving by slammed on her brakes and jumped out of her car, I blinked, trying to tell her to call the police, but all that would come out of my throat was a whimper. I was completely done. All of my fight and determination to escape had drained what was left of my energy. My vision darkened as I watched her reach for her phone. When I heard her say she needed an ambulance and the police, I finally closed my eyes and crumpled to the pavement.

One

ETHAN

I WAS bone fucking weary when I parked my Mustang in the driveway and hefted my large frame out of the car. I was more than ready to get inside and just let myself relax. It had been a damn long day.

I walked through the door and inhaled the delicious aroma of food wafting from the kitchen. Unbuckling my shoulder holster and shrugging it off, I immediately checked my service weapon out of habit, ensuring the safety was on. I then slid it into the drawer of the table next to the front door. I waited for the light to blink, letting me know the hidden safe had locked, before finally toeing off my shoes.

"Long day?" Brent was leaning against the doorway to the living room, wiping his hands on a kitchen towel. I took in his blue tee, gray sweatpants, and disheveled wet blond hair.

"You took a shower without me," I pointed out gruffly.

He pushed away from the doorway and sauntered to me with his usual sexy swagger. Everything he did was with that damn swagger. It was no wonder I had fallen for him.

"Yes, but I can still wash your back if you want."

When he reached me, he put his work-roughened hand on the back of my neck. I stared into his green eyes as I placed my hands on his waist before pulling him roughly against me. Our hard bodies slammed into each other almost as hard as our mouths. Our tongues tangled, wrestling for dominance, as usual. Neither one of us was soft, and neither one of us was willing to give in. It was always a battle in the bedroom, and it made life fucking fantastic.

"Mmmm. Dinner is done, but the stew can wait if you want that shower. You seem tense. Let me help you relax."

Yeah, we were both dominant fuckers, but we loved each other, and we both knew how to give just as much as we knew how to take.

My stomach growled at the thought of waiting for food, and I grunted. "I'll take you up on the shower. But food first, fucking later."

He stepped back after nipping at my lower lip. "Of course. I'm at your service."

I barked out a laugh and swatted him on the ass as he turned to walk away. "Like hell you are."

He threw a wink over his shoulder and kept walking. I followed, staring at his firm, round ass the whole way. I had to adjust my dick in my slacks. He never failed to turn me the fuck on. I could be sick with the flu, and he would waltz into the room, looking like a golden movie star, holding a bottle of nasty-tasting medicine, and I'd still get a hard-on the size of Manhattan. Not that he ever waltzed anywhere. Maybe stalk or stomp.

Once seated at the table with large bowls of stew and a plate of rolls sitting in front of us, he asked me what had gone on with my day.

"I got a call today. Domestic abuse. Turns out the fucker had been beating his wife and children." I paused and forced myself to swallow the bread that suddenly felt like a lump of lead in my throat. "His little girl had that look to her."

Brent narrowed his green eyes dangerously at me. "Did he..."

I shook my head. "I didn't get a straight answer from either the mom or the little girl. But if I had to place a bet on it, I'd say yes."

He slowly laid his spoon down on the table and folded his arms in front of him. Anyone else watching would think he was concerned about the little girl. They'd be right. But they wouldn't see what I did, what he hid so well. The rage that roiled like a stormy sea behind those mossy green eyes. A sea that would drag its victim down into the depths of the ocean and drown them until they were no longer alive.

"Did she press charges?" His words were forced out from behind clenched teeth.

I sighed and leaned back in my chair. "No."

He looked away and stared at the window covered in a plain blue curtain. "Goddammit."

I grunted out my agreement.

"Do you have his information?" His eyes burned into me with the question I knew to expect. I pulled a slip of paper out of my pocket and slid it over to Brent. It had a name, address, place of business, phone number, and any other pertinent information he would need.

Brent grunted and picked his spoon back up. We both went back to our dinner. Once we were done, we stood at the sink together, with him rinsing the dishes as I placed them neatly in the dishwasher the way I knew he preferred. The kitchen was his domain, and I had no problem following the rules he had set in place. Once the kitchen was tidy again, he turned to me and grabbed my tie.

"Shower time," he growled before slamming his mouth to mine with a brutal kiss. I knew telling him about the little girl would get him in a mood, but I also knew that it was necessary. I may have been a detective, but there was only so much I could do. The police's hands were often tied with bureaucratic bullshit. People didn't like to tell on their abusers, fearing that they would be in even more shit if they did. Sometimes, justice wasn't served because of some idiot fucking up and mishandling evidence.

When the innocent suffered, people like Brent were the real heroes.

I followed my life partner into our bedroom and began to strip off my clothes. As I removed each piece, he took it from me and put it where it belonged. I never argued his need for tidiness and for everything to have a place. Brent needed things in his life to be orderly. He couldn't live with chaos, or it would make his head spin. I understood it. I loved him enough to give in and let him keep the order in our home.

After he rolled my tie up and slid it into the drawer, he turned to me while pushing it closed. He eyed my half-hard cock. His grin was wicked, and he still had a hard glint in his eyes. Our night was going to wear me out in the best of ways.

"You aren't naked," I pointed out as I stepped into him.

"Give me two point three seconds, and I will be."

"Not soon enough." I backed away from him as he started reaching for me and headed into the bathroom. By the time I had the shower heads blasting hot water, he was behind me, running his hands over my abs before sliding them down to firmly grasp my cock. He rubbed his erection against the small of my back, and feeling it there, hot and hard, was enough to have my own cock ready.

"In," he whispered, and bit my ear roughly.

We stepped in together, our bodies staying in sync, never losing touch with each other. I placed my hands against the wall and let the hot water rush over me, relaxing my tense muscles even as they tightened for a different reason. Brent jacked off my cock with one hand as he grabbed the body wash with the other. Then, without releasing me, he popped the top on the body wash, and I hissed as I felt the cold liquid pour down my back.

"I'm going to fuck you, and you're going to be a good boy and take it." He growled into my ear as he ran his hand through the soap and brought it down to my ass, and rubbed against my asshole with his slicked-up fingers.

Like fuck.

I spun around and slammed him against the wall as he laughed in my face.

"Call me a good boy again," I challenged, grabbing his cock and jacking it roughly against mine. Our heads rubbed together, making us both let out guttural groans.

"Why," he grunted and ground into my hold, "when you do such naughty things when I say it?"

"I'll show you naughty." I let go of his cock and shoved hard down on his shoulders. "Suck me."

He looked up at me with a wicked smirk. Then, he opened those gorgeous, full lips and swallowed down my cock like it wasn't as thick as a long-necked beer bottle and as long as one, too.

I dropped my head back and groaned long and loud into the steaming shower. "Fuuuck. That's so fucking good, baby." I slid my fingers through his thick hair and gripped it tightly. There was no telling when he'd decide that he wanted control again, and his mouth felt too good to lose. I spread my legs wider and prepared for the onslaught of pleasure that only he had ever been able to give me.

I glanced down at him. His mouth was open wide, stretched to the limit as he sucked me deep, before sliding up to my tip to swirl his tongue over my hole. Then he swallowed me down again, just to repeat the process. Seeing his hand gripping his own massive cock, gaining his own pleasure from giving, was enough to have my balls drawing up tight.

I gripped his head firmly and pressed my hips forward, making him take my entire length as my cock began pumping my come from my balls. He swallowed with every pulse, the suction of his mouth making my toes curl with pleasure. I staggered back once the last spurt left my cock and watched with half-lidded eyes as he rose from his kneeling position and licked his swollen lips.

"My turn," he growled. I was far too sated to put up an argument, as he turned me back around to face the wall. Instead, I braced myself, relaxing as much as possible when a giant cock was about to enter my ass, and shuddered as he ran his fingertips over my hole. "I fucking like it when you get all loose and relaxed for me," he murmured as he placed his tip at my entrance. "It makes it so sweet when I get to do this…"

He pressed in slowly. He never took me in a way that would hurt me, the same as I was always careful with him. When his chest was flush with my back, he reached around and ran his hands over my abs and up my chest to pinch at my hard nipples before running them back down my body again. I was still too sensitive to have my cock touched again so soon, but that didn't stop him from running a hand over the length and then back up to my abs.

He pulled out slowly, then paused. I braced myself, planting my feet wide. He was careful entering me, but once inside, all bets were off. The air left me as he slammed back in. Gripping my hips hard enough to leave bruises, he pummelled my ass. Both of our groans filled the shower as he took his pleasure with my body. I loved the way his cock head felt as it rubbed inside my ass. It was enough to have my cock stirring again.

He always knew what I needed as he grabbed my now hardening cock. He began to pump it in his tight fist as he continued his brutal pace. It didn't take long before both of us were grunting out our releases.

Fully sated, I leaned against the wall and allowed Brent to wash my body. He took his time, careful to get every inch of me clean. Once he was satisfied he'd done a thorough job, he reached over to shut off the water and leaned into me, giving me a soft peck on the lips.

"All done."

After drying off and brushing our teeth, I let him lead me into the bedroom, where he pulled the covers back from their neatly tucked corners.

We slid in from opposite sides and met in the middle of the king-sized bed. I placed my hand on his hard abs as he lay on his back with his hands folded behind his head.

"Don't worry, Brent. You'll get justice for her."

His grunt of agreement was the last thing I knew as I drifted off to sleep.

Two

CASEY

I STEPPED off the bus into a small town somewhere in Texas; having lost track of where I was. I had ridden on so many buses, crisscrossing so many states, that I was tired of traveling. I looked around the busy terminal, trying to find a sign with a city name, but I gave up after being jostled too many times.

I grabbed my rolling suitcase and hefted my backpack over my shoulders. I had promised not to tell my mom where I was going. Though I missed her like crazy, I knew I couldn't call her. Calls were able to be traced too easily.

I stepped out into the sunshine and was instantly hit by a wall of heat and humidity. In our coastal town in northern California, it was almost always cool or pleasantly warm. It certainly had never gotten as hot as it felt right now. I already had sweat forming at my temples and was tempted to take my hoodie off.

After leaving the hospital and talking to one detective or FBI agent after another, I had retreated into myself. Finally, my mom convinced me to see a therapist to talk about my ordeal. The woman was nice enough, but I'd had trouble reliving my time in that basement. I'd given the police all the information I could, but it didn't matter. The man had disappeared without a trace.

Somehow, the Castle Killer had escaped without anyone knowing his identity. His neighbors didn't know him. The name he had given to his landlord was an alias and had been stolen from another man that had died in a car accident. The police didn't even know what he looked like because all I could give them was a description of his nose. And that might not even be correct because I had only seen him once and refused to look at him again.

With the serial killer on the loose and me as his only living victim, my parents and I had decided that it was in my best interest to get away. So they pulled every penny from their savings account, gave it to me in cash, and then put me on a bus with strict instructions to keep going until I felt safe. After spending almost two weeks on buses, I finally realized I would never feel safe.

I saw a diner a block down the road and began to walk in that direction. Perhaps something to eat that didn't come from a vending machine would help me decide if I wanted to keep going to another town or if I was ready to call it good. At the moment, I was famished and needed to sleep in an actual bed and not on a bus.

The bell jingled above my head as I walked in, keeping my eyes on the floor. Then, I heard a cheery voice call out to me and tell me to sit anywhere I liked. I pulled my suitcase behind me as I walked across the black and white tiled floor to sit with my back to the wall, facing the front, needing to see who was coming in. Even though I didn't know what he looked like, just the thought of him catching me off-guard was enough to have me want to vomit.

I slid into a soft booth covered in bright red vinyl and sighed, relaxing my shoulders. I pulled my suitcase against the wall next to me to keep it out of the way but within reach if I needed to leave quickly.

"Hey, there, darlin'. I haven't seen you around here before." The lady asked with a distinct Texan drawl as she handed me a menu and placed a glass of water in front of me, already sweating from the amount of ice in it.

"Hi," I said softly. "I, umm, I just got off the bus."

"Oh, yeah?" She perked up. "You here visiting family?"

I just shook my head as I pulled the menu in front of me and opened it to see pictures of hamburgers on one side and breakfast foods on the other. It all looked so good.

"Oh. Just passing through, then?"

I looked up at her and saw kindness in her brown eyes as she looked me over. I could see pity there, too, and knew she thought I was running from something. Well, she'd be right. But I was willing to bet it wasn't what she was thinking.

"I just needed to get away. I don't know if I'm staying or going at the moment. But I would love a cheeseburger and fries, please."

The bell on the door jingled, and we both looked up to see a man in dusty blue jeans and a dirty white t-shirt with the name Mason Construction on the front.

"Hey there, Brent!" she called out to the man with a huge smile. "Have a seat, hun. I'll be right with you."

He waved at her on his way to a booth, but stopped in his tracks when our eyes met. I sucked in a breath at the hypnotizing beauty of his eyes. He was tall, probably six-three or four, with dark blond hair and full lips. His body looked hard and muscular, likely from all the hard physical labor he did daily. His tee stretched tight across his broad chest, showing off his defined arm muscles that were covered in black ink. I couldn't tell what the art was, but I could see bits of it peeking out from the collar of his shirt, stretching up to his neck.

As he took me in, I realized that I probably looked like a mess. I hadn't had a shower beyond a quick scrub down in bus terminal bathroom sinks in almost two weeks. My clothes were wrinkly and smelly, I was sure. I probably had circles under my eyes from lack of proper sleep.

But the way he stared at me had tingles racing down my spine. I looked away quickly and picked up my glass of water with both hands. I gripped it tightly, hoping that no one would notice my trembling fingers.

"Alright, darlin', let me get your burger put in. Do you want a drink to go with it? My name is Grace, by the way."

I cleared my throat. "Water is fine. Thank you, Grace." She tapped the table and paused as if she wanted to say something else, but left. I chanced a glance over to see if that Brent guy was still staring, but I didn't see him anymore. I tried to tamp down the disappointment as I stared back into the ice inside my glass.

I didn't bother looking around anymore and watched the glass as if it held the meaning of life. Lost in thought, I jumped when a plate was placed in front of me.

"Here you go, darlin'. The fries are hot, so watch out for those." She slid a chocolate milkshake onto the table next. "This here is on the house. You looked like you could use something sweet." I blinked at the milkshake, touched by the gesture. Then, before I could thank her, the waitress slipped away to another table.

I ate slowly, keeping my head down, only glancing up when I heard the bells jingle, alerting everyone that a new customer had come inside the diner. Honestly, I didn't know what I was looking for. The killer could walk right up to me, and I wouldn't even realize who he was. It was the main reason my parents had been so desperate for me to escape. They were convinced he would never just let a victim go.

The burger was perfect, and the fries had just the right amount of seasoning on them. Maybe it was that I hadn't eaten such good food in weeks, or it really was that delicious, but I found myself cleaning the plate, leaving nothing behind but some smears of ketchup. The shake was the best shake I could ever remember tasting.

I realized I needed to use the restroom. I eyed my suitcase, wondering if I could trust it sitting at the table or if I should make a spectacle of myself by lugging everything with me. I finally decided that it should be safe enough, but I was going to ask the waitress to keep an eye on it for me, just in case. I looked around, trying to see where she might be, when I spotted the construction worker again.

He was talking on the phone. His conversation seemed urgent, and I had to look away quickly when I saw him glance at me from his seat across the room. I wondered idly where he had disappeared to earlier when I hadn't spotted him, then figured he must have gone into the restroom himself before taking his seat.

Grace came out of the back through a swinging door carrying two plates of food, and I watched her carry them over to an older couple. She spoke to them for a minute, then saw me watching and smiled. She came over to me immediately and scooped up my empty plate.

"Was the food to your liking, then?"

"It was great, thank you." I hesitated, then asked, "Would you mind keeping an eye on my bags while I run to the ladies' room?"

"Of course, darlin'. But just so you know, no one in this town would dream of taking what doesn't belong to them."

I didn't call her out on the lie. No town was that perfect. There were thieves, rapists, and murderers everywhere, but I thanked her anyway and slid out of the booth. Walking to the restroom would mean walking past the gorgeous construction worker. I kept my head down, not wanting to make eye contact with him or anyone else. Though I couldn't resist taking a peek from under my eyelashes to see if he was wearing a ring. A man like him had to be taken, even if he wasn't married. He was too beautiful to be single.

I spotted the dark band on his hand. It looked like one of those silicone ones, which made sense, considering his profession. It wasn't surprising. Even though I had no intentions of even talking to him, let alone trying to date him, I still felt some disappointment fill me. Whoever she was, she was a lucky lady.

I pushed the door to the ladies' room open, noting the theme of the restaurant carried on in here, and feeling relieved that it was empty. I quickly locked myself in one of the two silver-colored stalls. Once I was finished, I left the stall and washed my hands, avoiding the mirror. I hadn't looked at myself much since my escape. It wasn't that my appearance had changed. It hadn't. I still looked the same, though somewhat thinner. It was that I could see the haunted look in my eyes. I didn't want to be reminded of my ordeal every time I saw my reflection. It still wasn't over and I didn't want to be reminded that it might never be unless they caught the Castle Killer.

I splashed some water on my face, trying to clear my head. It had been a long two weeks sitting on buses. The poorly circulating stale air had made my skin feel dry. I patted my face with the paper towels I pulled out of the dispenser and took a calming breath before heading back to my table.

I was relieved to see my things were still sitting exactly where I had left them, and swung my backpack up over my shoulders. Then, grabbing the handle of my suitcase, I wheeled it over to the cash register and waited. Grace came over after just a minute and smiled. She seemed to always be smiling. It made me wonder if anything bad had ever happened in her life. I immediately felt terrible for my thoughts. I didn't want to be that person, the hateful one who resented anyone happier than I was.

"Hey there, darlin'. Your tab was paid, so you're all set."

I had to force my open mouth to close as the shock ran over me. "No," I shook my head. "That's not necessary. You don't have to do that."

She just shrugged. "It wasn't me."

"Well," I reached into my pocket, pulled out a five-dollar bill, and slid it to her over the counter. "At least let me give you a tip."

She raised her hand. "Tip's been taken care of, too."

I sighed and pushed it over another inch. "Then maybe I can pay you for some information? I need to find a hotel within walking distance that will be safe—" My eyes darted nervously around the diner; I swallowed and then finished quietly. "For a girl traveling alone."

Her eyes softened, and she got that same pitying look on her face again that she had before. "There's an inn a few blocks up the road that way. It is a bit pricier than the fleabag motel that way." She hooked her thumb over her shoulder with a look of disgust on her face. "But if you tell them Grace sent you, they will give you a good discount." She reached out and squeezed my hand gently. "Take them up on that offer, yeah?"

I pulled my hand away and gave a small, forced smile. "I'll do that. Thank you for the good food, Grace."

"Anytime, darlin'. Come back and see me soon."

I didn't say anything as I grabbed the handle of my suitcase. Instead, I just nodded once in acknowledgment and walked out the door back into the hot, humid air.

Once I was a couple of blocks away from the diner, heading toward the inn she had told me about, I realized I'd forgotten to ask what town I had ended up in.

Three

BRENT

I WATCHED the beautiful girl walk out the door without looking back. She had shadows in her eyes. Gorgeous, haunted blue eyes. Whatever had happened to her had left a mark. That was something I understood all too well.

The second I saw her, my world came to a crashing halt. Of course, I saw her beauty—it was unmistakable, but I also saw that whatever she was running from was bad. I wanted to gather her in my arms and protect her. At the same time, I knew I needed to find whoever had put those shadows there and then do what I did best.

I lifted my phone to call Ethan again.

"Hey, man. Yeah. She just left. Grace told her to go to Gladys' inn. See if you can spot her and make sure she makes it there, okay?"

"I can do that." He paused, and I knew what he was going to say next before the words came through my phone. "Are you sure about her?"

I watched until I could no longer see her back, her shoulders rounded as if she were trying to protect herself from something unseen. "Yeah. I really am."

"Fuck, Brent. Alright. I see her. She's a small little thing."

She was at least a good foot shorter than both Ethan and I. I thought of her. Of the way she would fit between us so well that we would be able to protect her from anything, if she let us. "Yeah, she's small."

He chuckled. "You seriously think a girl like her would be okay with two huge men? What if it is a man that she's running from? She might not even like men, you know."

I thought of the connection I'd felt every time our eyes had met in the diner. Of the snap of electricity that had raced through my chest. It was her. I was certain. She was the only one I'd ever want between myself and my partner. "Give it a chance. That's all I ask."

His sigh came over the line, and then, just like I knew he would, he agreed. "Okay, okay. I trust you, babe. Do you want me to try to talk to her?"

I thought about it. I hated the thought of her walking out there all alone when he could give her a ride. "Maybe test the water. Offer her a ride. But don't push her." I warned him. I didn't know if I could forgive him if he spooked her and ran her out of town before we had the chance to get to know her better.

He grunted. "Don't be an asshole. See you later." Then he hung up before I could add any threats.

Grace walked over once she saw me put my phone down. "She's sweet. Running from something."

"Yeah."

"I know you and my boy have been wanting to add a woman. This one is special, Brent. Take care with her. I'm rooting for you." She tapped her nails on the table. "Don't hurt her."

I tore my eyes away from the big glass window that she had walked past several minutes ago and jerked my head up to give Grace a look. "I would never hurt a woman."

"There are more ways than physical violence to hurt a woman, honey. Just keep that in mind as you and my son pursue her. That's all I'm saying."

I placed my big hand over hers on the table and stared at her. I let her see what I was feeling, not only remorse for being harsh with her but also the sincerity I felt in my vow to never harm the girl.

"I don't suppose you got her name before she left?"

Grace shook her head and looked out the window the same way I had done. "No. I didn't want to push. I'm just glad she took my advice to head to the inn instead of that rancid motel."

"I appreciate it." I unfolded myself from the booth and looked down at the woman, who, for all intents and purposes, was my mother-in-law. Ethan and I may not have ever gotten married, but we were a solid couple, and we had been for years. Grace was my family. I wrapped an arm around her, giving her a hug.

"Talk to you boys later."

"Bye, Grace." I kissed her cheek and then walked out of the diner. I had paid my bill at the same time I paid the girl's, so I didn't have to wait to see if Ethan had stopped her down the street.

I stood next to my truck and watched Ethan talk to her through the window of his Mustang. He could use a cruiser if he wanted to, but the bastard hated the idea and only used his own car. Being one of the only detectives in town allowed him a lot of leeway. It also had him picking up cases that most detectives wouldn't have to in a larger city. Like the domestic violence case last night.

I stuck my hand in my pocket and fingered the slip of paper there. As I watched the girl shake her head and back away, I clenched my fist around the piece of paper. Ethan waved to her and continued to sit in his car as she resumed her walk until she was just a speck in the distance. I didn't blame her for not wanting to get into the car of a stranger, even if it was a police detective. That was a smart move on her part. But it didn't stop my frustration from building.

I pulled the paper out of my pocket and smoothed it out so I could read the name and place of business again, even though I already had it memorized. There was only one way I knew how to ease some of the frustration simmering inside of me. I pulled my phone out of my pocket and dialed my foreman.

"Hey, Jack. I'm going to run some errands. I'll be back at the site in just a bit. Yeah, okay."

I thanked Jack, knowing he wouldn't mind not having me staring over his shoulder as the crew worked on the building we were renovating. I climbed into my truck and started the engine, turning at the corner to head over to the law offices of one Matthew Banks. The fucker was a lawyer. One that took cases for the low-life scum that littered our streets. I had done my research that morning. He was just as dirty as those he managed to get off on technicalities, just to let them peddle more shit on the streets to unsuspecting kids.

I drove around the building, looking for cars, cameras, back doors, and anything else that could help or hurt me if I wasn't so careful. His office was in a line of other businesses. A dentist, a florist, and a trading card shop. The flashy, red BMW parked at the side of the last storefront on the corner had to be his. Fortunately, there were no cameras to be seen. The fucker probably didn't want any witnesses to the kind of people that came in and out of his fucked up law office.

I drove on, heading back to where I knew Ethan was still waiting. As soon as I pulled over and came to a stop, I saw him climb out of his black car.

"Casey Smith."

I grunted. Casey was a real pretty name. Though I doubted Smith was real. "Gladys wasted no time getting you the information."

His grin showed off his perfectly straight white teeth, making me want to lean in and bite his lip. "What can I say? My aunt loves me."

I looked at him, really looking into his eyes, letting him see my sincerity. "You know you're enough for me, right? So if you want to end this now before it even begins, that's what we'll do. I know I don't say it often enough, but... I love you."

He reached out and grabbed the back of my neck. "Babe, I know you do. And we talked about this years ago. We both love the idea of a woman, even if neither one of us has ever been with one." He breathed out a low chuckle, the slight gust of air fanning over my lips. "We've both felt the need to have one as part of us, between us. We knew that this day would come, that one day she would come. Hopefully, we aren't wrong, and this girl is who we've been waiting for all these years. I trust your judgment. You know I don't say that lightly. I. Trust. You. We pursue Casey, and if it's right, she becomes ours. It doesn't take away from what we have together. It will add to what we have. Okay?" He squeezed my neck and placed his forehead against mine. "We do this together, and we will all be happy. Together."

I breathed out my relief at his acceptance and nodded against his hold. "Yeah. Together." He pressed a hard kiss against my lips and then backed away.

"We'll form a plan tonight. Miss Casey Smith won't know what hit her." He looked back in the direction of the inn. "She needs us."

I started the engine of my truck. "Yeah, she does."

I drove back to the work site, ready to get the day over with. I had plans for the evening that included getting rid of one nasty son of a bitch, then ending the night with dreams of bringing a sweet, damaged soul closer. Unfortunately, the day couldn't end fast enough.

I busied myself with what needed to be done at that renovation site. We had just finished setting up the flooring to be ready to lay the new wood planks when the alarm on my phone sounded.

"Alright, people, that's a wrap for the day. Get your shit and get out of here." I called out. Our days started early, and my workers were grateful to have their evenings clear for their families.

"See you tomorrow, boss!" Lydia, one of my best, called out as she picked up her tool belt and pulled her keys out of her pocket. I nodded to her and grunted to the rest of the crew as they called out their goodbyes.

I packed my own supplies into the toolbox that was bolted into the bed of my truck, and then locked the metal latch. After watching everyone else drive away, I started my engine. Instead of heading in the direction of home, I made my way back to the law office of the asshole that was about to regret ever laying a hand on his little girl.

I waited next to the side door, staring at the little red BMW. His wife drove a ten-year-old piece of shit that was held together with prayer and a string. The car that she was expected to transport this piece of shit's children around in. I hoped she traded the tiny car in on something more practical. But if I saw her driving it around town one day, I was sure it would be with a smile on her face.

As the door began to open, I straightened my shoulders and uncapped the needle, pulling the cap off and shoving it into my pocket with my gloved hand.

"Hey, asshole," I ground out as I plunged the needle into his neck. "I hear you like touching little girls."

Four

CASEY

I'D SLEPT like the dead. The sun was already shining brightly by the time I blinked my eyes open. I rolled over, facing the window, and stared at the filmy, pale yellow curtains. The inn was perfect. The room I was in was cute, with sage and pale yellow tones decorating it, making me wonder what the rest of the rooms looked like.

The place was called an inn, but it more resembled a quaint bed-and-breakfast. Except I had a private bathroom in my room. It had a regular lock and key on the door instead of the electronic locks most motels had switched to since before I could remember. Not that I had stayed in many hotels or motels. My parents were hard workers, but California was an expensive state to live in. My dad's job at the hardware store and my mom's cashier position at a local grocery store didn't exactly allow for many vacations. Our family getaways usually consisted of day trips to the beach when I was growing up. Just because I lived in a coastal town didn't mean I spent much time in the surf.

As I lay there thinking about my parents, I couldn't stop the pain that washed over me. They were good people that loved me deeply. It hurt to not even be able to call. So far, I had missed two, maybe three, Sunday dinners. I was already losing count.

"I miss you, Mom." I closed my eyes and sobbed into my pillow, allowing the pain and hurt out in a way I hadn't been able to while surrounded by strangers. It had been hard holding all that pain in for so long.

Yesterday, when I arrived at the inn, I was given a rate that I was sure was far below normal. I dragged my suitcase, along with my exhausted self, to my room and stripped down to nothing, so relieved to finally have a real shower. After a long, hot shower that went far to ease my aching joints, I had crawled into bed while the sun was still high in the sky. I must have been out the minute my head touched the pillow because here I was, blinking my wet eyes at the sun shining through the pretty curtains.

I thought of what I should do next. The thought of climbing back onto another bus had my body revolting at the memory of all the traveling and sitting for days on end. Of dodging men with lascivious gazes, ignoring questions from strangers that wanted nothing more than to pry into my life's history.

If I stayed frugal, I could continue to travel for several months with the money that my parents had given me. Or I could settle in one place. The money would run out quicker unless I found a job willing to pay me in cash. I thought of the diner. And then I thought of the man that had walked in before again, quickly clearing that image from my mind. He was taken. I was determined to remember that.

I could work at the diner. I was sure that Grace would work something out with me. Maybe. I wouldn't mind the work. I rolled onto my back and stared at the ceiling as the face of the detective that had stopped me on my walk to the inn invaded. He was a different kind of handsome. Where the construction worker was light, blond, and had green eyes. The detective was dark. His honey-colored eyes had been entrancing. I'd nearly been hypnotized by them. It was the only excuse I could come up with as to why I had stopped in the first place when he pulled up next to me, calling out.

I had paused, looking over at him, and my breath caught in my throat. One light, one dark. It was enough to give a girl wicked fantasies. He had been nice, his deep voice soothing. Even though he looked big and capable of causing harm, something about his manner told me that he would never hurt an innocent person. But even so, when he had offered me a ride to the inn, I had backed away, thanking him for the offer, and quickly continued on my way. I hadn't looked back, but I could feel his piercing eyes as they followed me.

If I were interested in a man, he would be the type that I would want. Someone large but kind. Either him or the blond one that I couldn't shake, no matter how hard I tried.

Taken.

I would keep telling myself that over and over until I stopped fantasizing.

I finally pulled back the covers and stood up, bending at my waist to stretch out my back. Hopefully, the stiffness will go away soon. I stepped over to the window and peeked out of the curtains, mindful of my nakedness.

The sun was beating down on the street and making the windows in the nearby shops reflect the light. From what I had seen so far, this was a nice town, and everyone I had met had been very kind. I still didn't quite understand how my room could be so cheap, but I couldn't look a gift horse in the mouth. I certainly wasn't in a position to argue.

I turned around and walked over to my backpack that I had left sitting in the chair in the corner of the room and pulled the envelope out of the bottom where the lining had been carefully cut away to allow for a hidden space to hide my cash.

I spread it out on my bed and counted the remaining amount, sorting it into piles. I still had a few thousand dollars—enough to allow me to keep going or to stay where I was. I looked back toward the window and decided I would stay... for now. If I couldn't find a job to pay me in cash, I would leave.

With my mind made up, I scooped all the money back into one pile and placed it back into the envelope. I thought about what would be safest; if I should continue to keep it in my bag or find a hiding place somewhere in the room. Undecided, I slipped it back into my backpack and figured I would look around for a good hiding place later.

I finally gave in to my bladder, urging me to pee. When I was done, I opened my suitcase and dug out my toiletries. Securing my toothbrush and hairbrush, I set about trying to make myself presentable to the world as I felt my stomach rumble in complaint. I had a granola bar in my bag and eyed it, but after weeks of vending machines and fast food, I just couldn't do it. I ignored the bar and dressed in a comfortable pair of jeans that weren't too dirty and slipped on a shirt that I hadn't worn yet.

Satisfied that I looked almost human, I hefted my backpack over my shoulders and left the suitcase where it was lying on the bed. I would unpack it later, after I ate, and asked at the diner if I could have a job. It was sure to be an awkward conversation.

It was already lunchtime when the bell jingled above my head. Grace looked up and smiled, almost looking relieved to see me.

"Hey, hun! Have a seat. I'll be with you as soon as I drop this order off."

I looked around to see the place was pretty full, with two other servers moving quickly around the tables carrying plates or freshly written order tickets. I spotted two tables that were open side by side and headed over to slide into the booth by the wall, leaving the table with chairs for someone else to claim. I sat facing the door and looked around. I hadn't really taken in the place when I had been here yesterday. Tired, hungry, and too worn out to appreciate the black-and-white checkered floors that reminded me of an old-fashioned diner from the fifties. The booths were red and comfortable, and each table had a napkin dispenser sitting with the condiments.

The walls had Coca-Cola memorabilia on them, adding to the nostalgic vibe.

There were six matching booths lined up along the wall and another six tables with chairs in the middle of the floor, with one more booth sitting alone on a short wall next to the hallway leading to the restrooms. The counter dividing the dining area from the workstation and open kitchen window had a few stools where a couple of men looked to be nursing coffees. A cash register sat at the end near the door. I loved the look of the place. It was inviting and cheerful. I could see why it was packed. With a well-kept and clean interior and fabulous food, it was probably one of the favorite places in town. Just a minute later, Grace walked up with a menu. "It's lovely to see you back. I'm glad you decided to stick around. Did you find your way to the inn, okay?"

"I did, thank you," I said as I took the menu from her. "The place is great."

She beamed at me. "Good! Would you like something other than water today?"

I thought about it and nodded my head. "I think a Coke would be great, thank you."

"You got it. I'll be right back."

I watched her hurry off and slip behind the counter. As she grabbed a glass for my drink, I saw her reach into her apron, slide her phone out, and send off a text with flying fingers before returning to her task. I went back to perusing the menu, trying to decide if I wanted the same juicy cheeseburger I had eaten the day before or if I wanted to branch out into one of the other options available. The top of the menu declared that breakfast was served all day, and I was a sucker for hash browns.

I heard the bell jingle again as I tried to decide between pancakes and hashbrowns or a burger with avocado. Instinctively, I glanced up and back down to the menu. Only to have my eyes shoot straight back to the door. My breath caught, and my eyes widened as I stared. Both men, that had been tramping through my thoughts unbidden since I had seen them yesterday, stood just inside the door. Grace walked over to them with a huge grin on her face and gave the detective a small hug, which he immediately changed to a giant bear hug. Once he let her go, she swatted his arm with a laugh and turned to the blond guy, lifting her cheek for the kiss he readily placed there.

I watched as they both leaned down to listen to something she whispered up at them before all three turned to look my way. I quickly ducked my head, suddenly very interested in what came on the burgers, but unable to read a word as my mind practically melted into mush. The sight of the two of them standing together, light and dark, was seared into my brain, and I didn't want to let the image go.

Individually, they had stolen my breath with how attractive they were. But together, they were too much for my heart to take. I hadn't known how tall the detective was as he sat in his vehicle, but seeing them side by side, it was easy to see that, though he wasn't quite as broad as his blond friend, he was just as fit under his suit jacket, and just as tall. More like a runner, I supposed. I wondered if he had tattoos, too, hidden under his suit.

I heard footsteps come my way and realized that they were headed straight for the table next to mine. The table was so close that if I tried to lean over far enough, I would probably be able to touch one of them—or both. My heart picked up in both excitement and dread. As much as I wanted to study them more, to see exactly what those tattoos on the blond guy's arms were, and to see if the cop's eyes were as golden as honey in the light of the restaurant, I didn't need the stress. They were taken. At least the blond was, and I wasn't that type of girl. I couldn't stand those people, the ones that thought it was okay to take from another.

Just as they reached the table, the bell rang, once again making me look up from my hiding spot behind the menu. A sweet looking older couple holding hands walked in and looked around.

"Oh, shoot. I hate telling someone they have to wait." Grace honestly sounded upset at the thought of making one of her customers have to wait for a table.

The dark haired detective placed his hand on her shoulder as Grace's worried gaze traveled from the one empty table and back to the new customers waiting at the door. "It's fine, mom. You let them have this table, and we can wait."

Grace hummed before saying something that had goosebumps rising on my arms. "Nonsense, son. Why don't you share a booth with Casey here? She's a sweet girl. I doubt she would mind if two handsome men sat with her for lunch. Casey," she called over to me softly, "Would you mind if my son and his boyfriend sat with you?"

I was so surprised at the words that I just looked up at her, speechless. The images that bombarded my brain were anything but wholesome. I had read plenty of books with two men together as a couple. It was some of my favorite reading material and had starred in many of my fantasies. Seeing these guys that looked like they had stepped off the cover of a book was enough to have my very overactive imagination putting them together in a bedroom. Any bedroom. Mine would do even if all I did was sit in the corner and watch.

The silence became awkward as the three of them stared down at me with a mix of smirks and a smile. Two guesses about where the smirks were coming from. I cleared my throat and shook my head, unable to get the words past my tight throat.

"Great! Here you go, guys. Let me grab you both some Cokes after I sit Mr. and Mrs. Brown." She patted her son's arm and walked away, somehow looking more pleased with herself than she had any right to be.

I expected the two guys to sit together on the opposite side of me, so I jumped, startled when a large body started to slide into the booth right next to me.

"Scoot over for me, would you, dollface? There's a lot of me to fit in next to you."

I quickly scooted all the way to the wall, practically plastered against the window. I glanced out of the corner of my eye as the one sitting next to me slid my menu in front of me. I could see the dark ink covering his arms and knew it was the blond construction worker that had taken over my side of the table.

"Ummm," I stopped and cleared my throat nervously, barely able to get my voice above a whisper. "Wouldn't you rather sit with your boyfriend?"

His deep chuckle radiated through me, making me need to hold back a shiver of pleasure at the sound. "You see how big that guy is? He's a seat hog. I'd be half on the floor if I tried to sit in the same seat as him."

I darted my eyes up to see the detective looking at me with serious eyes and a grin on his lips. Those eyes were just as golden inside as they had been in the sun. And the blond was right. He took up a lot of space for someone that wasn't as muscular as the one sitting next to me. He had his suit jacket unbuttoned, with an arm spread over the back of his seat. I could see the handle of his service weapon peeking out from a shoulder holster. Why that would make me hot inside, I would have to take out and inspect later, once I wasn't so overwhelmed.

"I'm pretty sure you take up more space than he does," I mumbled as I pretended to study the menu and questioned my life choices.

His thigh was pressed up against mine, and I was certain he was further over in the seat than he needed to be. I would ask for more room, but... did I really want to?

"Oh, sugar," the cop chuckled as he adjusted his weight in the booth. "I guarantee that he takes up plenty of space."

My cheeks heated at the implication. These two were too much. I was already overheated, and I didn't know if I could take sitting here with them for an entire meal.

The detective smirked. "I'm Ethan Hardgrove. He's Brent Mason." He jerked his chin over to the guy next to me.

"Nice to meet you," I murmured, completely overwhelmed. I wasn't sure if it was in a good way or not.

Five

ETHAN

SHE WAS A DELIGHT. Everything that Brent had said about her was true. I had always trusted him and his instincts, but he'd never been more right than he was about her.

She had a sassy streak inside her, one that two dominant fuckers like us would enjoy. It would offer up a great excuse to spank her ass and spoil her rotten at the same time. There was no doubt she was beautiful, but she was also kind and sweet. She didn't have to share her table with us. Though we had blindsided her without giving her much of a choice, but she could have pitched a fit and told us to fuck off. Instead, she had given a shy nod while her face turned pink. I didn't think it was from embarrassment, though.

Brent may have gotten to her first and been lucky enough to sit close to her, but I had the advantage of sitting across from her and being able to take in her gorgeous face. She was shy as hell. She hardly raised her eyes to meet mine, but when she did, the blue eyes I had wanted to see again since yesterday were filled with green and gold flecks I hadn't had a chance to notice before.

I took in every inch of her face, from her adorable nose with the bump on the bridge that told me she had broken it at some point in her childhood to the light-colored freckles that dotted her cheeks and over that bump. They were so light that they nearly blended with her natural skin tone. I was almost certain they would get darker when she spent some time in the sun. She had dark, golden blonde hair, and I could imagine myself fisting her thick strands as I took her from behind.

Her lips had a subtle cupid's bow, the bottom lip fuller than the top, giving her a pouty look and making me want to suck that lip into my mouth and hold it between my teeth.

"Here you go, loves." Mom set down three glasses of coke on the table with one straw, knowing Brent and I would forgo the straw for drinking straight from the glass. Before I could do it, the fucker that I was going to punish later slid the glass in front of our girl. I glared at him as I snatched the straw before he could and ripped the paper open. He didn't even give me the courtesy of looking up to see it.

"Did you figure out what you want to eat yet, Casey?" We all looked at her as she turned pink again from all the attention. I placed the straw in her glass as she shifted in her seat.

"I think I'll try the breakfast. Can I have two eggs over medium and some hash browns, please?"

"Of course, hun. Would you like pancakes on the side or toast?"

"Pancakes, please, and thank you, Grace."

She was quiet, but so polite. I just wanted to wrap her in my arms. She was too sweet for this shitty world. But she also had that cute little sassy streak that wanted to break free. Sugar and spice. My sugar. I looked over to Brent, and I could see the same thoughts rolling through his head. She needed us, and we were more than ready to protect her from anything and everything that would try to harm her sweetness. And she was sassy enough to keep her men from steamrolling her.

I was too distracted to even know what I was ordering, but Mom knew me well enough. She would make sure I got something I wanted. She was probably getting a kick out of this and had already told Dad what was going on out here while he cooked in the back. I was certain she would be heading straight back there to give him all the gossip.

"I noticed that you guys are both wearing matching wedding bands." Her soft voice was like a caress to my balls. I held my hand up, displaying the black silicone band that was a perfect match to Brent's. She didn't sound like she was questioning them, just curious.

"We've been together for a long time, sugar." I watched her closely, liking that she was asking about us. "We both tend to decide pretty quickly what we want in life."

She pulled her glass closer to her and stirred the ice around a few times before bringing the straw to her lips and taking a small sip before speaking again in that same quiet voice. "I admire that trait in a person. I have a cousin who could never make a decision, even to save her life. It took her over a year to settle on a wedding dress. They had to push the wedding date back three times. Shopping with her was excruciating." Her sad smile told me that she missed her cousin, regardless of her judgment.

"So, what brings you to Selene, Texas, dollface?" Brent's question had her placing her drink back down. Her hands went into her lap, and she looked down at them. I glanced at Brent to see if he'd noticed how her shoulders had rolled in. What was so painful in her past that she needed to protect herself from?

"My parents thought I could use a vacation." She said while keeping her eyes downcast and trying to sound nonchalant, but I'd been trained to read body language. Even if I weren't a detective, I would have been able to see the hurt she couldn't mask. Yesterday she had been wearing a hoodie, covering her body from prying eyes, but sitting in front of me in just a t-shirt, I had a great view of her arms. They were toned and smooth, not a single scar or bruise in sight. But I knew, from dealing with victims of violence, that many scars weren't always visible. Some were on the inside.

Brent chuckled, trying to lighten the mood. "Well, you certainly came to the right place. As you can see," he said, waving toward the window overlooking the hot street outside, "Selene has the best beaches on the planet. I hope you brought your bathing suit." His lascivious eyebrow wiggle, though cute, was lost on her since she kept her eyes in her lap, but the quiet giggle she let out sent another jolt of lust straight to my balls. This girl was a danger to my ability to restrain myself.

"I was supposed to travel the states for as long as I wanted." She finally lifted her head, but instead of meeting my gaze, she looked out the window Brent had just gestured toward and sighed. "I guess I needed a break from traveling for a little while." Good. She didn't know it, but there was no way we would be letting her get back on that bus. Not without one of us by her side.

"Here you guys go. Sorry it took so long. Honestly, I'm not really sure why we are so busy on a Friday afternoon." Our plates were slid in front of us, and we each eyed the food like a pack of hungry wolves.

"Don't sell yourself short, Grace. Everyone knows this is the best place to eat in three counties."

"You hush, Brent, you're biased. Casey, hun, do you need anything to go with your eggs? Hot sauce? Ketchup?"

"I'm good. Thank you so much." Casey gave my mom a genuine smile that lit up her beautiful face. I was glad she wasn't looking at me, or she would have seen the awe I felt at witnessing it. I wanted nothing more than to keep her smiling like that for the rest of our lives.

Mom reached over to a vacated table and snatched up the syrup before sliding it onto our table. "Well, I'll leave you to enjoy your food. If you need anything, just send one of these boys for it, okay? They both know their way around well enough." She winked as we both snorted. Of course we knew our way around. We had been coming here since we were kids, and it was the first job either one of us had.

Casey eyed her food with a hunger that I only hoped to see her eye my dick with one day soon. "Yes, ma'am. Thank you, it looks perfect."

With a grin, Mom was back to checking on her other tables. She was always run off her feet; ever since she and my dad bought the place when I was a kid, but it was obvious that she loved everything about the diner. I knew neither one of them regretted the hard work it took to keep the place going. Brent wasn't wrong, either. It was easily the best food in three counties, no contest.

We were quiet as we dug in. Though I enjoyed the hell out of my messy burger, I couldn't keep my eyes off our girl. When she took a bite of her pancakes and a drip of syrup got on her chin, it took everything I had inside me to stay in my seat instead of launching myself over the table and licking that spot off her soft-looking skin.

Once we were close to finished, and had slowed down to taking leisurely bites of what was left of our food, I finally asked what both Brent and I needed to know. "So, sugar, what are your plans while you're here?"

Brent and I both watched her carefully as she fidgeted in her seat. Finally, she cleared her throat and wiped her mouth with a napkin. "I, uh, I was thinking of looking for a job. I have some money, but it won't last long if I stay at the inn and keep eating out all the time." She looked around at the restaurant, which had emptied of most customers after the lunch rush. "I don't know. Do you think your mom needs help here? Even just a little bit? Maybe."

I smiled at her when she glanced my way, judging my reaction. "I think she's always looking for some good help around here. Those two," I gestured with my chin at the other servers, "are the last of my cousins that are at an age to help out. They both go off to college soon. I know Mom is going to be looking for their replacements. I could put in a good word for you if you want." My wink had a blush filling her cheeks again, and I loved that she was affected by me.

"Thanks. I think I'll talk to her about it today."

I could practically feel the relief coming off of Brent when she said what we had hoped to hear. As long as she stayed in town a while longer, it would give us a chance to woo her. It was going to take monumental strength to hold back our eagerness to get her locked down sooner rather than later. But we knew and had agreed after our talk last night that she needed us to be slow and steady. We couldn't rush her, or we would be the ones to make her want to leave. I wouldn't let that happen. I would lose my job due to holding up the bus she was on at gunpoint before I would let her leave again.

But there was another problem she had mentioned that would be easy to address.

"You know," Brent began thoughtfully. He even had his fucking finger tapping on his bottom lip, playing it up a bit thick. I wanted to kick him for making it too obvious. "If you want to save some money on renting a room at the inn, Ethan and I have a huge house with way too many bedrooms. There are several rooms we don't use at all. If you want, you could stay with us. You would be doing us a favor, really."

I glared at him. Not that he could see it because the asshole was staring down at our woman, practically begging her with his eyes to say yes. What the fuck happened to being subtle, fucker? I wanted her there, too, but we probably could have used Mom's influence to convince her.

When she glanced up at me through her lashes, I wiped the glare from my face and nodded as if the idea hadn't occurred to me until just then. "Yeah, that's a good idea, babe. She could have a safe place to stay with an alarm. She wouldn't have to worry about anyone trying to break into her room."

I held my breath as she bit the inside of her cheek, clearly being swayed by the idea of security. "Are you sure? You don't even know me. I wouldn't want to intrude. I'm sure I could find a cheap apartment... somewhere."

"Of course, sugar. This town is nice, but unfortunately, just like any other town, there are bad areas. The type of apartments that are reasonably priced aren't always going to be in the best neighborhoods." Fuck, now I was the one laying it on too thick. We both needed to back off and let her come to us on her own. It wasn't our intention to manipulate her, but fuck, as a cop, I knew all about what could happen to a young, beautiful woman on her own.

She nodded gratefully. "Thank you for the offer. I just need to decide what I'm going to do first. Would you mind if I said I'll think about it?"

"Dollface, you take all the time you need. Ethan and I will have the room for you whenever you are ready."

She relaxed back into her seat, letting the tension drain out of her. "Thanks, guys. I really mean that."

I slid out of the booth and waited for Brent to pry himself away from where he'd been plastered to her gorgeous little body for the last half-hour. I pulled a card from my wallet and handed it to her when she scooted out and stood next to us. It was the first time either of us had a chance to stand next to her. To say the size difference didn't make my dick hard would be a motherfucking lie. As soon as she took the card from my fingers, I made sure to pull my suit jacket in place to hide the monster that wanted to be let free.

"Give me a call at any time." I placed my finger under her chin and lifted her eyes from where she was taking in my card. "Day or night, sugar. Any time."

"Okay," she whispered, and I couldn't resist leaning down to brush a kiss on her cheek.

"Good girl," I whispered back. And I watched the blush heat up her cheeks as Brent leaned down and did the same.

Six

CASEY

I WATCHED the two guys walk out after stopping to say goodbye to Grace. I couldn't help but notice as Ethan passed her several bills when he kissed her on the cheek. I turned to grab my backpack and shook my head, certain he had paid for my food along with theirs. They were too nice. I wasn't sure what to make of their generosity or the offer for a room at their house.

I moved through the tables over to where Grace was rolling a bin of silverware. The smile she gave me when she looked up had a pang of longing rolling through me at the thought of my own mother. I hitched the bag further up on my shoulder.

"Hey, Grace? I wanted to ask…" God, how did I go about asking for a favor, like being paid in cash? I didn't even know if she'd hire me at all. What a mess. "You know what? It's nothing. The food was great. What do I owe?"

She paused in her rolling before continuing. I was starting to really hate the pity that I saw come into her eyes when she looked at me sometimes. Grace shook her head. "If my boy weren't the gentleman I raised him to be, I'd kick his ass myself." She gave me a wink, and I wanted to smile despite my irritation.

"That really wasn't necessary," I huffed. "Well, I appreciate the food, even if I didn't pay for it myself. Have a great day, Grace." I turned to leave, but stopped when she called my name softly. When I looked back, she was biting her lip. It was the first time I had seen her look unsure of herself. I barely knew the woman, but I got the impression she was one of the most self-assured women I'd ever met.

"I know you just got into town, and working is probably the last thing on your mind, but I find myself in need of more waitstaff. I'm sure you noticed how busy it was today?" At my hesitant nod, she beamed a smile. "I was hoping I could pressure you into working for me a couple of days a week. Unless you want more, I'm sure we could find more for you to do. But I was thinking it would do me a huge favor and give some relief to my aching feet if I could get you to cover a couple of shifts, and in return, I could pay you in cash for your time. Your tips are yours to keep, of course."

Was she fucking kidding me? I looked out the door at the cars driving by, but no sign of the men I'd sat with for lunch. I brought my gaze back to hers. I had strong suspicions that her son had given her the idea, but she looked so hopeful, and I didn't want to be rude. I sighed and nodded.

"I would be happy to. I would hate to be indirectly responsible for your aching feet."

She flushed under my knowing stare, but even though she knew I was onto her, she looked so relieved I couldn't be mad at her. I was certain that she thought she was doing what she could for the poor girl that stumbled in here yesterday looking like a pathetic mess. I had to be grateful for her kindness. I suppose I should be grateful for the kindness of her son and his boyfriend. I just wasn't sure about sharing a house with two strange men. Stranger danger had taken on a whole new meaning for me. I thought of the serial killer I had escaped from just a couple of months ago, and an icy shiver went up my spine. Those guys were nothing like that asshole. But was it smart to go to their home with the intention of living with them?

"So, what were you going to ask me?" Grace smiled as she resumed rolling the silverware.

I sighed and decided I might as well sit down. I slid my backpack off my shoulder and set it on the floor, then hopped up onto the bar stool in front of her. "Well, I was going to ask if you had a job opening but chickened out."

She laughed. "Well, I'm glad I didn't. I was afraid I would offend you."

I shook my head. "No, I really am grateful. I don't know why you're being so nice to me. I'm just some girl that wandered in here off the bus."

"That may be so, but I see you, Casey. You are a good soul." She side-eyed me as she hesitated. "I'm guessing you have a story to tell. You don't have to say anything right now. Just know that I am always here. My son is a cop, too, you know. If you are running from danger, there is no better person to protect you. And that man of his? Don't let his good looks fool you. That boy is one tough cookie. You want a shoulder to lean on; he's your guy."

I flushed and looked down at my fingers. Why couldn't my brain get the message that these two were off-limits? Her words had all kinds of images running through my brain: of them holding me, keeping me safe. Together. At the same time.

I cleared my throat. "Umm, Ethan offered to let me stay in their house."

"Did he now? Looks like I did manage to teach him right."

"You don't think that would be a stupid idea? Them inviting a total stranger to live with them? I could be like... a serial killer. Or something." I cringed inwardly at the thought of comparing myself to the actual Castle Killer.

"Honey, you ain't no serial killer. Like I said, I know you. You are sweet as pie. I bet your momma raised you right, too."

I smiled down at the counter. "My mom did her best, though I'm sure there were moments during my teen years that she despaired of ever having her child make it into adulthood without a record." I laughed. "I was a good kid, but I have to admit, my best friend convinced me to do a lot of stupid stuff."

"Then it sounds like you've had a good life, sweetheart. Those boys," she chuckled and shook her head. "It's a good thing you weren't hanging out with them in high school. Your poor momma would have spent every night on her knees praying for you."

My curiosity got the better of me, and I had to get more information. "What were they like?"

"As teenagers? Well, it's not my story to tell, but Ethan did his best to keep Brent away from his house as much as possible. When they got together, which was all the time, mind you, could they ever find ways to raise hell. In a small town like this one, there isn't much for teens to do but find trouble. I can't tell you how many phone calls I got from angry farmers. Did you know tipping cows isn't really a thing? It doesn't stop stupid boys from trying, though."

We both had to catch our breath from the laughter the image conjured. I wiped my eyes and realized that it was the first real laugh I'd had since I had been taken. The thought of it tried to steal my happiness, but I shoved the melancholy down.

"Seriously, though. If my boys offered you a room, you can trust that it will be safe for you. You should accept."

The doorbell jingled before I could say anything. "Think about it." Grace patted my arm as she walked past me to greet the new arrivals. I bent down to pick up my bag and slung it back over my shoulder. I needed to head to the nearest grocery store and pick up a few things that I could keep easily for snacks. I couldn't keep eating diner food all the time, even if I had yet to pay for it.

When Grace walked behind the counter again to grab some glasses, I figured it was a good time to say my goodbyes.

"When would you like me to come in to work, Grace?"

"How about you come by tomorrow morning around ten? I can show you where everything is. You can start slow, maybe get the drinks during the lunch rush. How does that sound?"

I nodded. "Sounds perfect." I started to walk out as she gathered the filled glasses to carry out, but paused. "Hey, Grace? How did you know my name today? I don't remember telling you."

She only looked slightly abashed, but admitted, "My sister owns the inn."

I watched as she sashayed past me and set her glasses in front of the customers, already chatting with them like they were old friends. Her sister? That was kinda... sweet. She was already looking out for me since day one. And it explained a lot about the rate I was paying for my room.

I shook my head and called out, "Bye, Grace!" I was immediately swallowed by the heat as I pushed the door open. I headed for the small grocery store a couple of blocks up. Relieved to find that it was close enough to the inn so I could easily carry what I needed without having to waste money on a ride.

I stepped through the doors and tried to ignore all the eyes that immediately turned my way, grabbing a handbasket while keeping my head down. I didn't like being the center of attention at the best of times. With my feelings still so raw, I just wanted to avoid everyone.

I walked quickly toward the fruit and grabbed a couple of bananas and apples, needing something healthy and easy. I thought of what else I could grab that wouldn't require a stove as I wandered down the aisles. I was searching a shelf of cereal bars when I felt a prickling sensation on the back of my neck.

I glanced around as surreptitiously as I could, peeking out from under my lashes. There were a few people that glanced at me as they walked past, but I didn't think that was the source of my sudden trepidation. Then I noticed a man standing at the end of the aisle. He was holding a box of cereal, but he didn't seem to be looking at it as much as he was trying to watch me. I grabbed the first box of bars my hand came to and turned, hurrying down the aisle in the opposite direction.

I still needed to get something to drink, but being watched had spooked me. I tried to shake it off, convincing myself that I was making more out of it than I should. I walked straight to the refrigerators, looking for a pack of individual orange juice bottles. I reached out to grab some, but felt that same eerie sensation of being watched.

I looked back at where I had come from and saw the same man again, this time pretending to look at the eggs, but doing an even shittier job of acting like he wasn't watching my every move than he had before. I decided I didn't need the orange juice and stepped away. Instead, I headed straight for the front of the store with the few things I had already grabbed. Out of the corner of my eye, I saw the man turn to watch me go.

My hand went to my pocket, where I had slid the card Ethan had given me earlier, and pulled it out. His name stared up at me. Just the thought of him and Brent was enough to calm my racing heart until I caught sight of the man following me to the register. I needed to find a phone. I needed to call Ethan.

My breath felt ragged, and my pulse was pounding as I practically ran to the register. I was going to leave my basket and forget about shopping today, but I needed to know where I could find a phone.

As I hurried up to the nearest register, the cashier looked up at me, startled. Her look immediately changed to one of concern.

"Ma'am, are you okay?"

I sat the basket down on the conveyer belt and leaned against the counter, resting my weight on both hands as I gulped air desperately. "I need a phone," I rasped out through my burning lungs. "Where is the nearest phone?"

The older woman pointed outside. "There's a payphone around the corner. I'm pretty sure it still works." She leaned forward. "Are you sure you're alright? Do I need to call someone for you? I can get the manager..."

I shook my head quickly. "No, I just need to call someone."

Someone stepped up behind me, and the cashier turned her worried eyes away from me and smiled. "Hello, Tom. How is Annie?"

"She's doing great. The baby has been keeping us awake, so she's been pretty tired." A deep voice came from right beside me, and I turned at the sound, gasping and stumbling back, knocking into the rack of candy behind me. I ignored the bars that fell to the floor as several sets of eyes turned to watch my freak out.

The same man that had been following me through the store was standing right next to me. My eyes were blurry with tears as I began shaking uncontrollably. Through my tears, I saw him reach out to steady me, but I jerked back, knocking a few more candy bars to the floor.

"Miss, are you okay? Do you need some help? I'm a doctor. I can help you."

My throat felt like sandpaper as I tried to speak through the vise-like stranglehold my fear had caused. "A d-doctor?"

He was a doctor. In this town. He wasn't the killer. He couldn't be.

My mind was a jumbled mess while I tried to process what was happening. I shrank back as I watched the man bend down to pick up something off the floor by my feet. He held up the small card. "Detective Ethan Hardgrove. Do you need me to call him for you, sweetheart?" His tone was low, and I knew he was trying to sound soothing, as if he were speaking to a wounded animal. All I could think was that I had never heard the killer's voice. Would it be low and deep like this man's?

My gaze darted around to see all the concerned and pitying stares. Some people were huddled together, whispering to each other. I jumped when I saw the man move to pull something out of his pocket, and I couldn't hold back a whimper.

"Easy, sweetheart. I'm going to make a phone call, okay?" He began to punch in numbers as I heard someone stifle a laugh. It was the last of what I could take. I turned and ran.

52

$$\mathscr{Seven}$$

ETHAN

I STOOD up from my desk with a snarl, causing my chair to roll back and crash against the wall. I slid my suit jacket back on, grabbed my keys and cell phone off the desk, and rushed for the door, ignoring all the eyes watching my hasty departure from the station. I had my phone to my ear before I made it outside.

"Get to the inn. Our girl needs us."

I slammed the car door hard enough to rattle the windows and tossed my phone into the cupholder. I had backed out of my parking space and floored it to the inn within minutes of the phone call. I bit back a growl of frustration.

Something had spooked our girl bad enough that she'd had a panic attack in the middle of the grocery store. All Tom could tell me was that she'd asked for a phone and had my card in her hand.

"Good girl," I whispered into the car's interior. I didn't like hearing my girl was scared, but I couldn't deny that I was happy as fuck that it was me that she had wanted to call. One thing was certain: we needed to find out what the fuck had set her off. We already knew she was running from something, but if we were going to help, we needed answers. Now.

As I pulled into the parking lot, I saw Brent turning the corner. I stood next to my car as he parked and stormed over to me, his mossy green eyes blazing.

"What the fuck happened?"

"I don't know. She was at the grocery store and freaked the fuck out. She had my card in her hand, so Tom, the pediatrician from the clinic, called me to tell me she ran."

He raked a hand through his blond hair and let out a frustrated noise low in his throat. "Fuck. We need to get her to our house where we can keep an eye on her."

I shot him a look. "We can't keep her locked up."

"The fuck we can't. She's obviously in some kind of danger. She will tell us. Today, so we know what to protect her from." He started heading to the front door, but I grabbed his arm, pulling him back. He turned to me with a growl.

"Look, we go in there, we have to be calm. She is already upset. Seeing you go all angry caveman on her isn't going to make her want to come home with us."

He glared at me, his chest heaving, looking like he wanted to throw a punch at my jaw. I would let him get his frustrations out if I needed to, but I would prefer to do it a different way. Unfortunately, that wasn't an option at the moment.

"Just calm down, babe. We need to show her that she can trust us to be her safe place. I'm upset, too. I wish we would have just taken her straight home after lunch. But this is Casey. She's skittish. Just... fuck. Just keep calm, alright?"

"Calm. Right." He chuckled darkly. "Yeah, I can be calm."

I gave him a look. From the outside, he was all movie star good looks and charm. There were few people that knew what lurked below his surface. He had too many demons inside of him. I had a feeling that Casey would be the one person that would be able to do what even I couldn't for him. She was going to be the one that could soothe the beast that was always raging inside of him.

He returned my look with a glare and raked his hand through his hair again. "I'm good man. I've got it under control. Right now, I just want to get to our girl and make sure she's alright."

I nodded, and together, we both walked through the door of my aunt's inn. Aunt Gladys came through the doorway from the back of the inn where her private space was. She was wiping her hands on a towel and had a smile on her face that brightened further once she saw the two of us standing in her entry.

"Please tell me you boys are here to check on that sweet girl."

I bent down to kiss her cheek. "Hey, Aunt Gladys. How is she?"

"I wish I knew. She looked so upset. She just rushed inside and went up to her room. I don't think she even saw me."

Brent kissed her cheek next. "Thanks for looking after our girl. I hope you don't mind that we take a paying customer away."

She waved a hand. "I just want that girl to be happy. There's something in her eyes that tells me she is holding something dark inside that she needs to let go."

Brent and I glanced at each other. Yeah, there was something there. And we would get to the bottom of it. We just had to be careful how we did it. It was instinct to corner her and demand she submit to us, but that was sure to be the fastest way to have her back on a bus and out of town before we could blink.

"We will take care of everything. Which room is she in?" I looked at the stairs as if I could see her in her room already.

"Room 2. The pretty one."

Brent pulled some cash out of his pocket and pressed it into Aunt Gladys' hand. "All your rooms are pretty, Gladys." I knew he would give her cash, for the same reason I had already arranged to pay the difference on the room rate that she had generously cut for Casey.

Her cheeks pinkened, but she slid the wad of bills into her pocket, already knowing by now that there would be no arguing with either of us when we offered her money. She gave us each a squeeze on the arm, then turned around to head back into her kitchen. From the smells coming from back there, I was willing to bet she was well on her way into baking a large batch of chocolate chip cookies.

We both headed for the stairs and took them two steps at a time, walking straight to the door with a fancy scrolled two on it. Before I could raise my hand, Brent had his fist up and was banging on it loudly. He ignored my warning glare, his jaw hard and determined. There was shuffling coming from the other side of the door, and I held my breath for what we would see once she opened it. I didn't like the thought of Casey upset, and all I had wanted to do since receiving that phone call was get to her and hold her close.

The door handle turned, and then the door cracked open, allowing Casey to peek around the wood. She didn't look overly surprised to see us standing at the door to her room. I watched as she swallowed and then lifted her chin. Before she could tell us to go away, I had my hand on the door and pushed it gently but firmly open. She took several steps back as we both entered.

The room was neat and tidy, but the first thing I noticed was her suitcase was closed and standing by the door. "Oh, good, you're already packed." Brent's words had her gaze flying up to his face before she abruptly turned around and walked to the bed. I hadn't missed the hurt look that flashed before she turned away, though.

"Uh, yeah." She picked up her backpack from the foot of the bed and slid it over her shoulders. "I was just getting ready to leave." She turned back to face us, her expression carefully blank. "I wanted to thank you guys for lunch again. I appreciate it. Can you tell Grace thanks for everything she's done for me?" Her eyes got glassy for a minute until she blinked and then fixed that blank stare back on us, walking toward her suitcase.

Before she could reach for it, Brent had his hand on the handle and was pulling it out of the room. "You can tell her yourself when you go in tomorrow for that job she offered you." His words were said over his shoulder as he continued to walk toward the stairs, her suitcase in tow.

"Wait! I need my suitcase!" Casey squeezed past me and marched up to Brent, where he had paused at the top of the stairs. "I'm heading to the bus station."

"Why?"

She swung around to look at me, an incredulous look taking over the blank one I hated. "Why? Because I made a fool of myself in the grocery store! I need to get out of here before everyone realizes I'm a nut job."

I couldn't help my glare as I stalked over to her. I put my hand under her chin and gently forced her face up to look at me. "Don't ever call yourself that again. Do you hear me, Casey? Everyone has moments of weakness. You obviously had something spook you, and it shook you badly. From what Dr. Tom said, you had been nervous for a while. Did you feel like you were being watched? Followed?"

I could feel her neck convulse as she swallowed hard. Her eyes got that glassy sheen again, and she stared up at me silently.

"Casey." Brent's growl came from beside us as he moved in closer. "Answer him."

Her eyes went to him, then back to me swiftly. "I, uh. Yeah, I felt like I was being watched." She jerked her head back and glared at us both. "But I don't see what right you have to question me about it."

Brent took another step closer. "We have the right dollface because we want to make sure our girl is safe."

I cleared my throat before he could say anything else and reveal what our intentions were. We had to ease her into it slowly, not shove her head first while she was still raw from her emotional trauma. "We are worried. Look, we already discussed you coming to stay with us, and I think now would be a perfect time for you to come to our home. We can keep you safe. When you are ready, you can tell us all about what spooked you and why. But not until you're ready. Okay, sugar?"

Her shoulders dropped, and her expression lost the look of defiance that she had been so bravely wielding. "I—" She looked off into the distance, and I could imagine she was weighing her options. Get back on the bus and keep running? Or come home with two strangers that offered her safety. I could see the moment she made her decision, and the tension that had been a ball inside me let go, allowing me to take my first relaxed breath since Dr. Tom's phone call. "Okay." She looked down at the floor, but instead of looking defeated, she looked relieved.

"Okay, what? I have to hear it, dollface." Brent stepped forward, standing shoulder to shoulder with me.

She looked back up, a small smile playing around her beautiful lips, even as they trembled slightly. "Okay, I'll become a guest in your home. I accept your offer."

Eight

BRENT

THE MOMENT the words left her lips, I wanted to shout, to rush her and wrap her in my arms. To kiss her. I did none of that. Instead, I took a page from Ethan's book and pasted on a grin. "Good girl," I practically purred, delighting in the pink that tinged her cheeks at the words.

I took her suitcase by the handle again, and this time, I didn't stop until I was at my truck, lifting it into the backseat of the dual cab. I closed the door firmly and turned around to see she was back to being shy, but hadn't reverted to reluctance. If she had, I didn't know what I would do with my sheer frustration. I had never been so eager for anything in my life. Ethan had always been there for me, always ready to fight my demons with me. This, not knowing if our futures would include her... it was killing me.

"Ready?" I didn't give her a chance to back out, just opened the passenger door and lifted her by the waist, depositing her in my truck. I wanted nothing more than to run my tingling hands over her body, but I would settle for knowing we were finally getting her into our home. It was the first step in reaching our forever together.

I shut the door after reaching across her body to buckle her in, hiding my grin at the adorable squeak she let out at my touch. I turned to face Ethan, taking in his relaxed posture and the grin that matched mine. Yeah, we were both beyond relieved at this first step.

I stalked over to him and grabbed him by the back of the neck, and slammed my mouth against his in a brief kiss that held a promise of what I wanted to do with him later. I yanked back and stared into his honey eyes before smirking and stepping back, letting my hands fall from his body. "Love you."

I turned around before he could say anything and stalked to the driver's side of the truck. It wasn't that I didn't like saying the words. Ethan knew I loved his sexy ass and had since we were teens. I was just uncomfortable with them. My home life had been nothing but fucking shit, shaping me into the man I was today. There was no love in our house. There was only filth and hatred. Ethan understood that, and he understood me.

I turned the key, fired up the engine, and backed out of the small parking lot, feeling Casey's eyes on me the entire time. Once we were a mile down the road and too far away from the bus station for her to change her mind, I let the tension I'd been hanging onto out with a heavy breath.

"You two are cute together."

I turned my head so I could glance at her out of the corner of my eyes, seeing her wistful smile. "Oh, yeah?"

"Yeah. How long have you been together?"

I grunted, turning back to the road as she played with the hem of her top. "Since high school. We were competitors, and then we became friends."

When Ethan had seen past the hard exterior I'd built for the world, somehow seeing the pain underneath. He had insisted I talk to him. He was the first person to have ever shown any concern for my well-being. Growing up, none of my teachers had ever seemed to notice all the bruises, or they just didn't care to. Ethan, though, he cared. It took our rivalry from being the best on the team to being a duo that worked together to make an unstoppable pair on the field. By the time we had made it to our junior year, we had been more than friends and didn't give one solitary fuck what anyone thought about it. The couple of times someone thought to give us shit, they learned real quick that we would beat acceptance into their shallow little brains.

"Competitors?"

"Yeah, we were both on the football team since our freshman year. We were both damn good and always tried to outdo each other on the field. Once we became friends, we started working better as a team and became unstoppable. Turns out, working together does more for your stats than working against each other."

Her little snort had me grinning and glancing at her again. The sun was shining through the window and lit her hair up. It made the dark blonde strands shine with every shade of gold you could imagine. It took my breath away.

Both of us knew we liked girls. We just hadn't had time for them when we were freshmen. Or we were just too awkward to get involved with one. I knew I held back because my head was fucked up. Falling into each other after spending our days and nights hanging out at his house, and later, taking his car out for joyrides when we got a bit older, was as easy as slipping on your favorite pair of jeans. Or slipping them off.

"So, you became friends, and then..."

I chuckled. "What do you want to know, dollface? You want to know which one of us took the plunge first?"

Her cheeks were rosy, but there was a twinkle in her eye as she stared at me. "Sorry, it's just... you guys together..." She turned her head to look out the window, obviously feeling shy from the turn the discussion had taken. "I just think you two seem to have a deep connection together. I wish I had that."

She said the last part so softly I could barely hear it over the sound of the radio playing a country song on low volume. I clenched my hands around the steering wheel, wanting nothing more than to reach over and grab her hand and drag it onto my leg. I wanted a connection with her; I needed her touch. I wanted to show her that she could have what we did. With us. Instead, I shrugged.

"He's been my best friend for years. It made us close. Solid. He knows me better than anyone in this world."

She looked back at me, and I glanced over to see her eyes were shiny, but her smile was genuine. "That's great. I'm glad you have that."

I finally gave in to temptation and took one of her hands with one of mine and gave it a gentle squeeze. Her fingers were small, delicate. So different from Ethan's. It had a jolt of lust running through me at the thought of having her under me, so small that she would disappear.

I let go and cleared my throat, placing my hand back on the wheel as I turned down our driveway. The first view of our sprawling ranch-style house had her sitting up straighter with a gasp.

"This is your house?"

I pulled in front of the doors to the garage and put the truck in park, seeing Ethan pull up the drive behind me in the rearview.

"Yep. Home sweet home."

I hopped out and rounded the hood at the same time Ethan parked his Mustang next to the truck. I gave him a wink and then opened her door before he could turn off his engine.

"Ready to get settled into your new home, dollface?" she already had her seatbelt undone, so I reached in and plucked her from her seat, letting her slide down my body to the hot concrete. She turned her face up to glare at me, shielding her eyes from the sun.

"You don't need to manhandle me. I can get in and out on my own."

I was still reeling from the feel of her soft tits pressed against my chest for those few seconds I had her in my arms, so all I could do was grin down at her. Ethan slammed his door, and she swung her head over to him, the glare dropping and a smile gracing her lips.

"Your home is beautiful."

"Just wait until you see the inside."

They stood there smiling at each other as I opened the back door to haul out her small suitcase. She couldn't have much. Our girl was going to need more of everything. I had a feeling that both Ethan and I would have fun spoiling her.

We all walked up the walkway together and waited for Ethan to unlock the door with his thumbprint. The lock beeped, blinking green, and then he swung the door open, heading straight for the alarm to disarm it.

"Wow, I've never seen one of those locks on someone's door before. I mean, I know they have gotten popular, but you know."

She was adorable when she rambled, which she seemed to do when she was nervous. Actually, I thought there wasn't much that she could do that wasn't adorable. I set the suitcase down, leaving it by the front door for now, and swung my arm around her shoulder, and led her through the entryway into the large living room.

"We are two hard-working men with plenty of money. Don't be surprised if the place is like one big man cave." I looked at the giant sectional black leather couch taking up the majority of the space. There was a black coffee table in the center of the floor, sitting directly in front of a TV stand with the largest flat screen we could buy inside the electronic store. I felt my cheeks heat at what it might look like to her. Definitely, like two men had decorated the place.

There wasn't a single girly thing in sight. No throw pillows or small blankets that women seemed to like. No knick-knacks or picture frames. The fireplace mantle in the corner of the room was bare. But the couch was fucking comfortable, and that was all we had bothered to care about. Until now.

Ethan cleared his throat as he came up to her other side as she stared at the room with wide eyes. "You can decorate it however you want. We know this place isn't very homey right now."

She swung her head to look at him. "What? No! This is your place. It's fine. Great even. I've just never seen a TV so huge before. Do you guys host movie nights or something?"

We both chuckled. I squeezed her shoulder and then turned her toward the kitchen. As we walked through the living room and into the large kitchen filled with black appliances and gray marble countertops, she shook her head.

"Casey." I picked her up and set her down on the large center island. "We want you to feel at home here. We also want you to stay as long as you want. If putting a fucking throw pillow on the couch will help that, that's what we want you to do."

I stood in front of her with my hands on either side of her legs, wishing I could just touch her the way I was itching to. Her hands were in her lap as she looked around, awe on her face.

"This kitchen..." She shook her head and looked first at me and then over to Ethan, who had leaned against the island right next to my hand. We were crowding her, but I was pleased to see she didn't seem to mind one single bit. "This whole place is amazing." She sighed. "I don't know why you're pushing me to change things. But if you want me to add some nice touches for you, I can do that. Just tell me what look you are going for. It might be fun to play interior decorator."

Her lips turned up as she started thinking about what she could do. She was wrong about us wanting her to spruce up the place for us, though. It had nothing to do with what we wanted, and everything to do with making her fall in love with the place and never wanting to leave.

And then, maybe she would fall in love with us, too.

Nine

CASEY

I WAS STILL overwhelmed and wasn't sure when I would be able to take a full breath again. My life felt like one insane event after another. Or, at least, it had gone from being your average life of a young twenty-something, trying to make her own way while still shamelessly hanging onto the comfort of her parents.

I was working in an old, dusty bookstore, loving every minute of chatting with the customers, and finding it my mission in life to find the perfect book for each individual person that came looking through the old tomes. I was making just enough money to say I was independent while still going to my parents every Sunday for dinner and accepting the little handouts that my dad snuck me while my mom pretended not to notice.

I had loved my relatively boring life. But then it was upended. In the worst way. I thought I was going to die. There was no better way of saying it—as I had lain there on the freezing concrete floor, there were times I *wished* for death. Escaping had been pure luck and desperation. Since then, each moment has been lived in a fog. I didn't know where my life would take me next. I didn't know if the Castle Killer would suddenly turn up one day to finish the job he had started. I didn't know when I'd get to see my parents again. And I didn't know why I was sitting on this comfortable bed more than a thousand miles away from where it had all gone wrong.

I stared down at my hands folded in my lap as I sat against the pillows with my legs crossed. I was ready for bed after having a pleasant dinner with the two men that had all but carried me to their home, not taking no for an answer. I was sure if I threw a giant fit, they would have let me go, but there was something about them. Something about the way they looked at me and the promises in their eyes. I didn't know what it meant. But for the first time since that awful night when I had been abducted and thrown in a cage, I felt... safe.

After giving me the full tour of their house, ending with my bedroom that was just a few doors down from theirs, we had our dinner of steaks, baked potatoes, and steamed broccoli. It was so domestic, yet it was exactly what I would have guessed two grown men would have. I hadn't expected the place settings at the table, nor did I expect that it would be Brent that seemed to slip into the role of caretaker. That wasn't to say that Ethan didn't pitch in. He did by making sure everyone had drinks and setting the table. They worked together like a well-oiled machine. I was jealous.

I swallowed at the thoughts invading my mind. I was jealous of two men that had been all but married for years. I should be scoffing at myself and reminding my brain that they were taken men in a committed relationship and to stop longing for something out of my reach. Instead, I was daydreaming about what it would be like if they opened their arms and pulled me into the center of them...

I ran my hands over my face in disgust and looked at the clock on the bedside table. It had been over a half-hour since I had said goodnight to them, closing my door firmly after reassurances that I knew where everything was. Once again, overwhelmed by their concern and generosity. I sighed and straightened my legs, scooting to the edge of the bed.

I needed to get a drink of water and use the restroom. I was used to having water at my bedside when I went to sleep. I rarely used it, but it was a comfort thing. Or a habit. Whatever it was, I needed a glass of water.

I straightened my tank top, nervously smoothed my hands on the smooth cotton sleep shorts I wore, and walked quietly to the door. I twisted the knob and quickly, without looking toward the end of the hallway, walked in the direction of the kitchen. I stopped in the bathroom, wincing when I flushed the toilet, then berated myself for being apprehensive. They'd invited me here, they wouldn't care if I went pee in their house.

Once I was done washing my hands, I flipped the light off before opening the door and slipping out towards the kitchen. I found a tall glass in the cabinet, having to stand on my tiptoes, leaning against the cold marble. Once I had it secure in my hand, I filled it from the fridge door dispenser. I took a small sip of the cool water, grateful for the soothing coolness it provided against my parched throat.

I made my way back through the dark house, grateful for the small bit of glow from the lamp turned down low in the living room. I suspected it was another kind gesture from one of them. Just another way to make sure I was comfortable getting around in their house. The thought had moisture brimming in my eyes that I quickly blinked away.

As I walked down the long, dark hallway, I looked up from where I had been watching my feet, and my eyes went to the door at the end of the hallway. My breath caught when I realized it was cracked open. I hadn't noticed before since I hadn't looked. But now I couldn't tear my eyes away.

I stopped in front of my door and lifted my hand to push it open so I could slip inside, but I paused when I thought I heard movement. As I stood there in the dark, my ears strained to listen for whatever I had heard before.

It was probably just one of them turning over in their sleep or trying to get comfortable! I chastised myself and turned, taking a step, one foot inside my room and the other still in the hallway, when I heard it again. A muffled moan. I gasped in the dark, my hand flying up to cover my mouth. Were they having sex? Every wicked part of me wanted to know. I wanted to crawl to the end of the hallway and push that door open so I could witness in person what I had so often read about in my books.

I needed to know who was dominant in their relationship. They had struck me as light and dark when I had first seen them together, and I wanted to know how true that really was. I wanted to know if Brent was as sweet in bed as he was out of it. I shook my head, a part of me remembering how forceful he had been at the inn. There was more to the lighter one than he showed the world, I was sure of it. Maybe he was secretly dominant, and the strong detective was the one that conceded his power behind closed doors.

I heard another grunt and curse, movement speeding up, the bed making noises that made it obvious what was happening in the room that definitely did not have a closed door. With rapid breaths rushing out of my aching lungs and my heart beating frantically, I turned and practically shoved myself into my room. Thankfully, I collected myself from my frazzled state before closing the door behind me. I dove toward the bed, sloshing water over my hand and not giving a shit. I set the glass down harder than I intended before sliding under the covers. I shamelessly dove my hand under my shorts and groaned when I touched myself. I was wetter than I ever remembered being, and it was all because I'd heard them having sex.

I didn't care that it made me a pervert for getting off on what I was imagining they were doing. I felt a need unlike anything I had felt before. With my eyes closed, I let my mind go wild with the images playing in my mind. I furiously circled my clit after using my own wetness as lubrication. It only took a few seconds to detonate, my back bowing off the mattress and my legs straightening, muscles so tight that my thighs cramped. It was worth it for the best orgasm I'd ever had.

I straightened my sheets and blanket, turned to my side, still breathing heavily from my orgasm, and let my eyes drift closed. For the first time in months, I slept without nightmares.

A knock on my door had me blinking my eyes open, staring at the gray walls of a room I didn't recognize. I jerked my head toward the door as a second knock came, and memories of the day before came rushing back.

"I'm—" I cleared my throat and tried again, calling out groggily. "I'm awake."

"Can I come in, sugar?"

Ethan's voice carried through the door, and I glanced down at myself to see that my tanktop had shifted in the night, one boob hanging out, and quickly adjusted the fabric so I was covered again. "Sure."

The door cracked open, and he poked his head into the room as I sat up, smoothing my hair back from my face and surreptitiously wiping my mouth to make sure there was no drool covering my cheek. He smiled with his eyes first as he took in my disheveled appearance, his lips following immediately, turning up into a grin.

"You're adorable. Do you know that?"

I blushed to my roots, knowing that I looked like a mess, having forgotten to tie my hair up in my haste to pleasure myself while thinking of their act of loving each other. He didn't make me feel bad, though. His face softened.

"We are getting breakfast ready and wanted to know if you would join us in the kitchen?"

"Uh, sure," I said dumbly as he stood there, taking me in. I could swear his eyes heated when I shifted, making my breasts sway under the light cotton of my top. "I'll be right out," I promised.

"Good girl." His words sent a shiver down my spine, but he was gone before I could turn any redder from the pleasure it gave me to be called that. I wondered if they knew what their words did to me.

I glanced over at the table where my water sat in a small puddle. I groaned and whipped off my tank to mop up the mess of water before it could do any damage to the wood. There was already a bit of discoloration there from the water sitting all night, making me feel bad. I hoped once it dried out, it would go away, or I was going to be indebted to them even more. A thought played in the recesses of my mind of what I could do for them to pay them back, but I shoved it way down. I could have my fantasies, but I wouldn't let them take over, or this arrangement would become extremely awkward.

I got up and threw on a bra, t-shirt, and shorts from the drawer. They had made sure I unpacked last night, not liking when I had said I would live out of my suitcase. Their eyes had gone hard, both of them. They had both ground their teeth, and it was like looking at two sides of the same coin. One dark, one light. They were so alike.

I finger-combed the tangles from my hair, making a pit stop in the bathroom to do my business and brush my teeth. I didn't want to take too long, hoping they wouldn't wait for me to start eating.

Once I got to the kitchen, Brent turned toward the coffeepot and grabbed a mug, filling it with wonderful smelling coffee.

"Morning, dollface. How did you sleep?" His smirk made him look wicked, and I thought of just how well I had slept after getting off to them.

My face burned as I reached for the mug and thanked him. "I slept very well, actually. Your bed is very comfortable." I realized how my words sounded and quickly corrected them. "Uh, the bed. In the room. My room. That you let me sleep in. It was very comfortable. Thank you."

To shut myself up, I took a large swallow and then nearly spat the coffee back into my cup as it scorched my mouth. A cup of orange juice was placed in front of me, my eyes watering from the pain, and I gratefully took it and let the cold liquid cool my burning mouth.

"Careful. Are you okay?"

I waved off the concern as nonchalantly as I could and slumped in the nearest chair. "I'm fine," I rasped out, embarrassed, not meeting their eyes. A bottle of coffee creamer was placed in front of me, and I saw it was a French vanilla flavor. I mumbled my thanks and doctored my coffee, careful to take a small sip instead of the stupid gulp I had done a minute ago. I groaned at the rich flavor, wondering how long it had been since I'd had a good cup of coffee.

I looked up when I heard two groans coming from both men to see them staring at me with identical looks of hunger in their eyes. I blinked, dazed at what I thought I was seeing on their handsome faces. There was no way I was seeing... desire. Was there?

I looked back down at my cup of coffee and tried to ignore the butterflies that suddenly took flight in my belly. After a few prolonged seconds, the men turned back to what they had been doing before the strangeness of the last few minutes. I sat there, resisting the urge to prod at my scalded tongue with my fingertip like a weirdo, and watched them through my lowered lashes. And if I sighed internally at the pure masculine beauty in front of me... well, I was only human.

Ten

BRENT

I HAD to quickly look away from the beautiful sight of our girl enjoying her coffee as if it were solely responsible for the orgasm she'd had the night before. Turning to face the stove, I adjusted my cock behind my jeans. I tried to make my erection more comfortable instead of the odd and painful angle it had been in when the blood rushed to it so fast it nearly tore a hole through the denim.

We were playing dirty. I knew it. Ethan knew it. All's fair in love and war, right? And we had decided that this was a war that we were going to win. If we had made sure to leave the door open a crack in order to pique our girl's interest, then I guess I would just have to apologize to her later for the underhanded tactics that we would deploy. After she's ours, wearing our ring, and has our baby in her belly.

I froze. Staring down at the eggs I was scrambling, and not seeing shit. A baby? It was something we had never discussed. Of course, gay couples have children all the time. We both knew that. But it wasn't something that we had ever brought up. Me as a father?

Sweat broke out on my forehead, and the hand holding the spatula began to tremble. I couldn't be a dad. What if I was just like *him*? But my girl. I closed my eyes, squeezing them tight. Picturing my girl, round with mine or Ethan's baby. It was something I never, not once, ever thought I'd want. But now? The thought terrified me and equally filled me with a longing so strong my knees shook.

Fuck.

"Hey, babe. Are you okay?" I opened my eyes to meet Ethan's whiskey ones.

"Yeah," I cleared my throat, and my face heated at the crack in the word. "I need to do something. Be right back." I shoved the spatula into his hand and practically ran from the room, not stopping until I was leaning over the sink in the primary bath. I stood there for a long minute. My stiff arms and sweaty palms bearing the brunt of my weight against the edge of the counter while I tried to focus.

I felt hot and cold all at once. Like the time I'd had the flu, and my whole body had been shaking with chills while a fever raged inside me. I felt just as weak now as I did then, too.

"Fuck," I grunted into the reflection in front of me. That man looked like he'd seen a ghost. He looked... scared. I jerked on the tap and splashed cold water over my face, not caring that I was getting droplets all over my work tee.

Casey was all I could think about. Well, her and the scary as fuck thought of a baby made from my seed. I held my breath as I met my eyes in the mirror. I realized I wanted it. I knew, I just fucking knew, I would never be like my old man. And if there were ever a time that I started to become anything like him, I had Ethan there to kick my ass.

I watched as the corners of my lips curved up. The tremors that had been wracking my body slowed down, and my heart stopped trying to jump out of my chest. A calmness not unlike the one I felt when I delivered justice came over me, making my breaths deeper and my senses sharper. While the calm washed through my veins, the surety of the future moved in. If Casey wanted children, I would be there with her every step of the way. Ethan would be on the other side of her, and with the two of us as her protectors, we would build a family.

I turned off the tap and pulled a hand towel off the rail to pat the moisture from my face. Filled with a new determination, I hung the towel back up and opened the door to see Ethan leaning against the closed door of our room, his arms crossed and a concerned look on his face.

"Do you want to talk about it?"

I grinned at him and stalked forward until I was pressed against him, instantly feeling my dick twitch at his closeness. I captured his mouth in a rough kiss that he immediately accepted, unfolding his arms and grabbing mine, holding me to him as our tongues battled for dominance.

I pulled back, savoring the taste of him on my lips. "Just coming to terms with things."

"Anything you want to share?" He cocked a brow as one of his hands glided over my hard chest. It was a gesture that comforted me just as much as it turned me the fuck on. There was no time to do anything with the pounding lust that filled me as we stared at each other.

"Just realizing that we could be daddies sooner than we ever thought." I winked, but I didn't think he saw it as his eyes glazed over and his jaw dropped in shock. I was chuckling when I pushed him out of the way of the door, and walked down the hall and back to our girl.

I could hear him choke out, "Daddies?" as I passed Casey's door and thought about how soon we'd be able to move her from that room and into ours. There was a possibility that she would want to maintain her own private space. If that were the case, I would make sure she knew the primary bedroom would be all hers. Ethan and I would take one of the smaller rooms.

I walked into the kitchen, still grinning, and noticed the scrambled eggs that I had been working on were in a bowl on the table, along with a plate of toast and bacon. Casey was sitting there staring out the window with a faraway look on her face.

"Hey, dollface. You okay?"

I picked up her plate and loaded it with more food than she was likely to eat, but I wanted to make sure she had anything and every-thing she needed. She could have all the food if she wanted. She turned her stunning blue eyes up to me and blinked before they seemed to focus on my face.

"What?" She looked down at the plate in front of her and looked back up, her cheeks full and flushed. "Oh, um, I was just thinking. I guess." She picked up her fork and started raking it through her eggs.

I took my seat as Ethan walked back into the room. He still looked like he'd been sucker punched, but didn't look freaked out, so I guess he was working on his own acceptance. "Do you want to talk about it?" I asked, parroting the words Ethan had spoken to me in the bedroom.

She stuck a forkful of eggs in her mouth and looked up at me, then turned her head to Ethan. She chewed slowly and pointed a finger to her face, making me chuckle. Alright, she didn't want to talk yet. That was okay. We needed to have a serious conversation about what was happening with her, but it could wait until later.

Ethan cleared his throat and started fixing his own plate. "So, we were talking about it this morning before you got up, and we wanted to hear your opinion on what you want to do today. I know my mom gave you a job. Do you want to go in with us when we leave for work? I don't want to strand you at the diner all day. I'd give you a car to use, but we only have the two."

Casey swallowed. "Oh, it's ok. I can't drive. If you want to drop me off, that's fine. I can take a cab back or something."

"You can't drive?" We were both staring at her in disbelief, forks full of food hanging mid-air as she shifted uncomfortably in her chair. I snapped out of it and shoved the eggs in my mouth. She reached for her toast and started tearing it into little pieces.

"Well, technically, I can. I just don't have a license." She shoved one of the small pieces in her mouth.

"Do you want to get your license, sugar?" Ethan asked as he continued to stare at her. I kicked my leg out under the table, trying to get him to take the intensity down a notch or five.

He grunted and took a bite of food as he glared at me, promising retribution with his eyes. She shook her head.

"I can't. I don't have any paperwork with me." She was shutting down on us while I watched. I suspected that her lack of identification probably had everything to do with the reason she'd run away from home. A lack of ID or a birth certificate would definitely stop her from being able to be put into any database that would be searchable. Ethan met my eyes from across the table. He had come to the same conclusion I had. It was frustrating as hell not to have the answers we desperately needed in order to protect her properly.

"That's fine," Ethan reassured and reached over to pat her leg under the table. The touch made her jump in surprise and then pink up again almost immediately. "I can usually get away from work when I need to. Just give me a call, and I should be able to pick you up and bring you back home."

She mumbled something as she shoved more food in her mouth, chewing rapidly this time. "What was that?" I asked as I reached over to place my hand on her other leg. I fought to hold back my grin as she startled again and began to shift in her seat. I watched her closely. If she were uncomfortable, I would pull back, but that wasn't the reaction she was having. No, instead of looking like she wanted to throw our hands off of her, she looked like she was fighting the attraction.

I gently squeezed her small thigh and pulled my hand back at the same time Ethan did. She took a shaky breath and reached for a piece of bacon. Thankfully, she didn't shred it like she had done with the rest of her food.

"I don't have a phone," she sighed and took a bite.

"You traveled all alone across the country and didn't have a phone with you?" Ethan asked, incredulity lining his words. "That's dangerous, sugar."

She stared at her plate and shrugged a shoulder. "I guess it was, but it's not like I had much of a choice." Her words were so quiet I could barely hear them.

I glared at Ethan, trying to force the words, *fix this*, into his head. He grimaced, knowing we had to tread carefully with her.

"That's fine. I can have a phone for you by this afternoon."

She jerked her head up, but before she could begin her protests, I cut in. "It's important for your safety to have a phone, dollface. We can just add you to our plan. It's no big deal. I promise." She looked at me for a long time before jerking her chin in a nod and turning back to Ethan.

"Okay. Thank you. That would be great."

My fingers twitched with jealousy as I watched him smile gently at her and reach over to tuck a strand of her hair behind her ear. I wanted to feel her hair on my fingertips, too.

"Anything for you, sugar." He winked at her and grinned at me. If she weren't sitting at the table, I would have flipped him off. Instead, I kicked his shin again. Then it was me grinning at him as he glowered back at me.

"Eat up, guys. The daylight is burning."

Eleven

CASEY

I STARED at the soda machine in horror as the Coke started spurting, then suddenly began to turn clear instead of the dark liquid it was supposed to be.

"No. No. No." I started looking around for Grace as I held the glass of really light colored Coke in my hand. She pushed out of the kitchen, holding four plates of steaming food, all balanced perfectly in her hands.

I watched as she hurried over to a table without so much as dropping a single french fry. It was like watching some kind of magic show, Grace bustling around the busy diner. She was always on the go, and she always had a smile on her face and a friendly word for her customers. I loved it as much as I was intimidated by it.

But I looked back down at the glass I was holding full of light brown liquid, nowhere near the color it should have been, and glanced helplessly over to the table of businessmen that were looking down at their menus. A small bit of panic was starting to edge in, making my hands tremble just slightly. There had to be a simple explanation, right? I had never worked in a diner before or anywhere that served drinks. The small bookstore I worked at didn't even sell coffee.

"Hey, hun. How's it going?" One of the other waitresses, a few years older than me, sidled up next to where I was standing in front of the soda dispenser, grabbing a glass to fill with ice.

I looked back down at my glass. "Uhh..."

"Oh, it looks like the Coke is out. Come on, and I'll show you how to replace the syrup." She smiled, turning around and walking to the swinging door that separated the kitchen from the dining room.

I sat the glass down next to the machine and hurried after her, relief washing over me. I had been nervous ever since I arrived. Changing into the t-shirt with the diner's logo felt like entering an arena filled with lions that I would have to survive. I knew I was being overly dramatic, but I didn't want to disappoint anyone. All I could picture was having to tell the guys that I couldn't cut it as a waitress and would need to find a different job. That I had let Grace down. After everything they had done for me, and the kindness Grace had shown me, I was determined to succeed and scared to death that I would screw up.

The other woman, Mandy, I think her name was, opened a door to a room I hadn't been in yet, revealing shelves of supplies. There was everything in there, from ketchup bottles and napkins to extra plates, stacked neatly and orderly. The industrial metal shelves filled the three walls, and there seemed to be enough supplies to allow an entire restaurant full of people to survive an apocalypse for a month.

At the bottom of one of the shelves were several brown boxes, each with labels of different types of sodas. She went straight for the one marked *Coke* and grunted when she slid the box out and hefted it into her arms.

"This is where the extra cases of syrup are. And, well, everything else we might need if we run out up front." I glanced at a large box of sugar substitutes and hummed my agreement. "Alright, let's get this bad boy hooked up, shall we?"

"Do you want me to carry that?" I offered, watching her grunt again as she elbowed her way through the door. I quickly followed her, shutting the storage room door behind us.

"Nah, it's not that bad. I've done this lots of times."

She was through the swinging door and back into the dining room, with me following behind her like a lost puppy, wringing my hands. I wanted to help, but I didn't know how. All I could do was watch helplessly as she dropped the box on the counter and turned to the soda machine.

Grace walked by as Mandy was opening the metal doors to the bottom of the machine.

"Oh, I was planning on checking the levels today. I guess we finally ran out of something, huh?" She gave me a smile and a wink as she grabbed a couple of coffee cups in one hand and a pot of coffee that I had just brewed a few minutes before. "You're doing great, Casey. Keep up the good work."

I gave her a wan smile back and looked down to see Mandy doing something with one of the boxes that were stacked on shelves I didn't even know were under the machine. She handed me the old box that felt empty and gestured to the new one behind us.

"Can you hand that one to me?" I sat the empty box down, exchanging it for the surprisingly heavy one that we had just retrieved from storage. I let out my own grunt as I held it out to her and watched in fascination as she did something with a tube. It happened so fast, and I wasn't sure if I would have been able to tell someone what she did if asked and bit my lip, hoping that this wouldn't be a common occurrence.

"There! See? Easy peasy. Now you can do it next time." She stood up and closed the door before wiping her hands on a towel. I watched as she dumped the glass I had filled a few minutes ago and put it back under the dispenser. There were several spurts of the clear liquid, and then, like magic, it turned brown again. She dumped that one too, then set the glass aside, grabbing fresh glasses and quickly, efficiently filling the three with ice and finally with soda that looked perfectly fine.

I sighed with relief and thanked her for her help. I hurriedly filled the drink orders for the table of businessmen. I wasn't taking orders just yet. I was simply helping around the dining room where I could, filling drink orders, refilling coffee cups, and bringing whatever items the customers were asking for. It wasn't difficult work, but I had a newfound gratitude for the work that servers did.

I walked over to the table with a small tray of drinks, nowhere in the same league as Grace's, who could carry all four glasses in her hands without spilling a drop. I smiled a fake smile at the table of men who didn't pay me much attention, instead continuing their conversations as if I weren't there. I was perfectly okay with being invisible. It hadn't occurred to me that I might have to talk to these strangers. It wasn't helping my anxiety any, constantly studying the men that walked in. Wondering if one of them might be a serial killer waiting to pounce.

The bell over the door jingled, and instinctively, I looked up to see Brent stroll in. I could barely contain the relief and the giddy feeling at seeing him. He was dirtier than he had been that morning. His blond hair was mussed up as if he had been running his hand through it repeatedly. I thought of him wearing a hard hat while carrying heavy equipment, hammering or sawing, and swallowed back the little wave of heat that zinged through my belly. He looked around the room, his eyes stopping once he saw me, and the corner of his mouth turned up in a grin. The look in his eyes said he was as happy to see me as I was him.

I nervously ran my hands over the apron I had tied around my hips and broke eye contact, looking over his shoulder. I tried not to let the disappointment at seeing him alone get to me. I looked back at him to see he was walking straight to me, that grin still turned up. When he reached me, he didn't pause, just bent down and kissed my cheek. I could have sworn he lingered there just a second longer than was necessary before straightening back up.

"How's our girl doing on her first day at work?"

I laughed nervously and glanced around to see several curious eyes on us. "I haven't broken anything... yet."

"That's good, dollface. Just relax. You'll be fine, I promise." He stood there staring down at me, and I fidgeted with my hands, feeling awkward.

"Do you want a table?" I wanted to facepalm myself. Of course, he wanted a table. It was his lunchtime, and he came to the diner. His smile widened, showing off his straight white teeth. The sight was mesmerizing, and I swayed slightly toward him, pulled into his orbit. He really was one of the most gorgeous men I had ever seen.

"Yeah, dollface. Why don't you walk me to my table?" He gestured his head to the same table he had sat at the first day I had seen him, the one closest to the kitchen and the hallway to the restrooms.

"Oh, okay. Do you want a menu?" I was nervous. Thrown off-kilter by the soft kiss he had given my cheek. I couldn't explain the need to show him I was a competent worker, but it was there none-theless.

He chuckled softly, walking with me to his seat, and I shivered slightly at the heat of his hand at my back leading me. He slid into the booth and grinned up at me, those mossy green eyes sparkling with mirth. I stood next to the table, staring down at him for a long beat before shaking myself out of the daze his eyes had put me in.

"Do you, ah, want something to drink?"

"Why don't you sit with me? Have you had a break yet?" He looked me up and down as if he were looking for signs of fatigue.

"Oh, umm..." I looked over at Grace, who was walking past with an arm full of plates steaming with food.

"Why don't you take your lunch, Casey? You're due for one." She looked at Brent. "She's doing great. I can tell she's going to fit in well here."

I flushed at her compliment and looked back down at Brent, who looked proud of me, making my cheeks warm even more. "I'll get our drinks before I sit down. Do you know what you want?"

After he gave me his order, I walked away, feeling the weight of his stare following me. It was overwhelming, but I couldn't deny how exciting it was to have the attention of such a handsome man.

As I was getting our drinks, Mandy walked up, grabbing a coffee cup. "That man," she sighed dramatically. "What I wouldn't give to be in the middle of that sandwich."

I looked at her, startled. "What do you mean?"

She laughed as she poured coffee. "Those guys were seniors when I was a freshman. Every girl in school wished they would be the one to turn either one of them straight. But we could all see they were committed to each other. Then we started dreaming of being the filling between them."

I glanced over my shoulder to see Brent still watching me. "Between them?"

She giggled. "Oh yeah. Any girl would have been happy to be the peanut butter to their sandwich. The meatball to their sub." She looked at me with a grin. "The cheese in their quesadilla."

My cheeks flamed. Yeah, I knew exactly what she was talking about. "They, umm, they never... experimented? With girls?"

"Nope. What a pity, right?" She sighed wistfully and then sashayed over to her table with the cup of coffee.

I picked up our glasses and turned back to the table to see Grace chatting with Brent. After what Mandy had said, I didn't know if I was happy that they hadn't brought in a girl to share between them or disappointed that it wasn't their thing.

I set our glasses down and started to sit across from him as he and Grace chatted, but I felt a tug on my hand and found myself being pulled into the seat next to Brent. So close I was plastered against his side, his arm against the back of the seat, resting against my shoulders.

"Umm..."

"Sit here, dollface. Ethan said he was going to try to make it to lunch again today."

"Oh, okay." I looked up at Grace, biting my lip, wondering how it looked to see me sitting cozied up to her son's almost-husband. She was beaming down at us, not looking the least bit bothered by the display.

"What do you want for lunch, Casey?"

"The special looked really good." Seeing the open-faced turkey sandwiches coming out of the kitchen for the last hour had worked up my appetite. They looked delicious and smelled even better. I had found out when I arrived that morning that the cook, Mark, was Ethan's dad and Grace's husband. While we were busy most of the time, Grace had taken a lull in customers to give me the history of the diner that they had purchased several years ago. They had made it a success and never looked back.

Ethan's dad looked like an older version of Ethan, tall and lankier, but just as handsome, with the same golden honey eyes that were kind. He welcomed me warmly, the lines around his mouth and eyes crinkling as he smiled broadly and gave me a bear hug that nearly broke my ribs until Grace chastised him. She pulled me away, warning that Ethan and Brent wouldn't be happy if he broke me. I knew she didn't mean it the way my thudding heart took it, but I still allowed myself to pretend that the guys cared about me as more than just a stray they picked up.

They were such good guys. I could see that now. There were no more doubts in my mind that they were trustworthy and that I felt comfortable with them. I would have to constantly remind myself that my fantasies were just that–fantasies. They didn't actually feel the same way about me as I did about them.

Grace left to go give our orders to Mark. I looked over at Brent to find his eyes trained on me, looking serious. "How is it going, really?" His concern was heartwarming, and I had to ignore the new round of butterflies bouncing around in my belly.

"I've been pretty nervous," I confessed. "I'm so afraid of screwing up. So far, it's been good, though." I giggled. "Except for when I thought I broke the soda machine." I looked back into his eyes, softened after their brief moment of concern. "Turns out it just ran out of syrup. Who knew?"

He chuckled along with me and squeezed my shoulder. "Grace loves you. You could probably drop ten plates, and she wouldn't even get mad."

I shuddered at the thought. "Well, I like her, too. But I don't want to drop any plates."

A warm mouth brushed a kiss against my cheek, and I inhaled quickly, realizing that Ethan had arrived. I didn't know how I missed the bells, except maybe I had been so wrapped up in the warmth of Brent's presence that I had blocked out everything surrounding us.

I looked up at him to see his gaze on me, his eyes full of warmth. Then he looked over to Brent before leaning over me. My breath caught in my throat as their lips met an inch from my face. They were so close that if I leaned forward just the tiniest fraction, I would have been a part of their kiss.

It was brief, just a press of lips, but a buzzing went through me, heading straight for my traitorous vagina. As they pulled away from each other, my eyes stayed glued to their lips, first Brent's, then Ethan's. He straightened back up, and I watched as he took his seat, a small smile playing across those lips I couldn't tear my gaze from.

It wasn't until Brent leaned in close to whisper into my ear that I finally took a shaky breath.

"Breathe."

Twelve

ETHAN

IT WAS hard to concentrate on lunch while Casey sat across from me with a dazed look on her face. The entire time she was eating, she kept her head down, looking for all the world like she was concentrating on her food, taking slow, small bites of the meal. But I saw her for what she was—a woman so desperate for friction that she couldn't stop adjusting her position in her seat. A woman that kept looking at each of us under her lashes. A woman that was turned on as fuck.

I imagined that if I closed my eyes and inhaled deeply, I'd be able to smell her scent. Brent and I carried on our conversation as if neither of us was tempted to yank her off the bench seat, throw her on the tabletop, and feast on her ripe cunt instead of the sandwich in front of me. Hungry for something else, I couldn't even taste it.

"Mrs. Banks came into the police station today to file a missing person's report," I casually stated. As if I were just recounting any other case I was working on. Technically, it wasn't my case, but I knew the officer that had filed the report. He would do his due diligence investigating the missing lawyer and close the case in just a few weeks. There would be nothing for him to find. Brent was that good.

There was an almost imperceptible pause that only I noticed before Brent took another bite of his burger with a grunt. After he swallowed his bite, he took a drink and looked me in the eye. "Was she upset?"

I hid my grin behind my own glass. "She looked okay, not very worried if you ask me." I glanced at Casey and then back at Brent. "Apparently, he had a mistress in another county over. Mrs. Banks assumed that he was staying with her. Either that or one of the criminals that he has on retainer got pissed and did something to him." I dipped a fry in my puddle of ketchup. "His little girl looked like she was having a good day. Doesn't seem like she's missing her daddy any. If you ask me, that family seems relieved that he's gone." I popped the fry in my mouth and wiped my hands on the napkin.

"They aren't sad or worried?" Casey's eyebrows furrowed.

"I had a domestic dispute call at their home a few days ago. Unfortunately, even though there were obvious signs that he had been abusing them, Mrs. Brady wasn't inclined to press charges."

"That's awful." Casey looked spitting mad at the situation and sad all at the same time. I knew how she felt. "You don't think she did anything to him, do you? I hate that the ones getting abused are often the ones that get in trouble for fighting back."

"It will be part of the investigation. But I would bet my life that she would never have raised her hand against him."

"If he was hurting her little girl, I wish she would have," she mumbled, and Brent grunted his agreement. It was a point of contention with him when the innocent weren't protected; especially by the adult that could put a stop to the abuse in any form.

"Yeah, I think we all do," I said softly, more to calm Brent's rising anger than anything. I had spent the last several years being the one to protect him, first from his family, then from the memories that plagued him. The only thing that settled his demons fully, though, was the satisfaction he found in ending the abuse of other innocents.

"When is your shift over?"

Casey looked up at me, giving me her pretty blue eyes fully for the first time since I slipped into my side of the booth. "Oh, actually, I don't know. I forgot to ask Grace how long she wanted me to work today." She looked around the diner as if she would find the answer written on the walls.

Brent's voice was gruff from the anger he was still holding back at the previous conversation. "Regardless of when, just call me when you are ready to leave. I'll make sure I can pick you up, okay?"

"Are you sure? I don't want to take you away from work."

He finally smiled. The tension in his muscles relaxing, no longer poised to attack a lawyer that we both knew had already disappeared and wasn't coming back. "I'm here for you any time, dollface. And if I can't get away, I'm sure Mr. Detective over there would jump at the chance."

Her face flushed as she looked from him to me and back again. "You guys are so nice to me."

"You are worth it," I assured her and pushed my plate away. "But we are both serious. Whenever you need us, all you have to do is call." I gave her a wink and reached across the table to capture her hand, giving it a gentle squeeze just to feel her skin under my palm. "Consider us yours to command," I told her. If I could, I would put her in my pocket and carry her around all day just to have her near.

She ducked her head, staring down at her lap again, and tucked a golden strand of hair that had escaped her ponytail behind her ear. She pulled ever so slightly on the hand I had captured, and I let it go with great reluctance. "Thank you." Her words were mumbled so low I could barely hear her over the din of the restaurant, but I couldn't miss the rapid beating of her pulse at her bared throat. Miss Casey Smith was deeply affected by the both of us. I hadn't felt like this in a long time.

We had promised each other we would take it slow, allow her to get to know us, to become comfortable before bombarding her with our desires. We had also promised that we would show her in other ways that we would be interested in more. Interested in her–as a woman. I figured we were doing a pretty decent job at both.

It would be so easy to just tell her what we wanted. But Casey wasn't ready for what we wanted. She was still obviously on edge. Even now, I could see her looking at the door and holding her breath as each person entered, as if she were expecting something terrible to happen.

I cocked my head and studied her carefully. I hated this game we were playing, even if it wasn't one that intended to harm anyone, but I couldn't help but wish it were that easy. Maybe it wasn't us that she would be unsure of. It occurred to me that there was a possibility that she would be more open to a relationship with us than we first thought, especially after her reaction to the kiss Brent and I shared. Instead, maybe we had to be more concerned with her being ready to run away at the first sign of danger. A girl like her would think she was doing the right thing by running away. To protect us instead of allowing us to protect her. It was something to give more thought to later.

I took one more sip of my drink and slid it back next to my plate. "I have to get going."

Casey practically jumped to her feet, sliding out of the booth and smoothing her hands down her jeans in nervous agitation. "Okay. Thanks for eating lunch with me." She looked over at Brent, who was sliding to the edge of the seat. He was face-height with her tits, staring at them hungrily, as if he hadn't just devoured a hamburger and a full plate of fries. "Both of you," she stammered out and stepped back to allow him to stand up.

I put my hand on the small of her back to steady her and marveled at how my palm seemed to fill the expanse of her waist. She couldn't step back without colliding with me, and she wasn't able to get out of the way as Brent stood to his full height, looking down at her as his broad chest brushed against hers.

Over her shoulder, I could see her nipples pebble at the contact through the thick material of her shirt and bra. I had to close my eyes and bite back the groan that wanted to escape.

"Was your lunch okay over here?" The sweet, cheery voice of my mother was enough to send an ice cold bucket of reality over my rising lust. My hand jerked as I reluctantly pulled it away from the warmth of her back. I turned to look at my mother and gave her a cocky grin before bending, kissing her cheek.

"Lunch was perfect as always, of course."

"Best in the state," Brent added as he kissed her other cheek.

She laughed at our antics and waved her hands at us, shooing us like we were teenagers trying to raid the kitchen while she was making cookies again. "Get out of here and get back to work." She looked at Casey, who was grinning. I loved that she got along with my mom so well, and Mom obviously had a fondness for her. I hoped it would be enough to help convince her to stay when the time came that she'd be ready to run. "Why don't you take the rest of the day off, sweetheart?

"Oh, are you sure?" She looked around the restaurant, which had mostly cleared out after the lunch rush. "I feel like I didn't do much today."

"Are you kidding? You were a huge help. Not having to be constantly refilling coffee and getting drinks made it feel like I was almost on vacation." She nudged at Casey's arm. "Go on. I'm sure your feet are tired from doing all that running around today. I remember what it was like when I first got started waitressing."

"Well, if you're sure," Casey hedged, obviously not wanting to disappoint Mom.

"I'm sure. Why don't you come back tomorrow when the boys are heading into work? We can do the same thing. Then, when you are ready, we can discuss longer days."

"Okay." She reached around her back and plucked the strings of her small apron, untying it and folding it in her hands. She offered it to Mom, who took it with a warm smile.

"I'll put this under the counter for you to use when you get in tomorrow."

"Thanks." Casey turned to us as we stood waiting. "Umm, will one of you give me a ride?" She was biting her lip, hesitation written clearly all over her.

We looked at each other, a silent conversation happening between our eyes before I turned back to our girl. "We already told you, you never have to worry. We will always be there for you, sugar. I'll give you a ride."

"I'll just go grab my bag from the back, then." She hitched her thumb in the direction of the staff room, which was nothing more than a small table with a shelf of cubbies for any belongings they had.

"I'll be waiting," I assured her, grinning as she ducked her head and hurried off through the swinging door.

Mom gave us both waning looks before smiling at us and heading behind the counter to put Casey's apron away and grab the coffeepot for more refills. Brent tossed several bills on the table, and we headed outside together.

"Tonight, we leave the door open." He grunted as we walked the few feet to where my Mustang was parked.

I grinned wickedly. "We left the door open last night." And little Miss Casey went straight to her room to get off on what she heard. There was no mistaking the sound of her muffled cry when she came last night. The walls aren't thin, but they aren't soundproofed either.

"Tonight, the door stays open... wider." His eyes danced with whatever mischief was playing out in his head.

"And we leave a light on," I added.

"Perfect."

Hearing the door open, we both looked to see Casey jogging toward us, her full tits bouncing under the diner t-shirt. Watching her, like a pack of wolves tracking our prey. Brent groaned low in his throat, sounding more like he was the wounded animal instead of the predator. He turned to me and grabbed me behind the neck, and slammed his hot mouth down on mine for a short, rough kiss. I knew we would both be on edge until we were finally able to claim her as our own.

I only hoped we would survive each other until then.

Thirteen

CASEY

I LOOKED DOWN at the small pile of dirty clothes. With a sigh, I gathered everything up in my arms and carried them down the hall to the laundry room. After only wearing the same few shirts and jeans for weeks, I was fairly sick of them. I had been able to take advantage of long layovers throughout my journey to make use of nearby laundromats, so at least I hadn't been wearing the same *dirty* clothes the whole time. But I was ready to trash them all and buy new things. Unfortunately, that would have been wasteful, and I needed to save all the cash I could.

After shoving them into the washer, I wandered into the office Ethan had told me I could use. I sat down in the comfortable chair and hesitantly hovered my hand over the mouse, not sure if I wanted to know the progress of the manhunt for the Castle Killer. If they had caught him, that meant I could go home. On the other hand, if he were still evading the FBI, well, I suppose it wouldn't be a terrible hardship to continue hiding out here.

Finally, I grabbed the mouse and opened up a browser, clicking on the search bar. With mechanical movements, I typed in *Castle Killer* and paused for a second before hitting enter. Instantly, multiple headlines popped up, making me swallow hard. I clicked on the first one and almost immediately wanted to throw up.

The picture they used of me was my high school graduation photo. It wasn't a bad picture, but I don't know why I hadn't expected it. With no known pictures of the man who was responsible for multiple murders, it was only common sense that they would plaster the pictures of his victims instead. As the only surviving victim, I made for a sensational story.

I stared, unblinking, at eighteen-year-old me with a mixture of dismay and horror. I didn't want my picture out there. I didn't want my name linked with his at all. It was making national news, and that meant that the people who knew me would soon know my story. With my chest tight and my eyes burning, I began to read what they had written.

Casey Rivers, age 22, is the only known survivor of the infamous Castle Killer. Currently, the whereabouts of the serial killer are unknown. The Castle Killer is known to have kidnapped, tortured, and murdered at least seven women between the ages of 20 and 25.

Casey Rivers was found, naked and covered in blood, wandering outside the dwelling of a man known as John Greene. A passing driver, Ann Benton, saw the young woman and stopped to help when Casey collapsed. It is known that Casey was missing for five days before escaping the killer. She was traumatized and dehydrated but otherwise healthy. The same day she was discovered wandering the streets, Megan Handford, also age 22, was found dead in a field on the outskirts of the once peaceful small coastal town of Castle Grove, California.

It has been determined that John Greene is not his real name, and sources say that he never showed his face to anyone. His identity remains a mystery.

Casey Rivers has not been available for comment. A source close to the family informed the media that she has not been seen for weeks and is presumed to be in hiding.

I couldn't read anymore. I closed out the browser and pushed away from the desk, making the chair fly backward. Without stopping to fix the chair, I ran to the bathroom and slid to the floor in front of the toilet, and heaved until there was nothing left in my stomach.

When I was finally able to catch my breath, I stumbled over to the shower and flipped on the water as hot as it would go. Struggling out of my clothes and whimpering when my shaking fingers had trouble with the button of my jeans. Finally, I got them unbuttoned and stumbled, trying to kick the jeans off, getting tangled over the shoes I had forgotten to take off first.

With a sob, I collapsed on the floor. I had to pull the jeans back up to reach my shoes, but I finally managed to completely untangle myself. Using the sink, I pulled myself to my feet, my muscles weak and barely holding me upright. With trembling knees, I stepped numbly into the shower, barely feeling the heat of the water as it rained down over my head.

As I looked down at my body, all I could see was the blood that had coated me that day. With another sob, I grabbed the body wash sitting in the corner and poured it into my shaking hands. In my haste, I dropped the bottle, and it made a loud thud when it hit the shower floor, startling me all over again. I furiously scrubbed at my flesh. I would never not see the blood. Megan's blood.

There hadn't been a time I slept since that day that I didn't dream of slipping through the rapidly cooling puddles, knowing that a woman had died within feet of where I had lain curled up in a ball. I had listened as she took her last breaths and would never get the sounds of her screams out of my head.

With heavy, wracking sobs, I fell to the shower floor and cried. It had been so long since I'd had the privacy to cry. When I first came home from the hospital, I had cried almost nonstop for days. It wasn't until I had seen what my tears were doing to my mom that I finally forced myself to hold it in.

But now I was alone and the whole ordeal came back to me, flooding my mind with every horrific, gruesome detail. I didn't know when it would ever stop. I just wanted it to stop. I didn't want those other women to be dead. I didn't want to know that Megan had died next to me. *Goddamn* that asshole for doing this to us.

I couldn't tell how long I stayed lying huddled on the shower floor. All I knew is that by the time my emotions had settled enough for me to stop crying, I was exhausted. I was also shivering in the cold water that was still raining down on me, the heated water long since depleted.

I struggled to my feet, my teeth chattering so hard I was afraid I would chip a tooth. My arms and legs were covered in goosebumps, and I wanted nothing more at that moment than to sink into a hot bath to warm up my insides, but I had royally screwed that up for myself. Of course, I wouldn't even need to warm up if I hadn't laid there like the emotionally wrung-out girl I was.

I moaned my frustration. At myself, my situation, and the cold that seemed to have rooted itself deep in my bones. I grabbed the nearest towel, and with numb hands, I rubbed the towel over my body as well as I could, my fingers stiff from the cold. The quaking in every inch of my body made it difficult to wipe the moisture away properly. Eventually, I gave up completely, just held the towel against my front, and stumbled as quickly as I could down the hall and into my bedroom.

I clumsily wrapped the already damp towel around my wet hair and collapsed onto the mattress. With another groan, I reached behind me, blindly searching for the edge of the blanket before finally finding it and pulling it tight across my shivering body.

It took a few more minutes for my body to calm down, and once the tremors subsided, my body edged itself toward sleep. I clenched my jaw tightly against the unwelcome and persistent chattering of my teeth. More tears welled with the intrusive thoughts that I would have to pack up and leave soon.

There was no future here for me. Not really. The only men I had ever really been interested in were already taken—with each other. I finally drifted off to sleep, knowing I wouldn't be able to watch them day in and day out and not have my heart crumble bit by bit a little more every day until there was nothing left of it.

***

The sound of my name being called out had me bolting upright in bed. My eyes felt swollen, and my body was still chilled. It took me running my hand through my hair to brush the tangled strands away from my face to remember where I was and what I had been doing prior to collapsing onto the bed in a state of depression. I ran my hands over my face, trying to wipe away the memories of what I had read in Ethan's office, when the door to my room opened.

I looked up to see the two gorgeous men that I was half in love with staring at me. I watched as their eyes changed quickly from looks of happiness to looks of concern, then finally to looks of such intense desire that I had to squeeze my thighs together to push back the sudden need I felt to pull them closer.

Shaking my head in an effort to push back the need I was feeling, I blinked up at them and noticed their eyes were laser focused, not on my face, but on my body. I glanced down, finding that the sheet had pooled around my waist, and my breasts were on full display to the room. With burning hot cheeks, I grabbed the sheet and yanked it up to cover my nudity.

"I, uh, I guess I fell asleep," I finished lamely as the guys continued to stare as if spellbound, like they could still see the shape of my breasts even though they were covered. I glanced down again to double-check. My nipples were hard as diamonds and clearly poking through the thin sheet. I cleared my throat.

Ethan was the first to blink, coming out of whatever fog he was in, while Brent just seemed to grow hungrier. It was as if the sight of my body had made him ravenous, and it was me that was on the menu.

"Shit, sorry, sugar. We should have knocked." He backed out of the room, having to grab Brent by the arm and yank him back with him. "We'll let you get dressed. Dinner will be ready in a little bit."

I started to say that I wasn't hungry, but the door closed with a loud click, cutting off my words and taking away the green eyes that said he wanted to rip the sheet off me. If I didn't know any better, I'd say that the two men were attracted to me. And more than just a little bit. The thought of what it could mean for their committed relationship, for me, for all of us if it were true, sent arrows of electricity through my veins.

Fourteen

BRENT

"FUCK!" I cursed as I ran my burnt hand under the cold water at the kitchen sink. I couldn't get my mind off the beautiful girl that had been haunting my every thought since I'd first laid eyes on her. I didn't know how much longer I could wait now that I'd had a glimpse of her succulent tits burned into my retinas. I knew it couldn't be much longer.

I shut off the water and dried my hands, ignoring the pain. I was having a hard time focusing on the stove, which led me to be uncharacteristically careless. At least I hadn't burned dinner. The steaks were grilled to perfection, and the zucchini was ready for our plates. The only thing left was to check on the rice.

As I stirred the rice to fluff it up after boiling, Ethan walked in with a hard look on his face. I threw down the serving spoon and gave him my full attention.

"What is it?" I asked on high alert as I braced myself for whatever bad news he had.

He pulled open the refrigerator door and reached in for a bottle of beer, unscrewing the cap and tossing it in the trash before taking a large gulp. I was becoming impatient as he took his sweet fucking time when he finally opened his mouth to speak, his words low to ensure they wouldn't go beyond the kitchen.

"I know who she is and what she's running from."

I stood there, waiting, ready to force him to talk, when he finally cursed and rubbed the back of his neck. I growled in frustration. "If you don't tell me right fucking now..."

"She's a survivor of a serial killer. The *only* survivor."

All I could do was stare at the only person I had ever loved before Casey had come into our lives. My mind was having a tough time trying to come to terms with what I had just heard. "A serial..."

He slammed his beer bottle down onto the table, making it foam up, the bubbles stopping at the lip of the bottle before disintegrating back down into the liquid. "Yeah, babe. A mother fucking serial killer."

I turned away from him and stared out of the kitchen window over the sink. Thoughts of what I was and the things I did were running through my mind. I looked down at my shaking hands and imagined them covered in blood. Her blood. I turned to leave, my feet taking long strides to get out of the kitchen. To leave the house. I didn't have an idea as to where I was going to go. Too many thoughts were tumbling through my mind too quickly for me to latch on to even one of them.

I needed to get away. To get away from her. The only constant thought was to find the person who had tried to murder her and show him what a real serial killer could do. But most of all, I wanted to get away so that my stain couldn't infect her. *A fucking serial killer survivor.* She would hate me.

"Stop!" His fierce growl had me pausing for a beat before reaching the door. I grabbed my truck keys and had my hand on the doorknob, ready to leave, when he grabbed me by the back of my clean t-shirt and slammed me up against the door.

"Don't you fucking *dare* walk out that door," he hissed in my ear. "Whoever had her is nothing like you, you fucking idiot."

I grunted harshly, my daze turning into a blinding rage in a heartbeat. "How could you say that? I am *exactly* like that. She ran away from someone exactly like me." Already the rage was being overtaken by something I could only describe as utter pain. It began to rip through me as I kept imagining what horrors she might have gone through. "It could have been me," I whispered.

He pressed his body solidly against mine, pressing me hard against the wood. "She *needs* you. She needs us. Both of us." He choked on the words. "He murdered seven other women just like her. He tortured them before leaving their naked bodies to be found. For no other reason than he is a sick fuck that gets off hurting innocents."

He slammed me back against the door, his words ringing in my ears even though he was whispering them through clenched teeth. "Does that sound like you? Does it?"

I choked, unable to answer him. My thoughts drifted to the bodies I had fed to his uncle's pigs in order to hide the evidence of my kills. I thought of the pieces that I couldn't feed to them, how I dissolved them in lye, burned them, then mixed what was left in the concrete I poured at my job sites. "No, I don't leave my victims to be found," I whispered.

"You fucking idiot. You don't have *victims*," He spat out the word harshly. "They are monsters that you take away from *their* victims. You do something that law enforcement can't when our fucking hands are tied. You *save* innocent lives. You don't take them."

Our heavy breaths were loud in the foyer as he growled the words in my ear. "I don't—"

"Shut up. Just shut up! Listen to me, Brent. That sweet girl in there, the one that we are both falling in love with? That girl we want to make ours? She needs us both. He is still out there, and he could be looking for her right now."

His words had me stiffening. Every muscle in my body went hard as stone, preparing to unleash the devil on the man that wanted to take her away from us. From me. I could take care of him. I could stop him from ever breathing air again, from hurting another living soul. It was me that could end him. Ethan would have to follow the law and take him into custody, where he would continue to live, to breathe, to eat, and to sleep. Where he could continue to want our girl. He would never stop. But I could stop him.

"Tell me what you know."

We walked back into the kitchen, and he pushed me down into a chair. He grabbed a second beer out of the fridge, uncapped it, and handed it to me. I gratefully took a large swallow and then a second as I willed my hands to stop shaking. I clenched my fist and closed my eyes as I tried to forget the blood I had imagined coating them just a few minutes ago.

He sat down heavily and sighed. "There was an article that she had read on my computer. It had a condensed story about her, her name, the town she was from..." he trailed off, staring hard at his bottle. "How long she had been kept. Five days, Brent. Five fucking days. She was found outside his house naked, covered in blood. She was dehydrated but otherwise healthy." He snorted. "Otherwise, healthy. That's what the article said. As if not being tortured meant she was healthy. Fuck! It explains so much."

"Her reaction inside the store."

He nodded. "The way she always seems to be watching; always looking around."

"How she kept her eyes on the door when she first got to town. Her back to the wall."

"Yeah, she was trying to stay safe, scared that he would follow her. The thing is, though, she doesn't know who he is. No one does."

"If he were to walk right up to her, she wouldn't even know it was him." An icy chill ran up my spine.

"She needs us more than we ever thought."

My mind circled back around. "But if she finds out what I am..."

"*If* she finds out what you have done, we will make her understand that you are nothing like him. You protect the innocent by removing the monsters from their lives."

I didn't believe for a single second that it would be that easy. If she found out, it would send her running. I couldn't let that happen, but at that moment, I couldn't think of any way to stop it other than to tie her to the bed. I closed my eyes and breathed through the thought.

A quiet voice spoke up from the entrance to the kitchen, quiet and hesitant. "Is everything alright?"

We both straightened up and pasted smiles on our faces. I turned in my chair and caught sight of her dressed in a baggy t-shirt that she had to have pillaged from one of our drawers. My smile widened and turned genuine as she fiddled with the hem.

"I hope you don't mind. I washed all my clothes earlier but fell asleep before I put them in the dryer."

"Of course not, sugar." Ethan stood up and walked over to her taking her hand, and leading her over to the table. She took the seat that had become hers since she arrived in our home, just yesterday. "You can take whatever you need from either of us whenever you need."

I stood up and grabbed the plates, set them at the table, and turned back to serve up the meal. "I think you look lovely in our clothes, dollface. You can raid my drawers anytime." My wink had her cheeks pink in the next heartbeat, and I had to hold back a chuckle at the way she blushed for us so quickly.

She picked up her fork and fiddled with it before sinking it into the white rice. "I thought I heard a commotion while I was in the laundry room. Is everything okay?"

I held up my hand, which was still a bit red from when I had grabbed the metal handle of the pan without thinking. "I just burned myself a bit, is all. No big deal."

She dropped her fork and reached over to take my large hand in her small one and straightened my fingers out so she could see the redness for herself. As she fussed over it, a warmth spread through me. Until Ethan and his family, I had never known a soft touch. My family had never cared about me before, other than to call me names. It was more likely that I would catch a fist to the gut or a slap to the face than ever have my mom or dad care if I had hurt myself. Seeing this small woman so concerned over a minor injury was enough to have my heart melt at her feet. I would do anything to protect her. Now and forever.

After a thorough inspection, she finally decided that I was going to live, and we went back to eating. We ate in companionable silence, with the occasional light topic coming up in conversation. Once we finished the meal, she insisted that she clean up, shooing the two of us to the living room to watch whatever game was on the TV.

While she was humming softly in the kitchen, we turned towards each other, and I let Ethan pull me to his side. My emotions were still raw. It would take a bit to settle me. That, or a hard fuck. He knew me well enough to give me what I needed, and my dick grew hard in anticipation. It would be a wild night ahead of us, and I planned to make the most of it. We were going to put on a show for our girl. By the time the night was over, she would be panting, ready to take what she'd know we wanted to give her.

I wasn't surprised when she walked out of the kitchen and announced that she was going to bed. I hated that she kept thanking us for our hospitality. I wanted her to feel like this was her home, too. As she walked down the hall and out of sight, I clenched my jaw.

Ethan's hand turned my face towards his. "Come on. Let's head to our room." He stood up and clicked the remote, turning off the game that we hadn't been watching. He stood and held out his hand. I batted it away, the frustration over everything becoming too much for me to accept his more gentle gestures.

"Yeah, let's go to bed," I snarled. I stood and pushed past him, stalking down the hall, passing by her closed door.

Fifteen

CASEY

THEY KNEW.

I didn't know how, but they knew. Maybe they had seen it on the news or read it on the internet. Or maybe Ethan had seen it in the search history on his computer. Brent tried to play off the argument I had heard by saying he had burnt his hand, but it was easy to see there was much more to it than that.

I sat cross-legged on the bed and went over my options. Did I stay? Did I go? If I left, I would have to continue running, and I would never find another safe place to land while I waited for the killer to be found. If I stayed, I could be placing these men in danger. It was obvious they would be able to handle the killer if it came down to it. I was sure that with Ethan's experience as a cop and Brent's job as a construction worker, they would both be able to protect themselves. Plus, they had each other. Could I allow them to protect me, too?

My mind spun round and round. I knew I wouldn't be getting any sleep, and that pissed me off. I hated the asshole that had done this to me. I was a twenty-two-year-old woman that had been content with her life. I had friends, a job I enjoyed, and a family that loved me. *How dare he take all that away from me.*

I closed my eyes and took several deep breaths, willing away the pain. I wished, more than anything at that moment, that I could talk to my mother. I wanted her to hold me and smooth my hair down the way she used to when I was a little girl. I wish I had a phone I could call her on. But of course, I couldn't. I couldn't put my parents in danger. I feared that neither I, nor anyone I loved, would ever be safe again as long as the Castle Killer was still alive. Even if he were in prison, I would always worry, looking over my shoulder, wondering if he could somehow get to me and finish what he started.

A groan and a loud thump had my eyes flying open. I was ready to bolt from the bed when another groan had me freezing. That wasn't a groan of pain. Or not completely. There was a lot of desire filling that groan. Were they having sex? I could hear them so much clearer than last night.

My breathing sped up as my mind raced with the possibilities of what they could be doing to each other. What I wanted them to do. I wrestled with my conscience as I considered what to do next. If I left the room to get a drink of water as I had done the night before and just happened to see them fucking each other, that would be their fault for not closing their door all the way, right?

I bit my lip, trying to force my limbs to stay in place, but my curiosity and lust won out. I slowly slipped off the bed and tip-toed to the door, placing my ear against the cold wood while my heart raced in my ribcage with anticipation. I couldn't make out the sounds I was hearing. It didn't sound like rhythmic movement the way I would have imagined if one of them were taking the other. Maybe they weren't going to actually have sex at all.

I slowly turned the doorknob, wincing at the slight squeaking of the metal as it turned. I pulled the door open a crack, but it was impossible to see from the small amount it was open. I would have to actually step into the hallway, taking the chance that they would see me and stop whatever they were doing. I pulled it open further, leaned my torso out, and glanced down the end of the hall to see their door was wide open. My eyes widened with the realization that they weren't even attempting to protect their privacy.

I could see Brent sitting on the edge of their huge bed, his hand gripping Ethan's hair tightly as Ethan knelt on the floor. They were both completely naked. Ethan's back was to me, his muscles on full display, shifting and bunching with his movements. Glancing lower, I could see where his back tapered into a narrow waist, and his naked ass was perched on his feet. From under his ass, I could just make out his heavy balls hanging, swinging from whatever he was doing to Brent. I mean, I knew what he was doing. I wasn't an idiot. But the movements looked like he was doing more than just giving head to his boyfriend. It looked like he was jacking himself off at the same time.

My skin heated and flushed as I watched, desire pooling in my gut and flaring out to every other part of me. It was a magnificent sight to see. A strong, virile man kneeling in front of another. Brent seemed to shove him down and hold him there by the tight grip he had on his hair, and sloppy gagging noises filled the silence.

Brent let up the pressure, and Ethan's head came up. He growled something that sounded like 'fucker', and Brent chuckled darkly down at him. There was a lamp on in the room, casting shadows at the end of the bed but lighting up enough of the room that I didn't have to strain to watch.

I felt like the worst kind of peeping tom and was about to back away into my room when the men suddenly stood up. My breath caught, and I hoped that they wouldn't be able to see me in the darkness of the hallway. At that moment, I couldn't have moved if I tried. My feet were rooted to the spot as I watched Brent grab Ethan roughly and all but throw him face down over the end of the bed.

Only seconds later, Brent's shapely ass thrust forward, and Ethan let out a deep, muffled groan. Their actions looked violent, but they both seemed to enjoy every movement, every second of their time together. The one time I had attempted to have sex when I was sixteen was a fumbling mess, neither me nor the guy really knowing what we were doing. The only thing that had stopped us from going all the way was the condom tearing and me becoming so terrified at the potential results of unprotected sex. Our night had ended with me giving the guy a sloppy blowjob and me feeling nauseous from the taste of his sperm when he came into my mouth. I had to jump up from the bed and find the nearest toilet to spit into. It had been traumatizing enough that I hadn't wanted to repeat it again for quite a while. Unfortunately, any dating I had done after high school hadn't produced enough desire to want to go home with the guy.

But these two were obviously in sync with each other. They looked like they were performing a choreographed dance. As rough as it looked, they weren't hurting each other. From the grunts and moans they were making, it sounded like they were enjoying every second.

Without realizing it, I had slowly crept down the dark hallway, inching my way closer for a better view. I stopped several feet from their door, plastering myself to the wall, and tried to regulate my breathing. I felt wet and achy, wanting to touch myself as I watched. I wanted *them* to touch me. I would have thought their roughness would be a turn off; instead, it drove my hunger higher until I finally slipped my fingers into the waistband of my loose shorts hidden underneath the t-shirt I had stolen from the basket full of clean clothes I had found in the laundry room earlier.

I bit my lip hard to hold in my gasp as my fingertip made contact with my throbbing clit. I watched as Brent's muscular ass pounded into Ethan's. I started moving my finger to the same rhythm, meeting him stroke for stroke. The pace was making me ready to come faster than I had ever come before.

I watched in fascination as Brent let go of one of Ethan's hips and reached underneath his abs. His arm muscles tensed and flexed with his movements. My fantasies had me thinking of ways that I could take care of Ethan as Brent fucked him. The thought of tasting him made my mouth water, and I knew that if given the chance, I would take him there. I didn't know if I'd be able to handle it better than I had before, but I was willing to give it a try.

Brent's hips started losing their rhythm, and I watched, fascinated, as he got closer to coming. I knew I would fall over the edge as soon as he did. My legs were shaking, and my breaths were heaving with shallow, quiet pants, trying my hardest to hold off from the orgasm that was barreling down on me hard and fast.

I knew he was about to blow, and I forced my eyes to stay open, not wanting to miss a second when every atom in my body froze.

"You like my hand around my dick? How do you think it would feel to have dollface in front of you, taking her hot pussy while I pound my come into your ass, huh?"

Ethan's long, drawn-out groan of agreement was enough to have my hand slipping out of my shorts as my clit throbbed in protest. What was he saying? Did they want me as much as I wanted them? My mind was racing. Even so, I couldn't stop watching, and my hands pressed into the hard wall behind me. Did they leave their door open on purpose just so they could put on a show? For me?

"One day, she will be right where we want her. Both of us taking her at the same time." Brent groaned so deep in his throat it sounded painful. "Making her ours." With those last words, he thrust deep one last time and grunted up at the ceiling. At the same time, Ethan groaned into the bedding.

Oh, my god. I had to go. Now, or I would risk orgasming in the hallway in front of their room. I slinked back down the hall to my room, my eyes not leaving the sweaty, heaving men. The last thing I saw as I pulled my head in was Brent's neck turning, the side of his face coming into view.

I quietly closed the door and leaned against it, panting like I had just finished a marathon. He knew I was there. He knew I had watched everything they had done to each other. Was it all just for show? Maybe it was some kind of act? Brent wanting to prove something to me? I didn't know what except for maybe not to spy on intimate moments. But maybe he actually meant the words. They had both seemed to have gotten off to the images that Brent had painted.

I crept over to my bed, not daring to make a sound. As soon as I was under the covers, I pulled my shorts off, kicking them off my feet and shoving them out of the bed until they were no longer in my way. I spread my legs wide and closed my eyes. Everything I had just witnessed replayed in my mind. I touched my hard clit and whimpered at the sensitivity there.

With the rhythm of Brent's pounding hips playing like a movie behind my eyelids, I restarted the same momentum as I had in the hallway. Only, in my mind, I changed things to match what he had said. Suddenly, I was between them, one in my pussy, one in my ass, as their hands touched every part of me.

I whimpered and slammed my legs shut as they tensed, trapping my hand as I furiously rubbed my clit. The orgasm came so hard and fast that I couldn't stop the scream from tearing out of my throat. I clamped a hand over my mouth, but it was too late. I had let the guys know that I had just come while lying just down the hallway. We all knew what we all desired.

I turned onto my side as aftershocks rippled through me. My leg was sore from how hard my muscles had tensed up. I had never come so hard in my life. Somehow, though, I knew that what the guys could do to me would make that orgasm feel like nothing. Even though it was probably wrong and could maybe be considered cheating, the seed had been planted deep. If the guys wanted me like they seemed to tonight, I didn't think I would ever be able to turn them down. It would be the experience of a lifetime, something I had only read about and thought only existed for women who were lucky enough to find guys to agree to it.

I thought about the guys and how they were in a deeply committed relationship with each other. I didn't want to come between them other than in bed. Would it cause problems? I wouldn't be able to stand it if it broke anything between them. Was it really cheating if they both agreed to it?

I fell into a deep, exhausted sleep as the what-ifs, both good and bad, played through my dreams.

Sixteen

ETHAN

I GROANED as I woke up, my ass sore from the pounding I had taken the night before and immediately horny when I remembered why. Brent had been insatiable, knowing that Casey had been watching us the entire time. Even though the worry had crept in afterward when he'd caught a glimpse of her face as she backed away, horrified at what she'd done. If she would have hung around just a bit longer, she would have known we were okay with it. Hell, we were both more than ready to invite her into our room and our bed.

Too soon, Ethan. I berated myself as a reminder that we were playing for keeps. She was our end game, and everything we were doing was to ensure that once we had her, she would be there to stay. Forever.

I stretched and turned under the tangled sheets, curving my naked body around Brent's hard one. Running a hand down his arm and down to his chest, reveling in his muscles that were no less incredible while he was at rest. Then I felt his pectoral tense, and I grinned, knowing he was awake.

He turned over, taking my hand in his and kissing it with a sleepy grin, his blond hair in a mess and covering his forehead. The sight of him like that, all sleep rumpled and relaxed, always made my heart skip a beat. This man had been mine since we were barely more than boys. He had been the one thing that I could always count on to be there with me through every stage of life. Helping get me to where I was today, just like I was always there for him.

"Hey." His rough voice sent shivers down my back and a tingle to my balls. My morning wood jerked, brushing against his.

"Hey," I grinned as I reached up to brush a lock of hair from his eyes. "Sleep well?"

He grunted as he leaned forward, crossing the few inches that separated our faces. His soft, closed-mouth kiss had my heart doing a little tango in my chest as it sped up for a second. He would never stop exciting me and making me sigh in contentment. The only thing that could make my life better than having this man by my side would be having our sweet girl in between us.

He brushed one more soft kiss against my lips before sitting up, exposing his hard dick as the sheet dropped into his lap. I eyed it, the hunger never far away, but rolled over so I could rise, too. With our busy schedules, weekdays didn't leave much time for morning activities. As we both headed into the bathroom and took our places at our individual sinks to brush our teeth, I noticed Brent looking down at the counter, a thoughtful look on his face.

I walked over to the toilet to take a piss with my toothbrush in my mouth and asked what he was thinking about, my words coming out garbled due to the brush and foam. He looked back at me as I flushed. He spit out the toothpaste and then rinsed. He headed to the toilet before finally speaking, gesturing to the double sinks in front of us.

"I could probably special order a triple sink. The counter is long enough to easily fit a third sink. No one would have to wait their turn." He turned to the large shower that was undoubtedly already big enough for a third body. He looked at me over his shoulder. "I'll put in the order today. I can have the plumbing done to add the extra sink once it comes in."

I nodded thoughtfully as I spread shaving foam over my jaw, watching him step into the shower through the mirror. Neither one of us spoke for a while as we got ready to head to work. Standing in the bedroom, I watched as he continued to look around with an assessing eye, and I knew that he was figuring out all the ways that he could make changes to add her into our home.

We hadn't prepared because it had never been a thing we had expected to happen. Yes, we had talked about it occasionally. Since we were teenagers, we had talked to each other about how we knew we were both attracted to girls. It had never been a secret between us. If anything, our relationship had been brutally honest from the beginning. It was how I had known about the demons that burned darkly inside Brent.

Being attracted to women and talking about the possibility of having one join us in a relationship was always a distant, almost fantasy-type dream. In all this time, we hadn't encountered a single woman we would have even considered it with. Of course, there were women over the years that thought she would be the one to tempt either Brent or me away from each other. There had even been a couple who asked to spend the night between us, but we had never taken them up on it. Not until this little slip of a thing came into our town with her big blue eyes filled with pain and scared of her own shadow.

I knew Brent had jumped in with both feet, even if I had been wary for a scant few minutes. Seeing him looking for ways to make Casey feel like she was truly a part of our lives had warmth spreading through my chest.

"Why don't you leave your shirt off for breakfast," I suggested casually. If we wanted to keep up the momentum, we needed to show our girl what we had to offer her.

He looked down at the t-shirt he was holding with his company logo on it. He had at least ten of those things. He looked back up at me. "Have you ever cooked bacon with a bare chest?" He raised an amused eyebrow at me.

I chuckled. "Why don't you make pancakes, then? I'm sure Casey would enjoy the view as much as I will."

He cocked his head as he thought about it. "I could do that." He nodded and tossed the end of the shirt over his shoulder, holding on to it and heading for the door. He stopped and looked back at me as I buttoned up my black dress shirt and began tucking it into my unbuttoned slacks. "But tonight, you get to eat dinner in boxers."

I laughed as his chuckle faded down the hall.

We were drinking our coffee when Casey came into the room, her eyes planted firmly on the floor with that irresistible shade of pink covering her cheeks. Yeah, our girl was still embarrassed by what she had done last night. It was obvious she had enjoyed it, though. Her muffled screams of pleasure hadn't been hidden any more than her quiet groans had been the night before. She was probably feeling out of sorts, thinking that spying was the worst kind of betrayal. It made me feel bad that we had put her in the position to begin with.

I stood up and made her a cup of coffee the way she seemed to prefer. I made sure to run my hand across her shoulder, my thumb brushing the soft skin above the neckline of her shirt as I walked by. Her little shiver and the goosebumps that rose on her arms were like a balm to my horniness for her. Before I sat back down, I leaned down and kissed her cheek, lingering there long enough to inhale her sweet scent.

"Morning, sugar. How did you sleep?"

The pink that had covered her cheeks when she walked in darkened with my question. I watched her squeeze her hands in her lap before lifting one to her cup. The little tremble couldn't be missed, but Brent and I pretended not to see as she brought the cup to her plush lips and mumbled behind the mug's rim.

"Good, thank you." She cleared her throat and looked like she was about to say something else when Brent took that moment to stand up, bringing her attention to his naked chest. Her breath seemed to catch, and she stuttered. "I—uh, I…" She took a deep breath and let it out slowly. Her head turned to me, and I couldn't miss the way her eyes kept darting to the side as Brent made her a plate of pancakes, slathering butter over the top and pouring a generous amount of syrup. "I was wondering if there was a clothing store near the diner that I could walk to after my shift is over?"

I couldn't stop myself from reaching out, taking her hand from her lap and gently squeezing it. "There is a store a few blocks over. But it's supposed to rain pretty hard today. I can drive you so you don't have to walk."

She looked over to the window. "Oh!" It was dark, with ominous gray clouds covering the sky. "That looks bad."

Brent shrugged as he sat back down after placing a fork directly into Casey's hand and kissing her cheek the same way I had. "Storms can get pretty violent around here." He gave her a smirk. "Don't worry, dollface. You have two big, strong men that will protect you."

She tore her eyes away from the storm brewing outside and looked at him with worry. "We don't really get violent storms back home."

It was the first time she even hinted at where she had come from. I decided to take the chance to let her know we now knew her story. What the media had to say about it, anyway. "Back in California?"

Her eyes got wide as they flew to me, then back to Brent. When she looked back at me again, her shoulders slumped. "You know."

"Sugar, look at me."

She raised her eyes from the table and turned to me. Her tears broke my heart, and I stood up from my chair to squat down next to her, invading her space so she could see every bit of sincerity inside me.

"You went through something horrific."

She blinked, and a tear escaped her watery eyes. It quickly made a trail down her now pale cheek and hung off her chin. I reached out before it could fall, gently brushing it away.

"Baby, we are here for you. Both of us. You can tell us anything. If you want to talk about it, we will listen. If you don't want to talk about it, that's okay, too. But know this, Casey. We will protect you. Always. We won't let anyone hurt you ever again."

A sob broke from her chest, and she flung her arms around my shoulders and began to cry in earnest against my throat. I let her get it out as I slowly rubbed her back and looked up at Brent from over her head. He looked stricken and at a loss for what to do. I gestured with my eyes until he snapped out of it and stepped closer until he was awkwardly patting her back. I had to hold back my chuckle. He looked as if he wanted to cry, too.

"Let it out," I murmured in her ear. "Let it out. Give it to us so we can carry it for you."

My words made her cry harder for another long minute before she pulled back and started wiping her eyes. Brent quickly reached over to grab a napkin off the table. Instead of handing it to her, he turned her face toward him with a finger under her chin. He gently wiped her cheeks dry.

"Dollface," he spoke quietly. "We need to know more about the man that kept you."

She nodded, blinking up at him. "I will tell you everything. But can we do it later tonight? I..." She looked around the kitchen, her gaze landing on the stove clock. "Can we talk about it after work?" She gestured at the clock. He nodded, still holding her chin as he stared down at her with concern. I knew he wasn't used to displays of emotions, he'd never been around people that showed anything but anger growing up.

"Of course." He swept his thumb over her cheek before letting it rest on her full bottom lip. "You'll be okay." It was a statement of fact. For him, there was no other option, one I wholeheartedly agreed with.

I stood back up and picked up her abandoned fork, pressing it back into her hand. "Let's finish breakfast so we can get you to work. I hear your boss is a real hardass."

She giggled at my wink. Brent looked relieved that her tears had dried up and almost collapsed in his chair, seemingly exhausted by the short bout of intense emotions.

Seventeen

CASEY

THE MORNING at the diner went by quickly. Grace had given me a couple of tables to get used to being a server instead of just running plates and drinks out. I had been nervous. It seemed like such a huge responsibility, but it wasn't as bad as I had built it up in my head.

I stood at the counter, feeling the solid weight of the new phone in my pocket that Ethan had slid to me before we left the house. I was rolling silverware after the lunch rush and staring out at the pounding rain. Grace walked up next to me and placed a tall milkshake down in front of me. She gestured to the storm outside.

"I'm afraid it's just going to get worse today. Mark has the radio running back in the kitchen and says they have just announced that we are on a tornado watch."

I whipped my head around to look at her. I was sure my face showed every bit of fear that suddenly cascaded into my belly. "Tornado?" I looked back at the rain, trying to see through it to the clouds as if a funnel cloud was about to form any second right over the street.

She pushed the glass closer to me. Needing a distraction, I picked it up and drew hard on the straw to pull the thick goodness into my mouth without taking my eyes away from the weather.

"Tornado watch. Right now, that just means the conditions are favorable to create a tornado. When it switches to a warning, then we will worry."

"What happens if it turns into a warning?" We didn't exactly get tornados on the California coast. I was more used to earthquakes and had felt my share of them. Tornadoes were new to me, and all I could picture was destruction, houses torn to bits with people inside. Trees uprooted, and cars tossed around like discarded toys.

"We have a basement under the diner large enough to keep everyone safe. Thank goodness we have never needed it, but it feels good to know that all our staff and customers would be able to wait it out if we needed to. If a warning hits, we close down. No sense in keeping everyone in danger working when they could get home safe instead. Of course, we will keep our doors open for anyone that doesn't have a safe place to go."

"And that's never happened before?" It was a relief to know that they hadn't had a tornado here before. But that didn't mean it couldn't happen, though. Right? I chewed my bottom lip.

"Well," she hedged, seeing my nervousness. "We have had plenty of warnings, so we learned to keep the basement stocked with bottles of water and things like candles. But we have not had an actual tornado yet."

"Yet?" I squeaked out.

She chuckled and patted my arm. "I just mean it can never be completely ruled out. It's better to be safe than sorry in any case. It will be okay, Casey. Once you have lived through a couple of decent storms, you'll be an expert."

"I don't think so," I mumbled before sticking the straw back in my mouth and indulging in the comfort the milkshake offered.

"I'm guessing where you are from, you don't get many storms?" She eyed me with curiosity. I shook my head.

"No, but we have had a few small earthquakes."

She raised an eyebrow, and I sighed internally. I hadn't meant for that to slip out. The fewer people that knew who I really was and where I came from, the better for me and the less likely it could get revealed where I was. I could just picture someone writing on social media that they had seen Casey Rivers, the girl that escaped a serial killer. Just one post would be enough to set the killer on my path.

"So you are from California? Or somewhere close to there?"

I nodded but gave her a pleading look to not go further with her questions. Thankfully, she caught on and gave me one of her sweet smiles. "Okay, sweetheart. No pushing."

"Thank you." My grateful words and her pat on my arm were interrupted by a woman stepping in with two young children, both around the age of seven or so. She folded up a large umbrella and leaned it against the wall next to the door, then she took her daughters by the hand and walked to an open table.

"Do you want this table, or do you want me to get it?"

I grinned at Grace's question. "I think I can do it."

She nodded. "I know you can. I'll get their waters. Why don't you take them their menus?"

I grabbed a laminated menu from the holder next to us and reached under the counter for two paper kids' menus and two sets of crayons. I paused before heading over to the table the woman had taken. "Grace?"

"Yes, Casey?"

"Thank you." I hurried away, leaving Grace to stare at my back with a look of sympathy on her face I didn't really want to see.

I set the menus down, making sure to push the small boxes of crayons over to each child with a smile. "Welcome to the Hardgrove Diner. What can I get you to drink?"

The woman looked up at me. Her smile was small, and there were dark circles under her eyes, but she looked happy. "I'll just have a water with lemon. The kids will each have a lemonade, if you have it?" I nodded.

"Of course. I'll be right back with the lemonades and a bowl of lemons for you." Grace walked up and placed the glass of water in front of the woman as I backed away from the table. Grace walked back with me and watched as I got two kids' cups out from under the counter and started to fill them with the lemonade. I could tell she had something on her mind, and I was sure I didn't want to hear it. Before she could come out with it, the door opened again, but the woman who stepped in didn't look happy to be there.

She was soaking wet from the rain, looking around at the mostly empty room. Her eyes landed on the woman with her two kids and narrowed dangerously. Grace tutted under her breath as she stepped back around the counter. Before Grace could say anything or intercept, she marched directly for their table and slammed her palms down on the tabletop, making the glass of water slosh over the top with the force.

Grace turned to look at me, a serious look on her face, her voice calm but firm. "Call Ethan, sweetheart."

I nodded, my eyes wide at the spectacle the woman was already making, just as she started to scream. I pulled my new phone out of my pocket and looked down at it in my hand, bobbling it for a second before finally opening up the call list. As I pressed Ethan's name, I could hear the woman asking where her son was as the young mother shrank back in her seat, and the kids started crying loudly.

"Hey, sugar. Are you ready for a ride?" Ethan's deep voice made me sigh with relief, already knowing that he would take care of whatever the problem was. As I whispered into the phone that there was a problem at the diner and Grace wanted him there, her screams just got louder.

Ethan's voice lost its cheerfulness, and it sounded as if he were moving through a busy office. "Okay, Casey. I'm on my way. Are you or Mom in any danger?"

"No. I don't think so. This woman, she's so angry. She keeps screaming that she wants to know where her son is. She's making the children cry, Ethan."

"Okay, sugar. I'm in my car. Let me call a patrol car. They should get there before I will. Be right there. Okay?"

I was nodding my head even though he couldn't see me while my eyes stayed glued to the table. "Yes."

"Good." Then he was gone, nothing but silence coming from the phone. I slid it back into my pocket and nervously picked up the two lemonades for the kids, not knowing what else I should do. But I hated how scared and upset they looked and had to do something.

Grace was trying to calm the woman down, asking her if there was anyone she could call for her, but that only seemed to make her more upset. She whirled on Grace and pointed at her face.

"I want my son! Do you think you can make this *woman* tell me where my son is," she spat out. Her chest was heaving, and her eyes were wild. She looked capable of violence, though she was dressed as if she were heading to a country club. Her hair was in wild disarray, and her face was void of any makeup, and I had the distinct impression that was unusual for her. I could tell she was a distraught mother, but she was taking it out on another mother, and in front of two crying children that looked scared.

I stepped forward as Grace continued to speak calmly. "No, ma'am. I don't know who your son is, but I'm sure if we all just settle down, we can find out." Grace placed a gentle hand on the woman, who was vibrating with her fury. "You're scaring the children, ma'am. I'm sure you don't want that, do you?"

The woman slapped Grace's hand away from her. "I don't give a fuck about anything except what this woman has done to my son!" She whirled back around to the now crying woman who looked helplessly at her kids while trying to calm them down, reaching across the table toward them. The angry woman reached out and grabbed the other by her hair, yanking her toward her. "Did you kill him?" She screamed.

The other woman sobbed hard, reaching up to grab the hand holding her hair. "No! I swear it! He just disappeared! He didn't come home. I thought he was with his mistress!" Her words were hard to understand between the crying of both her and the little children. I squeezed in between the women and set down the drinks before reaching out my hands toward the kids and gesturing wildly for them to come with me. Without hesitating, the first one slid out of the booth, taking my hand. Once she saw her older sister moving, she followed quickly.

Once I had them both in hand, we backed away, with me shielding the two of them with my body. The older woman spun around, her eyes zeroing in on me. "Don't you touch my grandbabies!"

Grace stepped in front of us, blocking her advance. "Ma'am, I'm going to ask you to leave," she said firmly.

"I fucking *dare* you to make me leave!" the woman roared out. "My son is missing! You aren't taking my grandbabies, too! They are coming home with me!"

The young mother cried out in denial just as the bell sounded over the door. I turned my head to see two uniformed police officers step inside, followed quickly by a serious-looking Ethan. As soon as I saw him, my shoulders immediately relaxed, and I squeezed the tiny hands holding mine. I turned around to face them and squatted down so we were face to face.

"It's going to be okay now," I whispered, wiping at their tears.

"Is Grammy really going to take us away?"

"I don't want to leave Mommy!" They both wailed at the same time as I continued to try to calm them down, keeping their attention on me instead of the commotion going on just feet away.

"Shh, it's going to be okay. I promise."

"I'm glad daddy's gone," the older one whispered, breaking my heart. Seeing the defiant look in her eyes and the way she hugged her sibling tightly made me glad he was gone, too.

Ethan had the older woman in handcuffs, trying to talk calmly to her while she continued to rage at everyone. When the young mother was finally able to get by, she sprang to her feet and ran over to us, her knees hitting the tiled floor hard without seeming to notice as she threw her arms around her girls.

"You fucking bitch! I know you killed him!"

"Ma'am, I promise you, we are investigating the case thoroughly. But Mrs. Banks was at a PTO meeting the night Mr. Banks disappeared. She has several witnesses, including the mayor, to corroborate her whereabouts."

"She's lying! He hated her, and she knew it! He was going to divorce her and take everything, and now she's driving his car around town. He wouldn't want her in his car." She had begun sobbing. I felt for her. Clearly, she was obviously worried about her son, but her behavior was out of line. I watched the two officers pull her from the diner with a sigh of relief.

I stood up and backed away from the small family as they hugged and calmed each other down. I felt a hand on the small of my back and looked up into Ethan's worried gaze.

"Are you okay, sugar?" I nodded and swallowed thickly. My shoulders slumped at the sudden end of the conflict.

"Why don't you go home for the day, Casey?" Grace looked outside and then over to Ethan. "The storm is getting worse anyway. You should probably hunker down for the evening. Just in case."

Ethan agreed, kissing his mom on the cheek, and led me to the door after I stripped the apron off and handed it over.

"Tomorrow is Saturday, Casey. You don't have to come back until Monday. Enjoy your weekend, okay?"

"Thanks, Grace," I said softly, glancing back at the woman and children one last time, and then took the hand Ethan offered before we left the diner and ran through the pouring rain to the shiny black Mustang.

Eighteen

BRENT

A RAINY DAY in construction meant there was basically not a damn thing to do other than get caught up on all the piles of paperwork that often got neglected throughout the week. It wasn't a completely wasted day since I was able to handle the phone calls needed for orders as well as payroll. It was a task that I had to do every Friday, anyway. But I hated not having my men and women at work. I would try to help them make up their hours throughout the week if they wanted by offering overtime.

I had just finished placing my special order for our new bathroom counter, a beautiful marble with room for three sink basins, when my phone dinged with a message. I dug the phone out from under a stack of invoices and opened it, not surprised to see a text from Ethan. The text made me frown and immediately sit up in my chair. Something had happened at the diner, and he was taking Casey home for the day. Not bothering to text back or call to ask what had happened, I stood up and grabbed my jacket, deciding that I was done for the day.

I ran through the rain as thunder boomed overhead and quickly made it to my truck, cursing the entire way. My hair was plastered to my forehead, and cold rainwater dripped into my eyes. I started the engine and put it into gear as the radio came to life with an emergency broadcast alarm blaring through the cab. I cursed again and lowered the volume until the recording came on, then turned it back up. You could never hear those damn recordings properly, and the sound was always garbled. But the warning of a tornado was clear enough.

With yet another curse, I flew through the parking lot of my office building and hurried down the streets, straight toward the house. I had planned to stop to get something for dinner on the way home, but there was no way I was staying out in this weather, not with a tornado warning for the county now in effect.

I pulled up into the drive, slammed out of the cab, and ran up to the front door. I was soaked from the run and stood for a second in the entryway, ready to run through to the bathroom, when Casey looked up at me from the couch, startled.

"Hey, dollface. I'll just be a second." Before she could jump up and say anything, I took off for the primary bathroom, leaving puddles of rainwater in my wake. I struggled to take off all my clothes, dumping the sodden mess in the bathtub, then jumped in the shower, sighing as the hot water ran over my rain-chilled body. The rain had felt good at first, washing away the heat of the day, but it quickly got chilly, especially while sitting in the cab with the air conditioner blowing.

I made quick work of washing down, ready to get back to the others. We needed to get into the basement for safety, just in case. It was always better to be safe than sorry when it came to tornadoes, and I was already taking too much time in the shower instead of herding them downstairs.

I shut off the water and grabbed a towel, rubbing myself down as I stepped into the bedroom to throw on some sweatpants. I tossed the towel on the end of the bed and stopped short when I saw Casey standing there with another towel at her feet. She'd obviously been wiping up the water I had left behind as I had darted into the bedroom. My cock went from limp and laying against my thigh to rock fucking hard in a nanosecond, almost making me dizzy with how fast the desire surged through me.

Her eyes were comically large as she stared at my cock. Reaching up to my navel, my piercings glinted in the dim bedroom lighting, probably scaring her even more than the size. I couldn't resist reaching a hand down to grip tightly as I felt a bead of precum forming at the tip. When I moved my hand from the base up to the tip and back down again, running over the piercings, she let out an adorable little squeal. Though she couldn't seem to take her eyes off the monstrosity that was my cock, she was already backing out of the door.

"I'm so sorry! I—I was cleaning up the water and thought, well, you were in the shower. I guess I thought you'd be longer." Her eyes darted down the hall, likely looking for an escape. Her eyes couldn't stop watching me as I lazily stroked my dick, using my thumb to run over the head to spread the ever-growing moisture.

She finally squeaked and turned to run down the hall but ran right into Ethan, who had appeared at the doorway. She ran right into his arms, and the lucky bastard wrapped them tight around her. I could just imagine the feel of those soft tits pressed to his chest as his hard as fuck cock pressed stiffly against her belly. My cock jerked in my hand.

"Whoa, you okay there, sugar?" He held her against him, and I watched as she shifted nervously against him, not missing the way her thighs pressed together. When her eyes came back to my cock, I couldn't hold back a grin and gave her a salacious wink.

Her face was beet red when she looked up at him. "I'm so sorry. I was just trying to clean the water off the floor."

"No need to apologize. Thank you for doing that." He leaned down and kissed her cheek, then lowered his head further to stick his nose in the crook of her neck to inhale her scent. I swear, if that asshole tasted her skin there before I could...

"Listen, I hate to say it, but," I said, looking out the window at the rain raging even harder than it had before, and I was glad I'd gotten home when I did. "There was an alert. That's why I came home so early." I looked back at the two people I wanted more than I could ever describe. To fall into the bed that was so close, I could reach out a hand and touch it. "We need to get down into the basement, just in case."

I reluctantly let go of my cock and turned to my dresser, not missing the little gasp from our girl as I flexed my ass. I suppressed a chuckle as I pulled open a drawer to grab and pull on a pair of sweatpants. I looked down once I had them around my hips. They would do absolutely nothing to conceal the raging hard on that stood out obscenely through the gray cotton. The front was stretched out with a wide gap that I could easily see down and to the head of my cock, which was still leaking precum and smearing it on my muscled abs. I shrugged and turned back to the door.

Ethan let go of Casey, who was doing a good impression of a tomato as her eyes darted around the room from my dick tenting the gray sweats to the bed where Ethan was picking up my towel, and to his ass, as he walked into the bathroom, grumbling about how I was a caveman. I shrugged. Honestly, we were both cavemen from time to time. Mostly, it was me grumbling about picking up after him. While I needed our home to be clean and orderly, sometimes we got lazy.

I reached out my hand and grabbed Casey's, pulling her along with me down the hall and toward the kitchen where the basement door was. "Let's get downstairs. We can relax and wait out the storm." I grinned down at her when she had to tear her eyes away from my dick again and blinked up at me with wide eyes.

"You said there was a warning?" She sounded worried. I supposed she wouldn't have much experience with tornadoes living in California, and knew it could be scary even if you grew up with tornado warnings all the time. I gave her hand a squeeze as I opened up the basement door with my other one, then gestured for her to go first after flipping on the light at the top of the stairs.

"There is. You can never tell with tornadoes, dollface. It's always better to be prepared and stay safe, just in case."

She nodded her head and then looked around the basement. "Grace was telling me about it at the diner today." She wrung her hands together and looked up at Ethan as he took the last step down into the basement with us and shut the bottom door. "I hope she and Mark are okay."

"I'll give them a call and check. But they are old hats at this. Dad wouldn't let Mom stay in the diner if there was a warning. I'm actually surprised they haven't called us already." He had a quick conversation in which he assured his parents that we were safe in the basement. I took the opportunity to lead Casey over to the small setup we had with a couch and a small tv with a game console. There was also a small fridge next to a cabinet with a bunch of snacks and even a microwave. Honestly, it looked like a teenage boy's playroom when I thought about it. When she looked around and then back at me with a small smile, I shrugged. It was a great way to pass the time.

I turned on the tv and sat down with her pressed tight against my side. My cock had finally softened to only a half-chub. But when I felt her thigh pressing against mine and the heat from her body, I started to inflate again. Being in this teenager's paradise was apropos, considering I was having as much trouble controlling my dick as one.

I slung my arm over her shoulder, tugging her body into mine, and let out a deep breath of satisfaction at having her snug against me. The TV came to life and immediately popped up on a news broadcast. There was a weather radar map with bright colors moving across the screen. There were several yellow circles, and the weatherman was pointing to the different locations, warning about the tornadoes that had been sighted.

"Mom and Dad are fine. They are hanging out in the diner basement for now with a few others that asked for shelter." He dropped down on the couch on Casey's other side and threw his arm on top of mine, his hand caressing the back of my neck, causing goosebumps to rise on my arms and a little more blood to pump into my cock. "Well shit," he said, looking at the tv. "Looks like there was a tornado in the town over."

Casey stiffened. "What does that mean?"

"Sorry, sugar. It means that a tornado touched down there. It wasn't a big one, so hopefully, no one was hurt. But it probably did some damage. Brent and I might have to go out there tomorrow to help with the cleanup."

"Does that mean it's over?"

"Not yet, baby," he murmured into her ear. If anything, her body got tighter, and her breaths came in pants as she started to tremble.

"Is it coming here?" She choked out as she stared at the pictures of damage from past tornadoes that were flashing on the screen. I was tempted to turn it off, but we needed to know what was happening outside.

"We don't know that, dollface. But I can promise you we are safe down here." My words didn't seem to help her anxiety at all as I watched her trembling get worse. I glanced over her head at Ethan. I looked back down at her then, leaned in to inhale the soft skin at the back of her ear then gave it a lick. "Would you like for us to distract you?" I asked, my voice husky from the desire and visions of what we could do to relax her and take her mind off the storm raging outside.

"Wh—what?" Her whole body shuddered as I nipped the tip of her earlobe, then soothed the sting with my tongue.

"We can take your mind off what is happening outside. Would you like that, sugar?" Ethan placed his hand on her thigh and rubbed small circles over her denim covered leg. I wanted to see her bare legs. I wanted to spread them and inhale her scent from her core. I had absolutely no experience pleasing a woman, but I could learn really fucking quickly.

"Take my mind... oh!" My hand covered her tit, and I palmed the weight, feeling her tight little nipple bead to a point in the center of my palm. Her gasp of shock and pleasure sent a jolt of electricity zinging down my spine. "I don't know. Wouldn't that be weird? You guys are..."

"We want you, Casey." Ethan finally spoke our truth out loud. I hadn't expected to feel the amount of relief I did hearing those words.

"We need you. Between us." I added.

We had both stilled all of our movements, barely daring to breathe in case we spooked her or pushed her too far. Her next reaction would be everything. It would either put a stop to our pursuit of her, or it would answer all our prayers.

I stared down at her, every bit of myself held tense, waiting for her answer. Sitting there, admiring her delicate beauty, the light sprinkle of freckles over the bridge of her nose, I watched her take great effort to control her heavy breathing, and her eyelids fluttered against her flushed skin. She was wrestling with herself over the fact that Ethan and I were a couple. This had to be confusing. But what worried me the most was her thinking we were playing around with her when what we really wanted was forever.

Finally, she spoke, her barely audible words holding both of us in a state of shock.

"Yes. I'd like that."

Nineteen

ETHAN

I WAS MOVING before the last syllable fell from her lips. I wanted to take it slow. I knew I needed to slow the fuck down, but there was nothing about the situation that would stop me from reaching for my beautiful girl's shirt and lifting it over her head in one swift movement.

Her gasp only managed to stir up the lust the two of us could barely contain. I stared down at the swells of her breasts spilling over the top of her simple cotton bra and couldn't hold back the deep groan that rose from the back of my throat. While I took her in, I could see Brent out of the corner of my eye, sinking to his knees in front of her. Even seeing my partner drop to his knees in front of Casey's pussy couldn't keep my gaze from the beauty in front of me. I watched her take each deep, ragged breath as Brent settled in front of her. His movements had her flesh shaking and quivering. When he reached for the button of her jeans, she gave a full-body shiver and let a whimper escape the lips she was biting hard enough to turn white.

"Oh, sugar," I whispered as I reached to pull the abused lip from between her teeth. "Only we get to bite you." I lowered my head and took her mouth with mine, finally knowing how it felt to have soft, feminine lips against mine. She was the total opposite of Brent. I had to remind myself to be softer with her. With him, I was used to letting myself go since he could match me in both size and strength. Knowing that I had this much smaller person under me was enough to have me almost coming in my pants while also making my hands tremble with trepidation. It was a strange juxtaposition.

I was tentative at first, barely brushing my mouth against her soft lips, just a gentle press. When I started to lift my head to look at her, to gauge her reaction, it was she who grabbed the back of my head and pressed our mouths more firmly against each other. I couldn't resist swiping my tongue along her lips and nipping her bottom lip the same as I had done with Brent a hundred times over the years, but with less pressure.

Something about having this woman underneath me stirred a fierce instinct to protect her. I'd never felt this way with Brent. I knew he could take care of himself. Hell, he could probably break my neck with a flick of his wrist if he wanted to. It wasn't that I thought less of her or that she couldn't protect herself. She'd already proven that she could survive anything. Instead, I thought she was even more precious. I wanted to hold her tight and keep her safe from anything that wanted to harm her. I could be the shield, while Brent was the sword. I knew he wouldn't want it any other way.

I ran a large hand down her arm and back up to cup her cheek as I coaxed her lips open with mine. The moment she sighed, opening for me, I delved in, finally tasting a woman, finally tasting *her* for the first time in my life. As I slid my tongue along hers, I knew I was in trouble. This woman wasn't going anywhere. There was no way we could even allow her to go back to California or anywhere without us. If she had to visit family, one of us would be next to her, no matter the distance or travel to get there.

Our tongues were exploring each other's mouths, when all of a sudden, her body was jerked halfway off the edge of the couch. I snarled, looking down at Brent, ready to chew his ass out for taking my sugar's mouth away when my breath solidified in my lungs.

Casey's ass was hanging off the edge of the seat, her neck at an awkward angle at the back of the couch where it met the seat, and her hair was in wild disarray around her. But what caught my attention was her neatly trimmed pussy with dark golden hair glinting in the low light of the room. I think my mouth had started watering the exact moment I looked down.

I watched as Brent paused what he had been doing and stared at her core as hard as I was. He reached out a trembling hand, and I just shook my head as the fucker petted her pussy like it was an adorable kitten. Here was one of the biggest, toughest guys I had ever seen, someone that had pounded my ass until I couldn't walk on more than one occasion, and he was slayed–by a vagina. I shoved his hand away and snarled. "My turn." It really was softer than I had expected.

Giggles interrupted our shoving fight as we each tried to be the one to pet her pussy. We both looked up to see Casey holding her hands over her mouth, her eyes dancing with humor.

"Oh, you think that's funny, sugar?" I leaned down and nipped her inner thigh.

"I think she was laughing at us." Brent looked like he was about to do something evil as he glanced over to me and then back to Casey. "Weren't you, dollface?"

Casey's giggles dried up at the look on Brent's face. I could tell her that he was just playing, that he could be a bit on the sadistic side when it came to sexual games, but it was something she should probably learn on her own. He never dealt out more than I could take, and it made our sex life even more exciting than it already was. I knew he would be even more cautious with our girl while still taking her to the edge to find out what she could endure. I was a dominant fucker when it came to figuring out who was in charge, but when it came to pushing limits, he was in his element.

Casey glanced at me, then back toward him, and suddenly seemed to realize what position she was in. Her hands went to cover her body, her face heating with embarrassment. I took one of her hands without removing her forearm from her breasts and kissed her fingertips as Brent kissed the back of the hand covering her mound.

"Sugar, do you want to put your shirt back on? We can help you get dressed, or we can leave the room to give you privacy." I watched her eyes go wide, and then what could only be disappointment filled her face. "Or..." I paused as I kissed the back of her hand. "We could show you how honored we are that you would allow us to touch you. To kiss you." I punctuated each sentence with a kiss.

"To make you feel good. To make you forget about the world outside these walls." I was tempted, so very tempted, to say more to her. It was hard as hell holding back. But we were lucky she was giving us even as much as she was, and I was determined to enjoy it.

Slowly, her body released some of its tension. Then both hands began a slow retreat. It was as tantalizing as any strip tease, watching with held breath as her flesh reappeared. She seemed confused as we each continued to stare at her. Brent was still on his knees in front of her legs, trapped by her jeans, and I was leaning over her body from my perch on the seat next to her.

Finally, she spoke, giving us the greatest gift in the world. "Please..."

It was all we needed to hear. I cautioned myself to slow down. But nothing could have stopped me from yanking the cups of her bra down. I immediately latched onto one soft pink nipple, making me wish I had two mouths so I could taste them both at the same time.

Her gasps and whines were the greatest background music. Hearing Brent's grunts only added kindling to the raging fire that was building inside me. As I reached behind her to find the latch of her bra, I switched to the other nipple and drew it deep into my mouth. The inferno grew in the room when I tasted her flesh.

It wasn't until I had run my hand back and forth across the smooth cotton strap several times that the sweet giggles coming from our girl finally penetrated my lust-filled brain. I let the nipple fall out of my mouth and looked down in confusion. Casey reached for my hands that were behind her still, causing her breasts to jut out, and I couldn't resist diving back down for another taste.

I pulled back again when our hands got in the way. It took me several embarrassing seconds to realize what she was giggling about. "What the fuck?" The clasp was in the front. I stared hard at the plastic contraption until I realized how it worked. A simple twist had the clasp separating, and then nothing was keeping my new favorite toys contained anymore.

I reached out to pinch one nipple and was about to lick the other when her back completely bowed off the seat of the couch. I looked down to see Brent had finally gotten her jeans off, and her legs were completely bare. I never thought I would be the kind of man that would lose his head over a woman's naked legs, but I might as well be back in the eighteenth century, panting after a peek at her ankle. Luckily, Brent was no better.

I watched as his mouth and hands roamed over her calves, knees, and ankles. He didn't leave a single bit of her legs unexplored. While he licked and kissed all her bare flesh, I petted her belly, as obsessed as he was. I leaned down to take her nipple back into my mouth, keeping my eyes on his progress as he made his way up her thighs. When he spread her legs, opening up a path to her core, I nearly came in my pants.

I had to close my eyes tight to get back under control before I made a mess. When I managed to take it back and knew I wasn't going to spill at my first sight of a woman's pussy, I noticed the mess on Brent's abs. I couldn't hold back my chuckle. My partner wasn't so lucky in holding back. His eyes met mine, and he snarled at me. I knew I was in for another punishment with that one look, but I wasn't sorry.

But the very next second, when he smirked at me and then dove into her juicy cunt, I immediately regretted our positions. Lucky motherfucker. With her gasp and squeal ringing out in the room, I shoved his head to the side and took my own lick from above. I had barely gotten a taste when his growl rumbled out, and he shoved me back, retaking his place.

I groaned out loud. "Come on, man. You have to share." I didn't give a single fuck if I was whining. That one taste had me addicted, and I wanted it again. I wanted her covering my face and her wetness sliding down my throat.

His "fuck you" was muffled where he was buried in her pussy. I looked down and saw her nipple glinting from my saliva and gave a mental shrug. I would make sure I got a turn. The second he made her come, I was taking over, whether he liked it or not. I dove back down, feasting on both of her nipples, taking turns sucking, biting, and licking them.

When her keening wail rang out in the room, I switched back to her mouth, swallowing her cries and taking them into my lungs. I felt like a proud peacock, knowing that we had made her come. It may have been him eating her out for the first time, but I owned that shit, too.

As soon as her body went limp below us, I sat up. "My turn, fucker." Not taking no for an answer, I slid to the floor and shoved him hard, making him fall to his ass, ignoring his grumbles. My mouth covered her pussy, my tongue diving straight into her tight as fuck little hole.

I was in heaven, finally getting a face full of her wetness. It was something I had dreamed of, wondering what it would be like when I finally got her opened for me, and it was a million times better than I had ever thought it would be. This time, when I closed my eyes, it was to savor.

Her hands clutched my hair, yanking and pulling, but she could rip me bald, and I would be a happy man, knowing that I was already building her up to another climax. She went off like a rocket as I sucked hard on her little clit, then went back down to her hole, trying to get every bit of the wetness that was leaking out of her.

As she collapsed for a second time, gasping and panting, I gave her one final lick, not wanting to leave, but knowing she would be way too sensitive for another so soon after the two we had just given her. I sat back, grinning at her closed eyes and relaxed face. Somehow, two assholes that had no experience with women had just taken this beauty to heaven twice.

I moved to sit up with her on the couch again when a large hand stopped me by gripping my thigh in a rough grip.

"You're going to pay for that." The growled threat was the only warning I had before he pounced.

Twenty

CASEY

I WAS TRYING to catch my breath as the aftershocks from the not one, but two, incredible orgasms I'd had made my body shiver with delight. I had never felt anything like that before. Even when I had tried with my boyfriend, he had never made me feel so good. If he had, I may have been willing to try again while we were sober.

I lay there with a small smile curving my lips when I realized that something was happening on the floor at my feet. With a great deal of effort, I managed to haul myself up onto my elbows and looked down at the floor. Then my mouth opened in shock. Brent had Ethan gripped by the throat, his large hand wrapped around, gripping hard, but it didn't look like he was cutting off his air, just holding him still.

Brent's other hand was pulling Ethan's slacks open harshly. I thought he was going to rip the zipper clean off with how rough he was being. I swallowed hard at the primal display. Their mouths were pressed together, their tongues tangling in a harsh caress. Once the pants were open, Brent had Ethan's dick out and was roughly jacking it up and down.

I held my breath, letting my fingers slide to my breasts and pinched my nipples as I watched the show. When their mouths pulled apart and they were breathing hard into each other, I paused, waiting to see what they would do next. Brent's hand didn't stop as both of them turned their heads to look right at me.

I swallowed hard, stilling my fingers. "Should I…" I looked toward the door and swallowed again. "Should I leave you two…" I was, after all, the third wheel here in an already established relationship.

"Oh no, you don't, little girl." Brent reached up and snatched one of my hands and yanked, not hard enough to hurt, but definitely enough to get me onto my knees in front of where they were kneeling. "You ever suck a man's cock, dollface?" His voice was like sandpaper. It felt like a fierce caress down my back, making goosebumps rise over me.

I hesitated for a second before nodding reluctantly. I had. It wasn't my favorite thing to do, but it satisfied my then boyfriend. He had made it seem like an act that was expected, especially if I wasn't going to be spreading my legs. I had also spit it out, which he hated, but that shit was nasty.

"Do you want to suck our boy's cock here?" He asked while giving Ethan's dick another pump with his tight fist. I looked closely at what I could see. He was so much bigger than my boyfriend had been. It was long and thick, veins standing out against the dark pink flesh. I licked my lips and watched precum cover the tip. I nodded.

Brent leaned down, swiped up the drop of come, and leaned into me. He released Ethan's throat and took me by the back of the neck. He whispered into my lips, making another shiver race through me. "Good girl. Our boy here will fall in love with you if you wrap those pretty little lips around his hard cock."

I tried to ignore his words, putting them in a box and locking it up tight as just words said in the heat of the moment, but I couldn't deny that I wanted them to be true. As if mesmerized, I let him put pressure on my neck, lowering my head to Ethan's dick. I put my lips around his head. It was almost a surprise at how large he was. I had seen it, but feeling it fill my mouth was something else entirely.

For the first time, I was enjoying having a dick in my mouth. With Brent's hand directing me, it didn't feel like a chore or like I was being forced to please someone. Instead, it felt like we were connected, all three of us. It was my mouth on Ethan's dick, but it was Brent that was directing the show.

As I tried to take more in my mouth, I gagged against the intrusion. I was going to try again when Brent pulled me back. "It's okay, dollface. Just take what you can. Look at him. He's going to enjoy whatever you do to him." I looked up to see Ethan's jaw clenched tight, his eyes wild, and his hands clenched into fists.

"He doesn't look happy," I whispered to Brent. He chuckled before placing a hot kiss on my mouth.

"Baby, that's the look of a man in ecstasy. Trust me." He kissed me again, deeper. When he pulled back, he winked at me. "Want me to show you how to make him explode?"

I nodded dumbly, dazed by the kiss, and wondered how I'd gotten where I was, kneeling in the basement of these amazing men. I was the only one completely naked, but Brent was shirtless, his sweatpants with a large wet spot and tented in the front. Ethan was still fully dressed, his pants wide open and pushed down under his ass, giving full access to the heavy cock sticking from the open waistband. I glanced back at Brent's sweats and wondered if he had already come. But if he had, why was he still hard?

I didn't have time to continue to wonder about it when he took me by the back of the neck again and brought my mouth back to Ethan's dick. I took the head in my mouth again but pulled back when I realized I wasn't alone that time. Brent swiped his tongue up the side of Ethan's dick, and as I pulled away, he took my place and seemed to swallow Ethan's dick whole. His mouth went down so much further than I knew mine had been. Unlike me, Brent didn't choke or gag.

When he pulled off, I took my turn, dipping my head down and swirling my tongue around the underside of the head. I bobbed up and down a couple of times, starting to get the hang of having such a large cock in my mouth. When I pulled off, Brent was there, taking the cock almost fully to the root. Then he lifted back up until only the head was left in his mouth, and I dipped down and licked the large vein running up the front.

As we took turns and then began to lavish Ethan's cock with attention at the same time, his moans grew louder in the room. I felt him grip my head, not pulling my hair, just holding me firm, as if he needed to hold on to something. I looked over to Brent, finding a hand on his head as well.

"Fuck. Fuck. Fuck. I'm going to come. Brent..." Ethan's raspy voice called out to us, giving plenty of warning, and for the first time, I didn't know what to do. I knew I hated the taste of cum, but at the same time, I had an almost overwhelming desire to find out if Ethan's would be different.

Brent could see my hesitation, though, and let me sit back. He sank his mouth over Ethan's cock, and as Ethan shouted up at the ceiling, the tendons in his neck tight, Brent winked at me. I could see his throat working, swallowing Ethan's load, and I felt myself get jealous for the first time when it came to these men. I knew that I wanted to try. I wanted to know how he tasted, and I knew that with them, I wouldn't hate it.

Brent pulled back when Ethan slumped down and released his hold on the two of us. I blinked, holding back the irrational tears that had sprung to my eyes when I thought of the chance I had wasted. In one swift movement, Brent's fingers gently gripped my chin and brought our mouths together.

"Taste him, dollface." His whispered words almost broke me. Somehow, he knew the battle I was fighting with myself and was going to give me what I needed. Our lips met, and our mouths opened. When his tongue slid against mine, I could taste what I had denied myself, and I was right. It was different. It still didn't taste like chocolate, but it wasn't the awful flavor that always made me shudder and rush to spit it out. It almost tasted… good. I wanted another chance to get the full experience for myself.

"Not horrible?" I flushed as we pulled away and stared at each other. I shook my head as he grinned.

Ethan stood up, looking like a baby deer, as he swayed a little, uneasy on his own legs. He started pulling his pants back up but didn't bother zipping them, only pulled his boxers back into place before collapsing on the couch. Brent stood up and reached down, gripping me under the arms, lifting me as if I were a toddler instead of a fully grown woman, and plunked me down right on Ethan's lap. The grunt underneath me had me immediately trying to climb off his lap, but Ethan wrapped his arms around me, holding me tight to his chest. I relaxed into him, letting my body weight settle, knowing he could take it.

Brent looked down at his pants with a grimace and pointed to the bathroom. "I'll be right back."

Ethan's chuckle had me turning my head so I could look at his face. "Did he…?"

"Yeah, sugar, he did. It seems our boy couldn't hold himself back once he got a good look at your pussy." I reached my hand down to cover myself at the reminder that I was completely naked, but before I could, a throw blanket was pulled over the top of me and tucked in. "You don't need to cover yourself, but I'm sure you're probably chilly." I nodded gratefully and settled back in, looking at the tv that was still playing on silent.

The line of storms seemed to have moved quite a bit since the last time we looked, and the yellow circles had diminished, making me feel relieved that the worst was over. They had set out to distract me from worrying over the storms, and it seemed like they had done their jobs perfectly.

Brent walked back into the room, his pants still wet, but the worst of his mess seemed cleared up, too. He looked at the tv and grinned. "Looks like we are clear to leave. Are you two hungry?"

I felt my stomach clench with hunger at the suggestion of food, and I nodded. Brent held his hand out to me and pulled me gently to my feet, a far cry from how forceful he had been while in the middle of our... sexual interlude.

"That was the best way to pass a storm."

"Much better than just playing a video game," Ethan agreed as he stood up behind me.

I flushed as they led me back to the stairs while I was still wrapped up in the soft blanket. I couldn't help but wonder if that was all I was for them—just a way to pass the time. I shook my head. No. That wasn't them. They had been ravenous for me. The way they almost fought over me. The way they seemed enthralled by my body. It had given me the impression that neither one of them had ever seen a naked woman before, let alone had sex with one.

No, those two hadn't been using me. They had given me a wonderful afternoon without expecting anything in return. I had felt worshiped and cherished. If I never had another moment like that again with them, I would be happy I had gotten to experience it. But a girl could hope that there would be more down the road.

A lot more.

Twenty-One

THE CASTLE KILLER

WHERE ARE YOU?

No one gets away from me, Casey. No one. Women like you think you can do whatever you want to a man. You think you can take and take and take. Do you think you can take from me, destroy a man, without consequences? I will teach you that there are dire consequences. Just like I taught *her*.

I searched for you. I watched your childhood home, but you disappeared before I could get you. I know you aren't there anymore. I stood over your bed where you slept, peaceful, knowing that you had deceived me, taken from me.

I have searched for you, but it is as if you have vanished. No one vanishes. I will find you.

Twenty-Two

CASEY

STANDING AWKWARDLY at the top of the stairs, I was still holding the blanket wrapped securely around me. Not sure what to expect, and with no expectations about what life now meant for the three of us. I was still an outsider here, and I had no desire to cause a rift between the two of them. Watching them has warmed my heart. I loved what they had together.

Brent and Ethan weren't what I would have considered a perfect relationship in the past. They didn't hold hands all the time, and while they kissed, they didn't show much by way of public displays of affection, but the love they had for each other was plain to see. They seemed to have a well-established way about them. Brent was the caregiver. He loved to cook and provide a service there, while Ethan filled the role of protector. At least, that's how it appeared from the short time I'd been around them. I had a feeling that it went much deeper. These men were more complicated than that.

There was something I hadn't seen with my own eyes yet. I was sure that the more time I spent with them, the more I would come to understand. I couldn't wait to explore and experience it for myself. If I was invited to. I didn't think many were privy to the inner workings of their relationship. They were private men and didn't seem to care what anyone thought about them.

One thing was for certain. They were both dominant men, though Brent seemed to have a darker edge. Before I had gotten to know them over the last several days, I had thought about Ethan as the dark one and Brent as the light. But that was only the surface. Their opposing hair color had nothing to do with the darkness that seemed to lurk under the surface. Brent hid it well with his golden good looks. If I didn't know any better, I'd think that Ethan was the only thing that kept him from being the demon that lurked below his angelic strands. The thought had a shiver run through me. I wasn't sure if it was of repulsion or want. I couldn't lie to myself, though. I definitely wanted to have this fierce man protecting me.

"You going to sit down?" Brent's grin shook me from my thoughts as I watched the two of them move around the kitchen. They were opening cabinets and beginning the preparations for a meal. I glanced at the clock, noticing that it was already seven. I hadn't realized we had spent so much time downstairs.

I walked to the glass doors leading out into the backyard. It was darker than it would normally be at this time of day, but the storm clouds were still covering the sky. The worst of it seemed to have passed, and the rain was just a light patter against the cement patio that wasn't covered by the yawning. It was almost peaceful.

I thought about going to my room and finding some clothes to slip on instead of staying wrapped in the blanket, but changed my mind. I was comfortable, more comfortable than I ever would have thought, being vulnerable in a house with two large men. I felt safe for the first time in a long while.

I turned away from the rain and walked back into the kitchen, and leaned against the counter as the guys joked with each other.

Ethan flicked a towel at Brent's ass, making me grin at their antics. I wanted this. I wanted to have this moment for the rest of my life.

"Baby, come sit down," Brent called to me softly, jerking me back into the moment, and I stepped forward on bare feet. I sat down carefully on the wooden chair that Ethan held out to me and smiled gratefully. My stomach growled when Brent slid a plate in front of me with a large sandwich on it that looked delicious, reminding me I hadn't eaten for hours.

I picked up the sandwich, taking a huge bite, and listened as the guys began talking about their day. It felt... natural.

"How was your day, dollface?" I jumped at the question, once again getting lost inside my head. I placed the sandwich back down on the plate and reached for my glass of sweet tea.

"Oh, umm. It was fine. Seemed like the storm kept away a lot of the regulars. A woman came in with her two kids. Everything was good until an older woman came in and caused a ruckus. Grace had to call Ethan." I looked up at him to see his grimace when Brent looked at him with a dark look.

"Yeah, Mrs. Banks was on a bit of a rampage. She was accusing her daughter-in-law, the younger Mrs. Banks, of making her son disappear." I didn't miss the look he shot Brent's way, but I couldn't decipher the meaning. "We ended up having to take her out in handcuffs."

Brent's head swung to me and stared hard like he was searching for something. "Did she hurt you?" His demand had me shaking my head swiftly.

"No. She smacked Grace's hand and got rough with the younger woman, but she didn't do more than that. I was just trying to protect the children. They were so upset by the whole ordeal."

His eyes softened at my words, but hardened again when he turned back to Ethan. "Was she arrested?"

Ethan shook his head. "No. No one wanted to press charges. The officers had to let her go with a warning to stay away from the wife."

Brent looked back at me. "If she ever goes into the diner again, you call one of us immediately."

His tone brooked no argument, so I just picked up my sandwich while nodding my head. I didn't want to deal with the unhinged woman. She seemed capable of some serious violence if she wanted to. I swallowed down another bite of my sandwich. "Do you guys know what she was so upset about? Did her son run off or something?"

They shared another look, then Ethan glanced my way before focusing on his own sandwich. "I had a call last week about a domestic disturbance. He had been beating his wife, and we had suspicions that he was doing worse to his daughter. Unfortunately, without evidence and because the wife refused to press charges, we had to leave him."

Brent grunted. "Sounds like she needs to learn when to stand up for herself and her children."

I couldn't help but nod. That poor little girl. The thought of her father putting his hands on her sickened me. I couldn't help but feel glad that he was gone. "Well, at least he can't hurt them anymore if he's gone. Good riddance." I picked up my glass of sweet tea for another drink and smiled at Brent's approving grin.

We finished the rest of our simple meal and then worked together to tidy the kitchen. With the three of us, it seemed to only take seconds to have the dishes loaded into the dishwasher and the counters wiped down. As soon as I closed the door to the dishwasher, I stood awkwardly, not knowing what to say or do next. I clutched the blanket tight to my breasts and tucked a strand of hair behind my ear as I looked up to see both men staring at me, ravenously.

"So, I uh, I guess I should go to—"

My words were cut off in my throat when they both took a step toward me. Ethan cocked his head as he studied me, sweeping his gaze down my body from head to toe and back up again to meet my eyes with a cocky smirk. "Is that what you really want to do, sugar?

Do you really want to go to your room and wait until it's dark to sneak out into the hallway to watch Brent and I fuck again?" I gasped. I knew they had seen me!

"Or do you want to come to our bed and join us?" Brent took a step forward, the predatory gleam in his eyes making my heart pick up speed. "Let us take care of your little pussy so you don't have to do it yourself."

It was Ethan's turn to take a step forward. They were only a couple of feet away, close enough to reach out and touch if I leaned forward. "Is that what you want, sugar? Do you want our cocks? Us to fill you up?" His voice seemed to get lower, rougher. "We could make you scream."

"Or you could help me get our boy off again if you prefer?" Brent stepped forward again, so close I could feel the heat radiating off his bare chest. Why was his chest always bare? Why is it so hot in here? "Do you want to watch as I slide into his ass? You could use that talented little mouth on his cock the way I taught you while I pound inside him from behind."

Ethan looked at me with a searching look, seeming to read my thoughts. "Have you had a cock in your pussy, Casey?"

His intense look and softly spoken question in his gravelly voice had my heart almost leaping out of my chest. I slowly shook my head, watching as both of their eyes dilated and their nostrils flared, their gazes focused on me.

Brent lifted his hand and stroked a calloused finger over my cheek. My eyes wanted to close, to absorb the sensation, the tenderness, but I couldn't look away from the two men that were staring at me with such looks of hunger it made my body quiver. My brain warned me to run, that I was prey and these men were the predators prepared to attack. My heart knew that them attacking me would be the greatest thing I had ever experienced.

His finger slid to my chin, and he used it to tilt my head up, turning my face to look directly into his eyes as he studied me intently. "Do you want to?"

This was the moment. I had a life-changing decision to make. I either accepted what they were offering, or I walked away forever, closing myself up in my bedroom. I knew if I walked away, they would let me go without a word. They wouldn't judge me or question my decision. But I would regret it until the day I died. Even if I found a man somewhere in the future, had babies and grandchildren, and had a wonderful life, I would lie there in bed and wonder... What if?

So I stared right back into Brent's mossy green eyes and told him exactly what I wanted. "I want you, both of you, to fuck me. And I want to watch you fuck each other. I want to suck his cock, or your cock. I don't care as long as you let me be there."

There was a pause, a moment of silence that was only interrupted by the swift intake of breaths by the two men as they absorbed my words. Then there was a flurry of movement too quick for me to take in. Before I could comprehend what was happening, I was swept into someone's arms and was being carried through the house. I couldn't see what was happening, and I didn't know or care who was carrying me. I just threw my arms around his neck and buried my face in his throat.

I was coming to terms with the choice I had just made and telling my brain to shut the fuck up as it tried to warn me about the potential mistake I was about to make. Taking this next step with them would change everything. I already felt so much for them. Stepping even further past what we had shared in the basement would seal my fate. I would tumble over the abyss and fall in love with them. It may already be too late.

I was placed gently on my feet, and my face was cradled between two large hands. Ethan was staring at me. Somehow, I knew he had carried me here. Pretending I didn't already know them would be a lie. Brent stood behind him and to the side, staring at me just as intently as Ethan was.

"Casey," Ethan began, his voice low, as gentle as his hands were holding me. "I need to ask you one more time. Are you sure? I have to warn you; we are possessive men. We, uh," he glanced over his shoulder, then back at me, "neither one of us has ever been with anyone other than each other. But we want this. We want *you*. And, Casey," his eyes seemed to grow even more intense as he said the next words that stole my breath. "We don't want just tonight. Do you understand me? We want you. Forever."

Twenty-Three

CASEY

I COULDN'T DENY the multiple thoughts running through my head as I absorbed his words. Doubt. Denial. Joy. Disbelief. *Hope.*

Could it be true? Did they feel this connection the same as I did? Was it some kind of weird cosmic fate that had landed me where I was? If that was what had happened, fate was fucked up. Any thoughts of regret of what we had done in the basement were far, far away. There were only four words that I could form out loud.

"I want that, too."

My whispered words were so soft I could barely hear them, but the men didn't seem to have any issues. Before I could blink, the blanket was ripped away from my body, and I was lifted in the air. Looking up at the ceiling as my brain tried to catch up to my body. The bed dipped, and a very naked Brent was crawling over me. I turned my head to the side and watched as Ethan shucked off his clothes. If stripping was an Olympic sport, he would have won the gold medal as fast as he tore his dress shirt and slacks off.

I felt a hand against my cheek and turned away from the lust inducing sight of a man eager to get naked and looked up into green eyes darkened with desire. His mouth came down on mine, and I let my eyelids drift closed as I sank into the sensation of having my naked body covered by another. Brent's lips wouldn't allow me any hesitation, coaxing mine open and plunging in with his talented tongue.

I could barely comprehend what was happening. Suddenly, his mouth tore away from mine, and I felt two sets of lips kissing, licking, and nipping from my neck to my chest. Two mouths that each closed over a nipple, making me cry out at the dual sensations. Too soon, one of those mouths left my breast and made its way down my torso, then my abdomen, before settling between my thighs, spreading them wide.

The cold air on my pussy only lasted for a second before a heated mouth engulfed my clit, the tongue licking before going lower and pressing into my core. I cried out again to see the top of golden blond hair as Brent continued his assault on my breasts. I couldn't see what Ethan was doing, but I felt everything. With a scream, my whole body tightened as an almost overwhelming climax tore through me.

When the majority of the orgasm faded, I whimpered. "Please!" I knew what I was begging for, but the words escaped me. I was beyond coherent thought, only need. So much need. I wanted everything, but all I could do was beg, hoping–knowing–that they would be able to figure it out.

There was shifting on the bed, and I watched with rapt attention as the men moved their places. It was Brent that hovered over me, a lock of golden blond hair falling over his forehead and one eye. I lifted a hand to brush it away, not surprised to see that I was trembling.

"Are you ready, dollface?"

I nodded, enraptured by the look on his face. He was as swept away as I was by what we were doing. I reached up my hands to anchor myself on his broad shoulders. I couldn't deny that I was feeling a bit apprehensive. I had seen his size. Both he and Ethan were well-endowed, with Brent having several piercings. I wasn't so ignorant to think that he wouldn't fit, and I'd heard that the hardware on a man's dick could feel amazing, but damn, he was big.

He began to prod at my entrance. When he had just the head of his cock lodged inside me, my body tightened up at the intrusion as though my body seemed to want to keep him out.

"Fuck, you're tight." He panted and looked over at Ethan, who sat next to us, stroking his cock and watching intently. It was clear to see that he wished it was him pressing inside of me at that moment. "Help her out, man. I need to get inside her. Loosen her up for me." His words were a rough plea that Ethan seemed eager to accept.

Brent sat up, his cock still only about an inch inside me. I realized he was making room for Ethan when he leaned down and licked around the cock inside of me and then swept up to latch onto my clit. The thought of one man fucking me while another tasted the both of us at the same was enough to have wetness rush forward. Brent took that as the invitation it was to continue and slowly pushed his way forward.

The sensation of Ethan's tongue kept me from tensing back up. All I could do was throw my head back on the pillow and moan up at the ceiling as Brent continued to ease forward until he came flush with my opening. The pressure was unlike anything I had ever felt before, and I was so grateful when he stayed planted there, not moving, while I adjusted to him. I felt another lick around where we were joined and shuddered.

I lifted one leg to wrap around Brent's hips, leaving myself open for Ethan to continue his ministrations. Never in my wildest dreams did I actually consider that I would be here. It was a fantasy come true, but so much better.

Brent pulled back just as slowly as he had entered me, and I knew that Ethan was tasting me on his cock. I held my breath, waiting for what came next, but I had no way of preparing myself. Brent slammed back into me hard enough to drive me up the bed, causing me to cry out. Then he slid out again and again, each time driving back into me forcefully. I knew the sounds I was making were loud, and I would probably be embarrassed by them later, but I was lost in the moment. The sensations overwhelmed me, and I was certain I was going to black out.

Ethan continued to lick and suck the both of us as Brent stroked in and out of me. I had a fleeting thought that I was glad he wasn't pounding into me the way I had seen him with Ethan the night before.

"Fuck. I can't take it." Brent was on the verge of letting go, and I whimpered at seeing this big, strong man coming undone inside of me. Because of me.

Ethan slid up to my head, kissing me roughly on the mouth before pulling back to taunt me. "Your pussy has him in a stranglehold, doesn't it, sugar? I bet your pussy must feel so good inside. Do you like feeling all those piercings scraping against your walls?" His dirty talk had me tightening around the cock that had grown impossibly bigger. "You're about to make him come. When it's dripping out of you, I'm going to lap up every drop of you both before I give you another load."

It was the gravelly tone, more than the words, that caused my body to lock up with another orgasm. I vaguely heard a stream of curses as I felt Brent go rock solid before plunging deep inside me one last time, and then held still. I was so wrapped up in my own climax that I didn't pay attention to the sudden heat filling me. It wasn't until he slid out of me and Ethan immediately took his place between my legs and licked up the mess that we had made together that I remembered I wasn't on any form of birth control.

"Guys," my voice was breathy, and I had to clear my throat as my whole body jerked when his tongue swiped over my clit, then back down to flick over my core. "I'm not on birth control." Neither one of them paused as Ethan continued to lick and suck, groaning at what he was tasting. Brent lay beside me on the bed, his chest heaving, a forearm across his eyes. But there was no acknowledgment from either one of them. "Guys?"

Ethan sat up and crawled over my body, staring down at me as his cock found my entrance and slid slowly inside. My hands flew up to his shoulders to hang on as the sensations from just a few minutes ago seemed even more pronounced. I hadn't known I could be so sensitive, but yet still want more.

"Sugar, there is nothing we want more than to keep you forever."

My eyes widened as I took in his words. Before I could say anything further, his mouth came down on mine, stopping any protests. Did I have protests? I should. I barely knew these men. As much as I wanted to stay with them, wasn't it logical to get to know each other better before possibly bringing a baby into the mix? Not to mention, my life was on a precipice. If the Castle Killer found me, it wouldn't be just my life in danger.

Brent rolled over as I moaned, unable to hold back as Ethan pounded into me. He swept the hair back from my face. "We would never force anything on you, dollface. I can go in the morning to the pharmacy. It's whatever you want, baby. I promise. But just so you know, we want every part of you."

God, how were these men so perfect? It didn't seem real. At that moment, I would have given them anything and everything. But I knew I shouldn't try to think beyond what was currently happening. Ethan lifted my legs and put them together over one shoulder without stopping his thrusts. It caused a new, different sensation to zing through me. Every nerve inside my pussy felt alive as he stroked against my walls.

It was all too much, and I fell again, my vision going hazy while sparks danced behind my eyes. Ethan grunted low in his throat and stilled above me, and once again, I felt warmth fill me as his release coated my channel. Though I probably should, I was unable to dredge up a single bit of trepidation. All I wanted to do was roll over and close my eyes.

I must have drifted off, still lying there after the last of my orgasm faded because I was startled when I felt strong arms pick me up off the bed, cradling me against his body. I snuggled into who I knew was Brent and allowed my eyes to drift close again. I could barely rouse myself enough to help when he stepped into the large bathtub and sat down, bringing the water level up to my chest.

The hot water only served to quiet my brain and soothe the aches in places I'd never known could ache. Still in a post-orgasmic haze, I wasn't sure how long we sat there, Hours? Minutes? When Ethan reached down to scoop me up out of Brent's comfortable arms, I wanted to protest, but all I could get out was a small whimper.

"Shhh, sugar. I've got you. Let's dry you off so you can slide under the covers." I was zero help as he patted me down with a warm, fluffy towel. I felt like a pampered princess.

"I could get used to this." I hummed, my voice not sounding like mine. It was low, husky, and slightly slurred as if I had been drinking all night. I supposed I was sort of drunk, in a way. If you could consider being drunk on lust a thing.

"That's the goal, sugar." I just smiled, my lips barely tipping up in the corners.

I was carried into the bedroom and placed on the bed. I immediately turned onto my side in my usual position when two other bodies slid in on either side of me. I wiggled a little closer to the one on my front while hooking my feet over the calf of the one at my back. I was cocooned in warmth and safety, and I never wanted to leave it.

My eyes cracked open just a bit when I felt a weight settle across my waist, and I smiled. The last thing I saw before falling into a deep, dreamless sleep, was my two men with their fingers linked together while holding me tight.

Twenty-Four

BRENT

SOMETHING WAS TICKLING MY NOSE, I was hot as a motherfucker, and my arm was dead asleep and tingling. And not in a good way.

I looked over while swiping my free hand across my face, only to get tangled in golden strands. It was when I looked down at the head of the woman sleeping next to me that the previous night came back to me, along with all the memories. My cock swelled even further from just the morning erection state it had been in and jerked hard against my abdomen.

Fuck, she was glorious. Her hair was everywhere, covering the pillow below her as well as my chest. She was snuggled up to my chest, resting on the bicep that was screaming for me to move it to get some blood flow back into it. Her soft little breaths were wafting over my nipple, giving me thoughts of what it would feel like to have her soft little mouth wrapped around one.

Movement from the other side of the bed had me tearing my eyes away from the gorgeous girl that had wrapped herself around my heart. Ethan pushed up to one elbow and looked over at the sleeping beauty snuggled up to me, and chuckled softly.

"She's finally here."

I nodded, agreeing with his sleep roughened whisper. "But can we keep her here?"

He shifted, leaning over to place a light kiss on her cheek. "We'll do everything we can to make sure she wants to stay."

He carefully slid out of bed, slowly, as if any sudden movements would have a bomb setting off in the room.

"You want a little help?" He gestured toward my adorable trap. I hesitated for a minute. No, I didn't want to leave. I was uncomfortable as hell, and it was everything I had hoped for. But I nodded because I had to piss like a racehorse. He maneuvered the pillow to take the place of my arm while I slid out as slowly as he had, being careful not to pull any of the strands of hair that had wrapped around me like a boa constrictor.

As soon as I was free, I bent over to give her cheek a kiss, brushing back some strands of hair so they wouldn't tickle her face, grinning when she snuggled deeper into the pillow, hugging it the same way she had done my arm. We both walked into the bathroom, and I breathed out a sigh of relief as I used the toilet while he flipped on the water to get hot in the shower.

We grinned at each other when we stepped in together after brushing our teeth, immediately getting into each other's space. Our kiss was hard in a way that it wasn't with her. I relished the hard muscles under my hands, a rumble coming from my chest as I took in all that he was. Yeah, I fucking adored this man.

We broke apart, and he handed me the body wash after pouring some into his own hands. Together, we washed up, eager to get back to our girl.

"Will it always be like this?" I asked as I glanced toward the closed bathroom door.

"Wanting to get back to her? Not wanting to leave her even long enough to take a shower? Yeah, probably." He ducked his head under the water, rinsing the soap and shampoo from his body. "It's intense."

All I could do was nod in agreement. After rinsing off, I shoved him up against the wall. "Love you." His breathy response warmed my insides as I kissed him again before pulling away and shutting off the water. We quickly toweled ourselves off and walked back into the room to see our little princess sitting up in bed, blinking in confusion. As soon as she saw both of us walk in completely naked, her face grew red. The color starting from the tops of her breasts that were barely covered by the sheet she clutched.

"Hi." Her shy greeting was enough for my hard cock to turn to stone. I placed a knee on the bed and crawled up to her, forcing her to drop back onto the pillow.

I grinned before swooping down for a closed-mouth kiss. "Good morning, dollface. Sleep well?" Her face grew even redder as she nodded. "Good." I gave her another kiss as Ethan climbed up on the bed next to us and placed his own kiss on her cheek.

"I have to, umm, go to the bathroom."

I chuckled. "Yeah, I know the feeling. You can use ours if you want." I sat back, giving her space to sit back up and shuffle to the edge of the bed. "But, baby?" She looked back at me, trying to keep the sheet with her as she slid out of the bed, an impossible feat since both Ethan and I were on top of it, holding it in place. "Hurry back. We aren't done with you."

She nodded quickly and then darted to the hall instead of our bathroom. I watched as her ass cheeks jiggled with her movements and sighed. Nope, I would never get enough of her. I moaned as Ethan wrapped his hand around my cock, giving it long, leisurely strokes.

She returned quickly, wrapped in a towel, beads of moisture still clinging to her flushed skin. Standing just inside the doorway as she watched Ethan taking my cock down his throat. I gestured for her to come to the bed, but she shook her head. At my raised eyebrow, she explained. "I really want to watch you. If that's okay?"

Ethan pulled his mouth from my cock and glanced back at her. "Sugar, you can do anything you want to do." He stroked me from where he was kneeling over my relaxed body lying in the middle of the bed. "But, there's something I've been dying to try." He gestured with his finger while giving her a devilish look. I had a feeling I knew where this was going and braced myself as she took slow steps forward.

He grabbed the towel from her body, tossing it to the floor. For once, I ignored it and focused on the woman he pulled in and onto the bed, not stopping until he had her legs spread and her pussy perched over my face. A deep groan rumbled out of my chest as I looked up to see all that beautiful pink hovering over me. I didn't hesitate to reach for her hips, yanking her down to my mouth.

I ran the flat of my tongue over her entire cunt, tasting the wetness from her shower along with the moisture that was all her. After that first initial taste, I dove in, sucking and giving her small bites to her clit, letting her flavor burst on my tongue. Fuck, yes. Even though I could hardly breathe, I knew I could die a happy man at that moment. It didn't take her long before her legs started shaking. Before I could send her over the edge, Ethan pulled off and slid her body down until she was hovering over my erection.

My protest at losing my morning meal died in my chest when he grabbed my cock and held it up before lowering her slowly down. I had to clench my eyes closed as her warm, wet heat enveloped me. I felt her do a full body shiver as I stretched her wide, my piercings dragging over her walls. As soon as she was fully seated, I opened my eyes to see her above me, looking like the goddess I knew her to be.

I placed my hands on her hips as she rested hers on my chest. I lifted her a few inches, then allowed her to slide back down. Our groans mingled together as I lifted my hips to meet hers. As I continued the slow strokes, punctuated with a hard thrust, I heard a bottle of lube open. Images of both of us being inside her at the same time flooded my brain, making my cock jerk hard. I knew it was too soon for that and suspected the lube had a different purpose than getting her ready for both of our cocks. My suspicions were confirmed when I felt his fingers reach down between us to finger my asshole.

I spread my thighs wider, giving him better access while Casey took over the movements, lifting and lowering herself. She looked over her shoulder and widened her eyes as she realized what Ethan was up to. I felt a rush of wetness coat my dick.

"You like that, huh? Knowing that our man is getting me ready to take my ass while you ride my cock?"

"Uh-huh." Her breathy moan sent another flare of arousal through me.

Ethan pushed on her back between her shoulder blades and shuffled closer, making her lie down on top of me, her pillowy breasts pressing flush against my hard pecs. He lifted my spread thighs, placing them over his as he got ready to penetrate me. It should have been an awkward position; I was sure that there were easier ways to accomplish a three-way, but nothing could have stopped what was coming.

Ethan leaned over her, placing the tip of his cock at my ass, and pressed in steadily until he was in as far as our position allowed.

"That's it, sugar. Grind that pussy while I fuck Brent." His dirty words made her even wetter as she rolled her hips against the root of my cock. "Soon, it will be your ass I take as you ride him. Would you like that, sugar? Having both of your men's cocks inside you at once? Maybe one day we'll both take you here."

I felt him slide his finger between us, stroking along my cock and around the opening of her pussy. His words and actions almost had me going off as my fingers flexed in reaction, gripping her hips harder.

"I—I don't think..." she stuttered out as she shivered almost violently.

"Don't worry, sugar. If that day ever comes, we will make sure you are nice and stretched out for us." He turned her head to kiss her deeply, then separated from her mouth so he could take mine next.

I didn't think it was possible, but her whines and moans grew louder while her pussy got even wetter. She had no idea that he was just teasing her, but the thought of having both of us in her pussy at the same time was obviously a turn-on for her.

As Ethan continued to plunge in and out of me, Casey ground her hips, moving as much as her limited space allowed. She rubbed her clit on the root of my cock with every rocking motion. The whole scene was hot as fuck, and I knew I wouldn't be able to hold back much longer. The dual sensations were nearly overwhelming.

Before long, her body began to shake, and I felt her pussy start to flutter around my cock.

"Fuck, she's about to come, man. I hope you're almost done because as soon as she does, I'm going off, too." I growled out my warning before kissing her deeply, swallowing her cry of pleasure.

Ethan didn't answer, he just began to pound me like a man possessed. Every movement added additional pressure on Casey's rotating hips. When she froze, holding her breath for a long second, I knew that she was going to explode all over me. When she let loose, I was done. I lifted my chin toward the ceiling and shouted out my own release, letting jet after jet of hot cum shoot off inside her, until it began to slide out from between us.

Just a few more punishing strokes were all it took for Ethan to off-load inside me. He pulled out slowly, then collapsed in a panting heap next to me while Casey just lay sprawled on top of me with little aftershocks running through her body.

Pure. Heaven.

Twenty-Five

ETHAN

WE SPENT the entire weekend getting to know each other better. We didn't spend our entire days in bed, but it was close. Brent only left to run to the pharmacy for a morning-after pill and the largest box of condoms the store had. With most of the town knowing us, I was sure he'd had plenty of questioning looks, but he gave about as many fucks as I did. Let the entire town speculate on what we were up to. They could all eat a bag of dicks. What we did in the privacy of our own home was no one's business but ours.

I knew we were facing the first hiccup in paradise when I just asked about the scar on her back. I had a feeling it had something to do with her time in captivity, but her immediate reaction confirmed it. She jumped back from me as if I had zapped her with a cattle prod instead of just running my fingers over her wet, soapy back.

I wrapped my arms around her and just held her still, letting the steady fall of the water in the shower soothe her. As I felt the speed of her heart gradually decrease, I grew increasingly angry. Not at her, never at her. No, I was enraged at the person that tried to destroy her body and soul. All I had was the story I had found on the internet. I knew she wouldn't want to talk about it, but I also knew that it would help her if she told us what happened.

I turned her around by the shoulders and lifted her chin with a finger. "Sugar, I need to know."

She took in a deep breath and let it out slowly. Her eyes changed from sadness to determination as I watched. At that moment, I was so proud of her.

"I thought it would be okay." She shook her head at the memory. "It was stupid. They had warned the whole town about it. Especially young women. It was all over the news. You couldn't turn on a radio or a tv without hearing about the Castle Killer." She looked up at me, gauging my reaction. I just nodded without reacting, encouraging her to continue.

"So I stupidly walked home from work, the same as I did every night. I was only a couple of blocks from my apartment when a hand reached out from between two buildings and yanked me into the darkness. I didn't have time to scream or put up a fight." She raised her hand to her neck, and I held back a cringe. "I'm pretty sure he injected me with something because the next thing I knew, I woke up naked inside a large dog cage. You know, those ones that people keep in their homes?" I nodded to let her know I understood. All the while, my insides twisted.

"It was so cold. I remember laying there shivering so hard my muscles ached. I lost track of time. Eventually, I didn't feel the shakes so much anymore. That was nothing compared to when he showed up." She swallowed hard, and tears started brimming in her eyes. "There was another girl with me. Her name was Megan. Instead of being in a cage like me, she was chained to a metal table in the middle of the room. When he came, he would—" Her tears finally broke free, and she threw her arms around me as she started sobbing.

"The things he did to her! It was awful. I couldn't watch." She pulled back to look up at me. "I was a coward. I couldn't watch." She shook her head emphatically. "I couldn't watch."

I brushed the tears away. Wanting to hush her, to calm her down, but she continued as if she needed to tell the story. I had the feeling she hadn't really talked about it, not completely.

"After the last time, when her cries stopped. When he—when he killed her, before he left, he opened my cage door. He left me a bottle of water." She shook her head again. "At first, I didn't notice. But you know how those cages have latches on both the top and the bottom?" I nodded because she seemed to want me to understand. "He didn't fully latch the bottom one and left the lock off. I don't know. Maybe he thought I was too weak to get out, or he didn't think there was any way for me to fit through." This time when she met my eyes, hers were full of pride.

"But I did. It took me a while. I had to bend the bottom of the door open, and there was hardly any room to maneuver, but I was finally able to squeeze through." She reached behind her, touching that long pink scar. "It's kind of hazy. I remember pulling myself to my feet and not being able to stand very well. There was so much blood. I know I had to break the handle off the door. I think I was just acting on instinct. The next thing I knew, I was walking through a perfectly normal looking house and out onto the street."

After she stopped talking, I cupped her face and placed a soft kiss on her lips. "I'm so proud of you, Casey. That was very brave of you. It took a lot of courage to escape, even though you were so afraid."

She nodded, though her eyes said she didn't feel very brave. She let out another heavy sigh. "I moved back in with my parents. But after several weeks of the police being unable to catch him, my parents begged me to leave."

My body grew tight. They kicked her out? What the actual fuck? It was her turn to calm me. She rubbed her hands down the stiff muscles in my arms.

"No, it wasn't like that, I promise. They gave me some money and told me it would be safer if I went on the road and traveled far away.

I got on a bus and paid for my tickets with cash using a fake ID that my dad got me somewhere. I don't know where. I didn't ask. No phone, no ID, no trail. He couldn't track me."

I didn't like it, but it made sense. It was all they could do for their little girl. "The FBI couldn't put you in WITSEC?"

She shook her head. "They said they didn't have space and that I didn't qualify." Her shrug was helpless. "But it brought me here. To you and Brent," she whispered.

I brought my forehead down to hers and breathed her in. "Oh, sugar. I hate that you went through any of that, but I am so glad that you ended up here."

We stood like that for another few minutes until the water began to run cold. I helped her out of the shower, handing her a towel and using a second one to dry her hair. Once we were done toweling off, she smiled at me hesitantly. "Thank you for listening to me."

"Of course, sugar. Anytime you want to talk about it, we are here for you. Both of us."

She nodded, then gestured toward the door. "I'm just going to go get dressed in my room. I'll be out in a few minutes."

I watched her walk through the door and smile up at Brent, who I knew had been standing at the door since the beginning. She reached up and brushed her hand over his chest as if she were trying to soothe him the same way she had done with me. He pressed a hard kiss to her lips and then to her forehead without saying a word. Then, he, too, watched her walk away.

He gave me a hard look, and before I could say anything, he turned to stalk out of the room. Likely heading back to the kitchen to finish whatever needed to be done for our dinner. I quickly threw on a pair of sweats and rushed after him, hoping I could stop him before he did anything we would all regret.

"I'm not leaving," were the first words he said to me when I entered the kitchen. He was plating the lasagna that was still piping hot, the steam wafting up from the pan on the stove.

"Good," I grunted back.

"She's going to hate me. Fuck," he slammed down the spatula. "Sometimes I hate myself."

"She's not going to hate you." My words were hollow. Someone who had been through what she had might not understand the demons that raged inside of him. I did, and my family did. That was why my uncle allowed him to use his farm to dispose of the bodies. It was why my cousin provided him with syringes filled with a sedative. What Brent was having a hard time coming to terms with was that the people he killed weren't the same, and he wasn't the same as the serial killer that was after Casey.

"Why would I hate you?" The soft voice coming from the entrance to the kitchen had both of us freezing. She stepped forward, looking at both of us in turn, before her gaze settled back onto Brent. "Why would I hate you, Brent?"

He collapsed in the chair nearest him and just stared at her, unable to speak. I stepped toward her, holding my hand out, not knowing what I was going to say or do but knowing that this was about to go very, very bad. "Sugar..."

She fixed me with a look before turning back to where Brent was slumped in his chair, looking defeated. "Brent?"

He looked up at her, sadness and shame burning in his eyes. "I'm a killer, dollface. I kill people. I'm just like the man you are running from." He snorted, a distorted grin tugging at his lips. "You have shit luck, baby."

She shook her head and took a step back. "No. No, you're..." She glanced around the kitchen helplessly and waved a hand. Then she looked at me, a pleading look in her eyes.

"Maybe it's time that she hears your story, babe." My words were for Brent, but my eyes stayed locked on Casey as she swallowed hard. Her eyes swung back to where Brent was still slumped in his chair, staring at the floor. He shook his head and chuckled but didn't say a word.

Casey took a tentative step forward. Her voice was small,

pleading when she begged. "Please. I need to know. I need to know you're not…"

He raised his head and stared at her, all emotion wiped clean. "Not like the killer that kept you locked in a cage, intent on making you his next victim?"

The first tear rolled down her cheek, and his eyes zeroed in on it as it made its way to her chin. There was another flash of pain before he checked it. Her next plea came out as a choked sob, and she crossed her arms protectively in front of her.

I crossed the room and gathered her in my arms. She went stiff for a long moment before her strength seemed to give out, and she collapsed against my chest, letting me carry her weight. I walked us both over to the chairs and sat with her cradled in my lap. She hesitated, reaching out her hand, but then firmly grasped one of his and held it.

"Please help me understand."

He looked up at our girl, his eyes red-rimmed.

Twenty-Six

BRENT

"I HAD A SISTER. Her name was Elizabeth. She was my twin."

Casey let out a small gasp, not knowing what had happened yet but already feeling empathy for a girl she didn't even know. It made me slip further in love with her. I gave her hand, clutching mine, a small squeeze to let her know I appreciated her reaction.

"My parents aren't good people. They are pieces of shit, really. When they aren't drunk as hell, they are high as kites. Meth, crack, you name it, they'll snort it, smoke it, or inject it. They had been abusive since I could remember." I took in a breath to calm my nerves at having to expose the horrors of my childhood to such a precious soul.

"They were more likely to backhand me than to say hello. I had to steal food from the nearby convenience store to feed my sister and myself since neither one of them could hold down a job. I always tried to get their attention on me so that she would be safe. They'd been abusing her, too, though. I was wrong."

I gritted my teeth. The painful memories ate at me even on good days, and reliving them now was pure torture. Ethan's low voice had me pulling myself back out of the pit the pain tried to drag me into.

"It's okay, babe. Take your time. We are here with you." I wanted to snort, to deny that they could help me in any way, but I knew that they were already. Just by being here. Ethan had stood by my side for years, never judging, always giving me what I needed. I looked up at Casey's beautiful face. But would she?

"I found out that they had been touching her. Both of them. The sick bastards had been cornering her when I wasn't around. I had no idea why, but she started wetting the bed when she was around eight years old. I tried to hide the evidence and clean up after her, hoping that if I did that, my parents wouldn't find out and punish her. Then, when she was twelve, I walked in on my fucking father raping her while my mom sat watching, stoned out of her mind. That's when I put it together. All those times I had stayed after school to play ball with my friends. Whenever I went down to the convenience store. At fucking night while I was sleeping."

I stared at the floor, remembering that awful moment when my world jerked to a halt. "I beat the shit out of him that day. Just beat him until he was bloody and unconscious. I would have killed him if it weren't for the police showing up. Someone had called them because of all the screaming my mom had been doing. I hadn't even noticed. I was just so focused on caving his face in for doing that to my sister. They had me in cuffs before I could blink."

"But… your parents!"

"Yeah, my parents." I snorted. "It only took them a minute to look around our disgusting trailer to see all the drugs and alcohol. They had my mom in handcuffs next and my dad on a stretcher to head to the hospital with promises that he would be heading to jail as soon as the doctors made sure he didn't die. The cops listened to what I had to say." I looked over at Brent. "It was the first time I realized that cops weren't all bad the way my parents used to say. When I told them about my sister, one of them got up to look for her, to make sure she was alright. But it was too late."

A sob I hadn't known was stuck there, tore from my chest. I pressed a fist to my mouth and squeezed Casey's hand like it was a lifeline. I couldn't speak, couldn't say the words. Ethan knew, though. He finished the story the way I couldn't.

"Elizabeth had gone into the bathroom and slit her wrists. By the time the officer found her, she had already bled out. Child Protective Services came and took Brent to a foster family, and his parents went to jail, where they have been ever since."

I looked up and blinked back the tears, watching as Ethan stroked the hair from Casey's face. She was crying as hard as I was, and all I could do was blink instead of comfort her. My story had broken her heart. That she could feel the pain as strongly as I did wasn't a surprise. She was all that was good and kind.

"I can't stand to see bad things happen to innocent people. So... I kill the perpetrators." My words were so matter of fact. Void of any emotion. "That woman that you saw at the diner with the two kids? Her husband had been beating her. But he was also touching her daughter. I couldn't let him do that. Not to that little girl."

I could hear the plea in my voice. I was begging for understanding. I needed her to understand and accept who I was. Because I knew I wasn't going to stop. I couldn't punish my parents for what they had done. All I could do was try to save others from their monsters.

Casey suddenly pulled her hand from mine and stood up from Ethan's lap. I was expecting her to run from the room, call the police, and escape from our lives forever. What I didn't expect was for her to crawl into my lap and wrap her arms around my neck.

I hesitated only a second, then wrapped my arms around her and held her to me. I was probably holding her too tight, but she didn't seem to mind. We cried into each other's necks for a long while. I didn't even know how long we sat there, but I was exhausted by the time I raised my head and looked down at her. She was sound asleep, tears drying on her cheeks, and looking like an angel.

"Go," Ethan whispered as I continued to stare down at the

woman that had stolen my heart. "Take her to bed. I'll clean up the kitchen."

I nodded numbly and carefully stood up with her cradled in my arms. She sighed and pressed her cheek against my shoulder as I walked down the hall. Gently laying her down after I pulled the sheets back, making sure to place her just right in the center of the bed. Then I stripped off my clothes and lay down next to her, pulling her body flush with mine. She blinked open her eyes and looked up at me.

"Sleep," I whispered and kissed her lips with just the lightest pressure. I didn't deserve her. But I would fight to keep her with me always. And if the man that was after her came to claim what was ours, I would show him what a real killer was.

A short time later, Ethan walked into the room, shucking off his clothes before climbing in behind her. Together, we held her close. We would both protect what was ours.

***

I woke up in a similar state as I had the first morning, with hair covering me like jungle vines. It was easier to extract myself this time, since it seemed like it was Ethan's turn to be used as a pillow. I couldn't help the pang of jealousy. Not that I was upset she was snuggled up to my partner, just that I missed her draped over me instead.

As I stood at the side of the bed, I looked back before heading into the bathroom, surprised to see Casey blinking up at me.

"Do you enjoy it?"

Her quiet words had me pausing. "Do I enjoy what, dollface?"

"Do you enjoy killing people?" She bit her lip as she waited for my response.

I put one knee on the bed and braced myself on my hands as I leaned over, placing my face close to hers so she could read the absolute sincerity in my eyes. "Do I enjoy removing the worst kind of scum off the face of the planet? Fuck yeah, I do."

I kissed her hard on the mouth, then backed off the bed again and headed straight for the bathroom. I was brushing my teeth when she walked in wearing one of my T-shirts. She stared thoughtfully at me for a long minute before breaking the silence.

"I just want you to know that though it scares me, I don't blame you for doing what you do. In a way, I understand." She hesitated, shifting on her feet. "I want to understand. The next time you... do what you do, I want to be there. To watch."

I threw the brush down on the counter and turned to her incredulously. "What? No! Fuck no." There was no way I'd want her to see me like that. "Why the fuck would you want that?"

She looked down at her hands as they tangled in the shirt hem, twisting it and then smoothing it back out. "I want to know you aren't like him."

Him. The serial killer that had planned to kill her. "I already told you, Casey." I jerked open the shower door and twisted the handle of the shower hard in my agitation. "I'm exactly like the man you ran from."

I felt her place a hand on my back, making me freeze. "I don't think you are."

"You don't want to see that. I don't want you to see that. You say you understand, but all you'll see afterward is a killer. You won't see *me* anymore." I shook my head and turned away from her, stepping into the shower and shoving my head under the water. When I pulled back to look at her, she was lifting the shirt over her head and placing it on the counter. She stepped inside with me, and I automatically stepped aside, making room for her under the spray.

"That's not true. I'll see you're still the same man that I..." She stopped herself and looked down at my chest, breaking eye contact.

I placed a finger under her chin to raise her eyes back to mine. "The man that you what, dollface? Tell me."

She blinked, her face turning pink. I didn't think it had anything to do with the heat of the water. "A man that I am falling in love with."

I stroked my thumb over her soft cheek. "Only falling?" I asked softly.

"Maybe more than that." Her quiet confession had me dipping down to take her mouth in a deep kiss. I picked up her slick body and shoved her up against the tiled wall.

"That's good, dollface. Because both Ethan and I were just waiting for you to catch up." I lined my cock up with her entrance and sank inside slowly, watching as her pupils dilated and her breathing grew shallow. "You're ours now. We aren't letting you go. Ever."

Once she adjusted to my invasion, I pulled back. I didn't give her soft and sweet. There was very little of what I did to her that could be called making love. I fucked her hard and rough against the tile wall. I held the back of her head so she wouldn't hurt herself, but the hand that I had gripping her ass as I pounded into her, would likely leave a bruise. I was just depraved enough to look forward to seeing my fingerprints on her for days to come.

It wasn't until I made her scream—twice–that I finally let myself go, pouring all my frustration, guilt, and love into her. I got down on my knees as she leaned, slumped against the wall, breathing heavily. I lifted one of her shaking legs and put it over my shoulder, holding her steady with the other, then cleaned my cum off her inner thighs with my tongue.

Twenty-Seven

ETHAN

I DROPPED Casey off at the diner, heading to the police station after giving my mom a kiss on the cheek and saying hello to my dad in the kitchen. The office was quiet since not a whole lot of crime happened around our small town. For the most part, it was petty theft and physical violence. That wasn't to say that we didn't have our fair share of criminal activity. It was the whole reason we hadn't wanted Casey to stay at a hotel. But it was nothing like the larger cities, and I was grateful for that.

I strode across the room to my office, which was little more than a coat closet. I had been proud when I had earned the office, but I ended up keeping the door open most of the time to keep from feeling like I was being buried alive in a coffin. I sat down at my desk and started reviewing the files that hadn't been on my desk Friday.

"Hey, Detective."

I grunted, barely glancing up from the files. One of the officers that had been hired when I had been promoted to detective rapped on the doorframe before leaning against it. Jared was a good guy, one

I was happy to have my back if the situation ever called for it. "I wanted to make sure I updated you. First thing this morning was the final day of the court case for that guy that murdered his pregnant wife."

That got my attention, and I set down the papers, looking up at him. That had been a fucked up case, and I couldn't wait to hear how long he was being sentenced for. "How long?"

"Yeah, that's the problem. His lawyers found some kind of mishandled evidence. The judge declared a mistrial." He looked as pissed as I was. He'd been the officer on scene to arrest the guy, which was why he'd been at the trial. I had been following closely—for obvious reasons. The guy had been thrown into the county jail without bail due to the nature of the crime and his chance of being a flight risk. Brent had been livid, wanting to mete out his own brand of justice.

"That motherfucker walked?" My hands were clenched into fists on my desk, and I had to resist the urge to throw my computer screen across the room.

"Yeah, he fuckin' walked. You should have seen the smug smile he gave the courtroom. The poor woman's mom was crying her heart out. He just walked past, givin' her a fuckin' wink." He shoved his hands in his slacks, turning around to stare out across the office full of cops typing away at their computers, likely filing a million copies of every report to cover their asses and the entire department. "I have never wanted to throat punch someone so much in my entire life."

I cleared my throat as I thought of what Brent would do once he got his hands on the guy. He would wish for a simple throat punch within minutes of encountering Brent. "Nothing we can do about it," I said gruffly, picking the file back up. "We keep an eye out for him to fuck up again. Hopefully, we catch it before he hurts the next woman. Or worse."

Jared rapped his knuckles on the door again before backing out.

"Right. Okay, I'm getting to work. Just wanted to make sure you knew."

"Thanks, Jared."

I let the information go to the back of my mind for the time being. What Jared or anyone else didn't know was that the guy likely wouldn't live to see the end of the week. He might have been smug, thinking he literally got away with murder, but he would have been better off taking his sentence. I didn't think he would be as satisfied knowing he was about to be pigshit.

The rest of the day went by quickly. I had a few house calls to make and follow-up questions on open cases I was in charge of. One of those calls was to the younger Mrs. Banks. She assured me that she was doing fine. The children seemed happy enough, sitting on the floor nearby and playing with toys.

The questions I had to ask were all bullshit. I hated wasting my time and hers, but if I didn't do everything like a real investigation, I could put Brent in danger; I had to follow the rules, cross the T's, and dot every fucking I. We were standing in the foyer of the large, lavishly decorated house and I shook her hand. Before letting go, I looked into her eyes, searching.

"Are you doing okay, Mrs. Banks?" Her color was good, and the shadows that once lived in her eyes seemed to have faded. They weren't gone, and she still looked apprehensive, ready to jump at any sound, but I was certain that wouldn't change until quite some time had passed. She would never get a body to bury along with her fears. All she would have to heal was time. But eventually, she would be free.

She swallowed and blinked up at me, moisture filling her eyes. "I'm good, detective."

"And your daughter?"

Her shoulders seemed to roll in, hunching in on herself. It was the reaction of someone trying to protect themselves. I hoped it was also one of shame. If there was any question that her husband had been hurting the child, that reaction would have been all I needed. I would be keeping an eye on both her and the girl to make sure she didn't fail her daughter again.

"She's good." Her soft whisper was filled with pain. Good. I nodded, dropping her hand, and left the house. Not everyone deserves a second chance to prove they could be better. I hoped I wasn't making a mistake with her.

I dropped the paperwork back off at the police station, ready to call it a day, and headed straight to the diner. I snorted when I pulled up to the front to find Brent practically fucking Casey's mouth with his while pressing her up to the side of his truck. I honked once, making Casey jump like she'd been jolted with a cattle prod, and laughed when Brent didn't even stop inhaling her tongue as he reached behind him and flipped me the bird.

I pulled up next to where his truck was parked and waited for either of them to come up for air. When Casey was finally able to focus her glassy eyes, her face broke out into a happy grin. She pushed past Brent, ignoring him as he grumbled, and skipped over the few feet to where I was waiting with my window down and the car idling.

"Hey," she breathed out once she reached me.

"Sugar, when you say hello, you say it with a kiss."

She nodded. "Okay." Then proceeded to say hello until the fucker I had been in love with since we were hardly more than boys pulled her away and carried her back to his truck, setting her in the passenger seat. He slammed the door, giving me the evil eye, and started to stomp around to the driver's side. When I honked my horn again, he stopped, throwing his head back to growl at the sky. Then he turned back around, stomping straight at me with a murderous glare.

Once he ducked his head down, our mouths clashed together in a rough kiss that left us both breathless when we finally pulled apart. He nipped my lip once before pulling his head out of the open window. Still bent down, our foreheads touching, he grinned coyly.

"See you at home."

"See you at home," I said, not breaking our eye contact until he turned around and walked back to Casey.

I watched his ass move in tight jeans that pulled just right across his hips and thighs until he was about to turn the corner around the end of the truck. I put my Mustang into drive and revved my engine like an annoying douche just to watch Brent shake his head.

"No stopping on the side of the road for pussy!"

His finger went back into the air, and I could see Casey with her hand over her mouth as she covered her giggles. I honked one more time, then took off for home, fairly certain that he would actually make it the entire way without stopping to fuck our girl. But the chances were never going to be zero.

***

I knew I was about to stir up a nest of hornets. But I also knew that to heal themselves, this might be the one thing the people I loved needed more than anything.

Or it could ruin everything. For all of us.

I looked at both of them, taking in their beautiful features and enjoying their happiness. We were good, but we weren't great. Casey was laughing about some story Brent was telling that happened on the construction site. She looked so much more relaxed and freer than she had since we first met her. It was a beautiful look, one that I never wanted to leave her gorgeous face. As much as Brent was going to hate what I was about to set into motion, nothing else would have the power to forge an unbreakable bond.

"Hey, Brent? Remember that case last year about the man who murdered his pregnant wife?"

"Fuck. Yeah, I remember." His reaction was pretty much what I had expected, the smile instantly slipping from his face, replaced by a vicious scowl.

Casey looked back and forth between us. "What case? What happened?"

I twirled my fork in the noodles on my plate and speared a piece of meat with it before answering. "There was a couple that lived near my mom and dad. Someone called in a domestic disturbance one night. It wasn't the first call. But the woman always refused to press charges. When the call came in this time, she was around six months pregnant. She was dead when they got there. The husband claimed she had fallen down the stairs during an argument." I put the fork in my mouth and chewed thoughtfully, giving it a moment to settle in for them.

"There were obvious signs of a struggle all over the house. Tables overturned, and things were broken. It looked like she put up a good fight."

"So, did she actually fall?" Casey's eyes were misty. Our girl had such a big heart.

"They found a suitcase by the front door. Maybe she went back up the stairs for something. I don't know. But the evidence indicated that she'd been strangled. It wasn't a broken neck or anything else that would be indicative of a fall. The worst part was the coroner found bruises on her abdomen and bruises on her arms."

"He hit or kicked her pregnant belly, and she tried to protect it." Casey deduced, her voice breaking slightly as her tears breached their dam.

I nodded slowly as I tracked her tears rolling down her cheeks. "Yeah, that's what the evidence showed."

"So, how did he get away with it?" She demanded. Her food was sitting forgotten on her plate, and a glance at Brent showed he was angrily pushing his around with a fork. "The defense attorney found evidence today. Well, he found out that evidence that would have helped seal his case closed was mishandled. I don't have all the details. But the judge had to call a mistrial because of it. He gets to walk away like nothing happened."

"But that's unfair! Can't they just start over?"

"That's not how it works, sugar. "Double jeopardy doesn't allow a person to be tried for the same crime twice. But the court system could try him again," I paused, not wanting to lie to her, but not wanting to give her hope, either.

"It depends on the circumstances. I imagine the case will eventually go back to court. The only problem is the evidence that was considered mishandled in the first case won't be allowed to be used in the second trial. Considering that evidence was enough to let him go this time, it's unlikely that the prosecution will be able to gather enough new evidence to replace it."

"So, that's it? A man can kill his pregnant wife and get away with it?" She looked over at Brent, who was glaring daggers at his plate. "You have to do something!"

He slowly lifted his head and cocked a brow. "You think I don't want to put that fucker into the ground?"

She swallowed hard but held his glare. "I think that you are the only one that can get justice for that woman. What if he does the same thing to someone else?"

He nodded. "You're right. The system is fucked up, and too many innocent people get the shit end of the stick." he waved his hand in my direction. "Ethan does all he can but often gets tied up in red fucking tape, or the victims are too scared to press charges."

She straightened her shoulders back and fiercely held his glare with one of her own. "You're going to kill him."

The words hung in the air like a heavy weight as I watched them both struggle with their emotions. Finally, Brent slowly nodded. She mirrored his movements.

"Good." She picked up her fork and stabbed at a noodle. "I want to be there when you do."

Brent's fork clattering to the table and falling onto the floor was loud in the silence. I held my breath as I waited for his outburst.

Twenty-Eight

BRENT

"ABSOLUTELY NOT. Fuck no! Have you lost your goddamn mind?" My thundering boom made her flinch, but she just popped a fucking noodle in her mouth and stared back at me. Not saying a word, just casually chewing her food like she hadn't just said she wanted to commit a felony with me.

I shoved back my chair and gripped my hair, yanking hard. I turned to Ethan and pointed a finger at him. "You!" He just lifted one eyebrow at me. That fucker had *planned* this. He didn't have to tell her; he knew how her fucking bleeding heart would react. Ever since it had happened over a year ago, I had wanted to drain that motherfucker dry for what he did, not only to his wife, but to the baby inside her.

I stood up and stormed out of the room. Fuck! Casey wouldn't let this go. She had all but begged me that morning to let her experience a kill. Now this shit had dropped right into her fucking lap. Ethan may as well have tied it up with a bow. I should have told her no, I

195

wasn't going to do anything about it. But of course, I was. *Fuck! Shit! Damn!*

If I didn't take her with me, she would be hurt. It could end what we were building as easily as I would end that man's life. If I let him get away with it, it would eat at my soul. If I let her watch...

No.

No, that couldn't happen.

I paced the living room as I warred with myself. More than frustrated, I threw back my head and roared. "God fucking damn it!" I stormed back into the kitchen and stood there with my chest heaving as I watched the two of them. Casey had her hands folded in her lap, calm and seemingly unbothered by my temper tantrum. Ethan was watching her like he needed to rush to her if she fell apart.

Even though she appeared calm, I could see tiny tremors in her hands that she was trying hard to hide. I stalked over to her and dropped to my knees on the hard tile. I cupped her hands in mine and begged one last time.

"Baby," I pleaded. "You don't want to see it. After everything you have gone through, do you really want to see a man murdered right in front of your eyes?"

She lifted her head and stared at me with so much determination I knew I had already lost. "No, Brent. It wouldn't be a man. It would be a monster. A monster killed seven women, and he wants to kill me. *That* monster killed two people. I want him stopped before..." Her breath hitched, exposing a small crack in her iron-willed determination for the first time. "Before he kills someone else."

I let out a heavy sigh and dropped my head into her lap as I continued to cradle her hands. "Fine."

Her breath hitched at my resignation, and then she pulled her hands from mine. I felt her tug on my hair and allowed her to raise my head up, cradling my jaw in her small hands. I was still fucking pissed, and I was sure she could see it in my eyes, but she didn't flinch away. Instead, she lowered her mouth to mine and placed a soft kiss on my mouth. "Thank you." Her whispered words against my lips almost broke me. I knew at that moment that she was going to rule me. One look of her big blue eyes, one smile of her soft, plush lips, one flash of her gorgeous as fuck body, and I would drop to my knees to do anything she asked of me. And I was helpless… because I wanted to.

I stood up and scooped her out of the chair. I glared at Ethan, who was trying, unsuccessfully, to hide his smug look. "Get in the bedroom. I'm going to pound your ass into the mattress while you fuck our sneaky little girl. Fuck!" I started stomping off to the bedroom. "You are both getting punished tonight!"

Casey wrapped her arms around me, putting her face in the crook of my neck, and giggled, causing goosebumps to erupt on my skin. As much as I wanted to be angry at being fucking manipulated, I just wanted to fuck it all away. There was only so much I could take before I exploded. A good fucking would calm me when I couldn't cut a mother-fucker up.

I tossed Casey on the bed, not waiting for her to stop bouncing before I was tearing my shirt over my head. "Strip!" I barked out while going for my belt. I watched as she sat up and shoved her golden hair out of her face, and gave me a disapproving look. It reminded me of a spitting kitten, and she was too cute to do anything else but laugh at. But I knew that if I did, she would show her blunt little claws.

She pulled her shirt off, exposing her plain cotton bra, reminding me that she still needed new clothes. I wanted to see her in satin and lace. She deserves nothing but the finest against her skin, showing off her curves.

I shoved my jeans down my legs, kicking off my shoes before I ended up tangled in my eagerness to get the both of us naked. I looked behind me to see Ethan entering the room, the buttons of his dress shirt already undone and the ends hanging open to reveal his smooth bronze chest, making my cock throb with anticipation.

Looking back at Casey, I grabbed her by the ankle and yanked her all the way to the edge of the bed, smirking at her squeak of surprise. In an instant, I had the yoga pants that she had changed into after getting home off and tossed to the floor somewhere behind me, not giving a shit where they landed. I ran a finger over her bare pussy, already glistening with wetness.

"Naughty little dollface. No panties?"

Her face heated as her chest heaved with her heavy pants. "I am running out again."

"Hmmm." We couldn't put off a shopping trip much longer. One of us would have to take the time to buy her some more shit. I jerked her thighs open for my hungry mouth, practically swallowing her pussy whole, lapping at her wetness, and then spearing my tongue inside her. "Fuck, you taste so much better than I ever thought a woman could." My gruff words growled against her flesh and had a violent shiver rushing through her. Seeing her reaction to both Ethan and me whenever we got our hands, mouths, or cocks on her was a dream come true.

The bed jostled, and I looked up from where I had unconsciously closed my eyes, mesmerized by her scent and taste. I watched Ethan take her mouth in a hot as fuck kiss, reaching down to fuck my cock with my fist as pre-come began to leak from the tip. I swiped my thumb over it and used the wetness as lubrication for my strokes.

"I need to get inside of you." I couldn't wait anymore. I needed my cock inside of her before I exploded all over the side of the bed and the floor. Pulling back and standing to my full height, I lifted her legs high into the air. Ethan immediately grabbed one of her thighs, helping to open her up for my cock that was already sliding through her pussy lips, getting wetter. I started to slide into her, notching myself just inside. I waited until she stopped to look at me, her breasts heaving with the effort of her breaths. "Brace yourself," I warned before plunging in deep and hard.

I threw back my head, and my eyes closed again at the sensation of being inside something so warm, so wet, and so tight. Her walls clenched around my cock, and she let out a small scream. I only paused long enough to allow her to get used to my invasion before giving her all of me.

Over and over, I thrust inside her. Bringing my gaze down, I admired the vision of her passage stretched tight around my cock. "Fuck. Look at that gorgeous pussy taking all of me." Ethan let go of the nipple he'd been sucking on and glanced down, watching my cock get covered with her wetness each time I withdrew and plunged back in. His groan at the sight had Casey clenching around me and my cock jerking in response.

"I have to taste that," he growled and leaned in to swipe at her clit before tonguing my dick, licking the pussy juice off with each stroke. He alternated between sucking at her clit and licking my cock; sending both of us on a climb so high and so fast towards our releases that I just knew when we finally broke and fell back down, it was going to ruin us.

I felt his hand reaching around under her thigh, the back of his hand rubbing against my nutsack, and I almost came right then at the added stimulation. I was in sensory overload and knew she needed to come soon, or I was going to be leaving her behind.

"Fuck, man. Make her come. I can't last much longer."

He tilted his head so I could see his face, slick and shiny, and a wicked grin on his mouth. "Working on it." At Casey's gasp and sudden shudder, I finally caught on to what he was doing.

"Fuck. Are you fingering her asshole?" His chuckle reverberated on my dick, making me desperate to come, holding back with every thread of my strained control.

"Am I fingering your asshole, sugar?" There was a sudden movement against my balls, and my whole body tightened at the exact time Casey froze. We both broke. Her scream and my shout of pleasure echoed around the room as she squeezed my cock so hard with her spasming pussy that it felt like my come had to force its way out.

I pressed a few more shallow thrusts into her as I flooded her, making sure every last drop emptied out of my balls. I finally withdrew, my legs no longer able to hold me up. I collapsed onto the floor, my back against the bed and breathing so hard one would think I had just finished a marathon. Fuck, I was thirsty.

I felt Casey's leg brush against my shoulder and opened my eyes. Reaching up with what little energy I had left, I ran my hand over her soft skin and leaned in to press a kiss to her calf. My mumbled "love you" was so low even I could barely hear it, and I vowed to tell her to her face as soon as I was able to stand again.

"You guys are shit at using condoms, you know," Casey panted out somewhere above me. I kissed her leg one more time before heaving myself back up, having to use the bed for leverage.

"Goddamn, I think you sucked my soul out through my cock, dollface," I grumbled as I crawled weakly to lie next to her, snuggling into her side. Seeing a breast next to my face, I couldn't resist temptation and stuck my tongue out for a taste. That taste alone had my cock twitching. I leaned up on one elbow and sucked as much as I could into my mouth. Pulling off, I looked at her sheepishly. "I'm so sorry, dollface. I didn't mean to. I'll be more careful, I promise."

She let out a huff, grabbing my head and shoving my mouth back to her breast as I chuckled against her silky skin. "If you aren't, you might be getting more than you are ready for." Ethan and I shared a look. I think she would be surprised at how much we were ready for when it came to our girl.

Ethan grabbed the hair on the top of my head and jerked my face up to look at him, a snarl immediately on my lips. "If one of you doesn't take care of my cock, I'll be shoving it into the first hole I find."

Casey and I glanced at each other with wicked grins. We moved at the same time, pouncing on Ethan. It was quite a while later, when we were all tangled limbs and exhausted but well satisfied bodies, that I remembered the forgotten condoms... again.

Twenty-Nine

CASEY

I COULD BARELY HOLD in my excitement. I was full of jittery nerves, scared out of my mind, but strangely excited for reasons I couldn't explain even to myself.

Brent climbed into the cab of the truck next to me and pressed the button to start the engine. He put his hand on my bouncing thigh and began to drive away from the house, the path of the circular driveway lit by lights embedded along the sides. I was too wound up to take in the beauty of their landscaping tonight, though.

He gave my thigh a squeeze, then gave me the side eye. "Dollface, what the fuck are you wearing?"

I glanced down at my black yoga pants and the black t-shirt peeking out from under my black hoodie. I had my hair pulled back into a low ponytail and tucked under a black beanie. Unfortunately, all I had was the one pair of beat-up pink sneakers. I looked over at him, wearing pretty much what he did every day. He had on a pair of jeans that were worn and faded around his thick thighs and other stress points, looking like an expensive pair of jeans that someone would pay hundreds for.

"Ummm, blood?" Blood didn't show on black, right? Wasn't he afraid that his clothes would get ruined? How many pairs of jeans did he go through? I liked the way he looked in those jeans, and I hated the thought of having to throw them out.

"What?" He sounded like he was fighting back a laugh, so I huffed out a breath and crossed my arms. I turned my head to glare out the window. "Dollface?"

I sighed. "I thought killers would wear all black."

"I'm pretty sure that's cat burglars, baby." His chuckle had me turning to glare at him, thankful the dark interior hid the pink in my cheeks.

"Well, blood doesn't show up on black clothing." It was my best and only reasoning, really.

He turned his head and grinned at me before facing the road again. "I wear coveralls to protect my clothes."

"Oh." Well, I felt dumb. My heart also sped up as I thought about the Castle Killer and what he would wear. As I thought about it, picturing it in my mind, the dark eyes that I could barely see morphed into green ones, and suddenly it was Brent's eyes staring back at me through my memories. I shuddered and wrapped my arms around myself to ward off the sudden chill. I slammed my eyes shut, trying to erase the disturbing image from my mind.

I jumped when Brent's hand moved, rubbing along my leg and squeezing. "Hey. You don't have to do this. I can take you back home right now."

I was already shaking my head. My mind was made up. "No, I'm fine. It's nothing."

The truck rolled to a stop, and Brent threw it into park. He turned to stare at me for a long moment while I tried to hold his gaze steady until he finally turned away, opening his door and climbing out of the cab of the truck. I drew in a deep breath and then finally opened my door just as Brent came to stand next to it. He held out his hand, helping me hop down from the seat. Once my feet were on solid ground, I looked around in confusion.

"Where are we?"

He continued to hold my hand, lacing our fingers together as he led me to the door of the small office building that read Lassiter Construction. "My office."

He pulled out a key, unlocked the door, and flipped on a light illuminating the room. There was a small desk, front and center, with two doors against the back wall. I assumed one was the restroom. The other one had to be his office. When he headed straight for one of the doors, flipping on that light, too, I figured I was correct in my assumptions. There was another small metal desk and a large filing cabinet against one wall. The entire office was void of any warmth. At least the front room had a couple of plants in it.

"Well, this place is homey. What are you doing?"

Brent grunted as he stepped behind his desk and flipped on the computer. He sat there for a few minutes, clicking the mouse and typing away at something. It didn't take long for him to stand back up. "I'm running a couple of programs that will look like I will be here for a while. I have a whole group of people that will vouch for me if I ever need an alibi, but it doesn't hurt to make it look like I was here in the office trying to catch up on payroll." He opened a door revealing a small storage closet, and pulled out two different bundles, placing them in my arms.

He walked back through the office and out into the main room. I watched as he opened the bottom drawer of the desk to reveal a small safe. After punching in the code, he pulled out a key that was one of many in the safe. He slammed the lid of the safe shut and then stood up, nudging the drawer closed with his foot. "Ready?" I swallowed but nodded, my heart beating against my ribcage.

Without saying another word, Brent opened the front door, glancing around, noting the empty street. I followed him out, then walked over to his truck and waited while he locked the office back up. He grinned at me and gestured with his head to the side of the building. "Over here, dollface."

I followed him with a healthy dose of curiosity, wondering what I would see. There was mostly disappointment when I realized there was a fenced-in lot in the back that held different types of heavy machinery and a large shed-type structure. After unlocking the gate, he led me over to an older model white pickup. For the most part, it was in decent shape and had the business logo on the door. I watched in fascination as he pulled the large magnet off and walked around to the other side, repeating the process. He unlocked the passenger door with his key, tossing the magnets into the center of the bench seat.

"In you go, baby."

I climbed up into the spacious cab, noting that it didn't have a backseat and smelled faintly musty. I blushed when he took the two packages from me, setting them in the center of the long seat, and pulled the seatbelt across my lap before kissing the tip of my nose. The long bench seat was vinyl and had several cracks, but it was still comfortable. When he climbed into his own side, I just had to ask.

"Why are we in this truck instead of yours?"

He put the key into the ignition, grabbed the handle close to the dash, and pulled it, maneuvering it into place. I blinked at it for a good minute before I realized it was a gear shift. He grinned.

"My truck is great. It has all this nifty technology with all kinds of computer chips. It has satellite radio and even a built-in GPS."

It took me only a few seconds to let his words settle when my brain clicked on. "The police would be able to track your vehicle and place you at the scene of the crime."

"Exactly."

He drove through the gate, not bothering to close it behind us, then pulled onto the road and headed in the general direction of where Ethan and Brent's house was. The houses were nice in the neighborhood he drove through, though not quite as large and spread out as the one they lived in. He came to a stop along a curb that had dense trees next to it and shut off the engine. I sat there staring expectantly, knowing that he was going to give me some kind of order, and I was right.

He turned to face me, his features hidden in the shadows, but I could see his eyes peering at me. Even in the gloom, it was obvious he was serious, and there would be no arguing. "I want you to stay right here. Do not leave this truck for any reason. If I don't come back within thirty minutes, I want you to slide over into this seat, turn on the truck and drive back home." Before I could make any protests, he held up his hand. "Promise me now, dollface, or we leave and never do this again. I won't put you in danger, and this is the most dangerous part."

He waited, and would have waited all night for me to relent and agree. As much as I didn't want him in any danger either, I had to agree. I would only make things harder for him. "I promise." My whispered words were quiet in the cab of the truck. The only other sound was that of the ticking engine as it cooled. He breathed out a sigh of relief, reaching over and snagging me by the back of the neck.

"Thank you," he breathed out against my lips and took them in a fierce kiss that left me gasping. When he let me go, he reached for one of the bundles he'd had me carrying and ripped it open, pulling out a pair of black gloves that he slipped on. Next, he placed a black baseball cap over his head. I raised an eyebrow at the choice of color. I could just make out the smirk on his lips before he turned and slipped out of the truck, closing the door quietly behind him, barely making a sound.

The night was quiet, and all I could do was let my imagination go wild, wondering what he was doing. I imagined a million different scenarios. Did he lure the man out of his house? Did he break in, somehow dismantling the home alarms that were surely installed? How would he get him out?

It seemed like time slowed to a vicious crawl as I waited with anticipation, my anxiety growing with every second that ticked past. The only way to tell time was from the numbers from the small clock on the radio. We had left our phones at the office, of course, for the same reason we couldn't take his other truck.

I drummed my fingers on my legs as I stared hard into the night. Taking in every shadow on the darkened residential street and wondering if I was seeing actual movement or if it was just tree limbs moving in the slight breeze. It was impossible to keep my leg from bouncing.

When the time ticked over to twenty minutes, I was slowly edging toward panic. I had promised to leave him behind, but could I really do that? What if he needed help? The man he had gone to retrieve was a heartless murderer. I had no doubt that he would kill Brent if he felt as though he might be in danger, and he wouldn't even blink. I knew Brent had a syringe of something, but I was unaware if he had armed himself with any weapons. All I could picture was the other guy having a gun. Nothing could stop a bullet from going through a man only dressed in jeans and a t-shirt.

I was so busy imagining a gunshot ringing out in the quiet neighborhood that when a thump and a muffled curse came from the back of the truck bed, I screamed out into the cab, jumping and turning around in the seat. Before I could even make out anything, the door swung open, and Brent was climbing inside. I stared at him with wide eyes, my hand covering my heart that was racing out of control and ready to pop right out of my chest.

I could see the flash of his white teeth as he grinned at me. "Ready to go, dollface?"

With my whole body trembling, I nodded, not sure if I wanted to strangle him or kiss him.

Thirty

CASEY

WE DROVE FOR A WHILE, taking a back road out of town. The low hum of a country station on the radio that started to get staticky as we got further away from town was the only thing filling the silent void in the cab. He finally turned down a bumpy old dirt road. I had to hold on to the handle above my window as we bounced along to keep from banging against the door. With every jostle over the many potholes, I clenched my teeth tighter until the headlights illuminated a tiny rundown shack in the middle of the woods.

I didn't say a word as we came to a stop just outside the old wooden door. The whole place looked like it would fall over in a harsh wind. We descended silently from the cab of the truck, and I stood there with my hands shoved in my pockets as I watched Brent messing with something in the truck bed. It was so dark outside that without the headlights still on and pointed at the treeline next to the cabin, it would have been pitch black. It was the perfect scene for a murder. If it were a movie, some masked man would probably sneak up behind me and stab me through the heart.

I jumped as Brent passed me, heading for the door, his arms holding something I couldn't make out. I followed him as he made his way up the creaky steps and opened the unlocked door. Standing just inside the doorway, I was barely able to make out anything, straining to listen as Brent moved around. He seemed to know what he was doing, like he had the layout perfectly memorized.

A quick flare of light and the sound of a match being struck had my head jerking around to see Brent lighting an oil lamp. He turned the dial on it, and it suddenly brightened enough to light up the small space, allowing me to get my first look around.

The cabin was small enough that it couldn't even really be called one. It was definitely the shack I had first taken it for when the headlights had bounced over it. Everything was wood, from the walls to the floor. Even the single table pushed against the wall was wood. It was the size and shape of a dining room table that someone with a large family would have, but it was rustic and uneven. I supposed it more resembled a picnic table instead of a dining table.

I watched Brent pick up a roll of plastic and, with quick efficiency, rolled it out across the floor, covering the entire small one-room space. He walked over to the table and lifted one end onto the plastic, then moved around it to do the same with the other end. I moved forward to help, but he waved me off.

"I got it, dollface. If you want, stand on that end of the plastic to keep it from moving as I get the table into place.

I did what he asked, practically tip-toeing over. I smoothed the thick sheet of plastic where it had been bunched up around the legs, pushing it up against the wall with my pink sneakers. If I didn't know any better, it would look like we were getting the room ready to be painted.

He continued to edge the table over into the center of the room, careful not to shove it and risk tearing the plastic. The whole process only took a few minutes. When he laid a sheet of plastic over the table like a tablecloth, I looked around. I shivered when I realized we had created a kill room.

He had made sure there would be no evidence once he was done, and if I had to bet, I'd say the shack was expendable. If it came down to it, he would set the whole thing on fire, getting rid of any trace he'd ever been there.

"What do you do with the plastic once you're done?"

He looked up from adjusting the new tablecloth and pointed outside. "There's a metal barrel out there. I stuff it inside and pour gasoline on it. Within a couple of minutes, it's nothing but a melted, charred mess. It stinks to high heaven, but it works." I nodded.

He walked over to where I was still standing against the wall and cupped my cheeks with his hands. "You know I love you, right?" I blinked up at him, sudden wetness filling my eyes. "Ethan and I both do. We wanted you to be ours the very second we saw you. We have been waiting for you our whole lives. I don't want to live without you, dollface. I can't live without you. If I were to ever lose you…" He put his forehead against mine and ghosted out a breath against my lips. "If what I'm about to do bothers you, I need you to leave. Climb into that truck and don't look back, okay?"

I nodded as we stared straight into each other's souls. I knew it was too late to turn back now. He had already taken the guy. It was impossible to just take him home and pretend that none of this had happened. Brent had to see this through, and he had to do it in the way he always had, with no evidence left behind.

"Brent?" I breathed out, not letting my eyes leave his even as a tear rolled down my cheek to slide over the back of his hand. "I love you, too."

His eyes flared, and then he was kissing me with so much passion I couldn't help but melt into him. "When we are done here tonight, I'm going to take you back home and fuck you in the shower. Then both of us are going to fuck Ethan until we all pass out, okay?"

"Okay," I breathed out, then he pulled away, giving me one long look filled with promise before turning back to head outside. I slumped against the wall, realizing that somehow, through all the darkness, I had found my light.

Brent came back in a few minutes later, carrying the man over one shoulder and a metal bucket in his hand. He dropped the guy on the plastic covered table, his head dropping with a thunk. He was nothing interesting. At first glance, I would never have thought he was the monster that he was. He was average in every way, from his height to his brown hair. He wasn't muscular, nor was he over-weight. He looked like he was getting soft around the middle, but that was the only description I could have given anyone if they'd asked me what he looked like. For a monster, he was rather insignificant.

Brent stepped back inside without me even realizing he had left again as I had studied the man that had killed his wife and unborn child. Next to the man's feet, he laid out a small black bundle before unrolling it. Out of pure, morbid curiosity, I pushed away from the wall and stepped closer. They were tools.

There was a set of pliers, a screwdriver, and a straight-edged razor that glinted in the light. There was also a wicked-looking knife that I would have guessed was for hunting. It had a sharp edge on one side of the blade with serrations the last couple of inches on the top. I shook my head as I took it in, then looked back at the rest of the tools. They looked so innocent compared to the knife, but I had a feeling it was the other items that were the most dangerous.

Brent took the top off of the small bucket, and I could see it was filled with some kind of liquid. It smelled awful. Brent handed me one of the bundles.

"Put this on, baby."

I opened the package and saw a set of gloves that looked just like the ones he was wearing. I took them out, setting the rest of the items on the ground at my feet, and slipped one hand in before pulling back off again. They were huge on me. I picked up the next item to see a pair of canvas overalls, the kind someone might wear while painting a house. I shook them out and found a velcro opening. As I began slipping into the huge cover, I saw Brent doing the same.

The inside of the canvas had a rubbery texture that I guessed was to keep them fluid resistant. It made sense why he wasn't worried about blood getting on his clothes. These overalls would keep him completely dry as he did whatever he planned.

I bent down to see whatever else was in the bundle and came up with booties to slip on over my shoes, but there was more than one pair. I held them up. "Why are there so many?" He winked at me as he held up a pair from his own bundle, then proceeded to lift up each leg of the table, placing it in and setting the table back on the floor with a thud. "Wow." I was impressed. I doubted there was much he hadn't thought of, and from what I could tell, other than the knife and the razor, there was nothing in the room that a construction worker wouldn't have on hand. Except for the body.

I put the hat on over my hair and slid back into the large gloves. Everything was large and baggy on me, but I was fully covered and protected. Brent picked up the razor and stepped to the head of the table. With quick efficiency, he grabbed the guy's thinning hair and started shaving it off, tossing each handful into the bucket. When he was done, he set the straight razor back down and picked up the knife.

I watched as he cut the clothing off the man, dropping it on the floor behind him. When he got to the man's underwear, he looked over at me, making me roll my eyes. Men. "Just do it. Trust me; I don't plan on looking at his junk." He grunted in annoyance but sliced through the cloth before adding it to the rest of the pile. Even though I didn't want to, my eyes drifted to the man's penis, making me grimace when I took it in. I knew I didn't have a whole lot of experience with penises, but his was ugly. Small and shriveled, it didn't look anything like my men's did.

I darted my eyes away from the sight and met Brent's that were narrowed on me. I threw my hands in the air. "What? It was there! Trust me; I'm not impressed. If that were the first dick I ever saw, I'd probably swear them off for life." It was his turn to roll his eyes as he picked up the pliers and stepped back to the head of the table.

"What are you doing now?" The man was stripped naked, his hair shaved off, and Brent looked like he was about to start removing teeth.

"There are few things that pigs won't eat. Hair and teeth are two of them." He gripped the pliers, fitting them to the first tooth. With a hard yank and twist, it was pulled out. He held the tooth up and clamped in the pliers. "They can't digest them, which means if their pen was ever searched…"

"It would be full of human teeth." I watched as he dropped the tooth into the can of liquid. I swallowed hard, saliva filling my mouth and acid churning in my stomach. I took a deep breath and pushed back the nausea that wanted to take over.

It took him several minutes, but eventually, every tooth was removed from the man's bloody mouth. I had been battling the urge to run outside and bathe a tree in my vomit but jumped in alarm when the man began to stir. He let out a pitiful moan, his hand trying to reach up but dropping back down to the plastic.

"Brent," I whispered with wide eyes. The guy wasn't restrained in any way, and I was scared that he would jump off the table and run out the door.

"Don't worry, dollface. He isn't going anywhere."

I stepped back against the wall and watched as Brent carefully and methodically made the man suffer while reminding him of why he was there. Before the man stopped breathing, he was nothing but a moaning mess, begging for forgiveness that would never come.

As I stood there watching the systematic torture of this stranger, I learned many things about myself. I learned I didn't have the stomach for torture and struggled to keep my nausea under control the whole time. I also learned that I didn't equate Brent with the Castle Killer. Brent had told me he enjoyed killing these people, the murderers of innocents. But watching him, I didn't think that was true at all. Brent was serious the entire time, not smiling. He didn't taunt the man as he hurt him. What he did was calmly explain what he was doing and why, as if he were teaching a class. The man had zero doubts as to why he was about to die.

If there was a glint of anger in Brent's eyes, I could hardly blame him. He'd been through a lot in his life, lost a lot. There was no joy in what he did. Perhaps he had some sense of satisfaction that there would be one less monster in the world, but he didn't enjoy the pain he caused, not in the way a cold-blooded killer would.

Ultimately, I realized that I could accept that this man walked a razor-thin edge of humanity. Could I accept that Brent did very bad things for very good reasons? That his morals were firmly in the gray area?

As he lifted his head to check to see if I was alright, a worried expression on his handsome face, I knew, without a doubt, the answer was yes.

Thirty-One

ETHAN

I STAYED UP DRINKING A BEER, pacing, doing some paperwork, and having another beer—anything to distract me while I waited for the two of them to get back. I never, ever went with Brent on one of his kills. Plausible deniability was a real thing. It wasn't because I didn't want to be tried as an accomplice, but so I wouldn't be forced to testify against him. Since we weren't legally married, there would be nothing I could do if I were called to the stand, so it was better not to know any details.

The thought stopped me in my tracks as I stared off into space. Casey would know. She would be able to describe, in detail, what and how he did it. Unless they got married. It answered the burning question that had been rattling around in my brain whenever I thought of the future. Texas may allow same-sex marriages, but they certainly haven't begun to allow more than two people to get married yet. No state did. It wasn't anything I could see changing any time soon.

That left only one answer to the question: Brent would have to marry our Casey.

I was still grinning when they finally slipped through the door well after one in the morning. Casey looked exhausted but somehow still wired. I stood up from the couch where I had been staring into the dark screen of the tv and stalked over to her, cradling her cheeks in my hands and staring into her eyes.

There were no signs of her being upset. I could find no signs of trauma or fear in the crystal blue depths of her irises. I blew out a heavy sigh of relief and turned to look at Brent without letting go of her face. "How did it go?" It was all I would ask. All I could know.

"No problems."

I nodded and looked back at Casey. "You okay?"

She lifted her hands up to hold my wrists and gave me a small smile. "I'm good. I just need a shower." She shifted her eyes to glance at Brent, who had stepped up to my side. She looked back at me. "Want to join?"

I kissed the tip of her nose, then kissed Brent's lips, telling him without words that I was glad he was home. "I want nothing more." Kissing her nose one more time, I bent down, placing my shoulder in her middle and scooping her up over my shoulder too quickly for her to do anything more than gasp in shock.

She smacked my ass hard as I walked down the hall with her, so I retaliated by reaching up to find the waistband of her yoga pants and yanking them down her hips. She seemed to be stunned into silence, and I could swear she was holding her breath. I had a lovely view of her ass and easy access, allowing me to take a nice big bite out of the cheek closest, then soothing it with my tongue while ignoring her squeals.

"No sex tonight!" I declared, walking past our bed and turning into the bathroom. "You two need your rest. We all do." I slid her down and pushed her against the door to the shower. "As much as I would love to give you your first double penetration experience tonight, we all have work in the morning."

She turned a fiery red and smacked my shoulder while trying to hold back her giggles. "I can't believe you would say that!"

Brent walked in, already bare chested and working on his belt buckle. "Why not? You know that ass is ours, right?"

She spluttered as she looked back and forth between us. "I thought you were talking about things in the heat of the moment. People say all kinds of things they don't really mean when they have sex."

I flipped on the water, making sure I leaned most of my body into hers, letting her take in every hard inch of me. "Sugar, nothing we say to you will ever be in the heat of the moment. Everything I have ever said to you has been nothing but the truth."

"I love you!" I froze and slowly turned back to face her when she blurted out the words I'd been craving to hear from her lips. She was fiddling with the bottom of her hoodie, her yoga pants still pulled down to her upper thighs, and she was bright pink. I reached up to gently pull down the lip she was in danger of biting straight through. She held my gaze, and I couldn't help but be proud of her bravery.

"Say that again." My voice was raspy, so I cleared my throat and tried again. "Sugar, I'm going to need for you to say that again."

Her eyes softened, losing the trepidation, and she lifted a hand to cup my cheek. "I fell for you so fast, both of you." She reached out blindly, and Brent didn't hesitate to take her hand in his. "I am so scared of the future. You know that. I don't know what's going to happen. If that man finds me…" she swallowed as both Brent and I growled our denial that it was even possible. "I want to spend the rest of my life here, with both of you. As long as you'll have me."

I wrapped my arms around her and jerked her body against mine. "Forever," I snarled against her lips before taking her mouth in a harsh kiss. I pulled back and looked at her. "We are all taking the day off tomorrow." My declaration was punctuated by her giggles as I lifted her in my arms. She tried to wrap her legs around my waist, but her pants at her thighs wouldn't let her spread her legs far enough.

I turned to Brent, holding her out, her legs still dangling. "Wanna help out, babe?"

His smile turned wicked before he gripped the sides of her pants and yanked, not stopping until both her pants and her underwear were completely stripped off and across the room somewhere. She immediately wrapped her legs around my hips as soon as I brought her body flush with mine.

"I can't leave your mom without help after she was kind enough to take a chance on me." I rested my forehead against hers and looked into her eyes but smiled at the hesitation and worry I saw there.

"Of course not, sugar. We will celebrate our official relationship tomorrow after work." After Brent finished stripping our girl, I stepped under the hot spray with her and watched as she tilted her head back, exposing her neck and chest. I took advantage by running the flat of my tongue from the top swell of one breast, up her neck, and then stopped to nip at her ear. Keeping my mouth there, I whispered. "We need to talk about you marrying Brent, too."

She froze, then tilted her head back down to look at me with wide, shocked eyes. "What?" Her breathy whisper could barely be heard over the sound of the water. I looked over at Brent to see he was working to get his shoes and socks off. Knowing him, he would carry them directly to his closet to be put away in their proper place before joining us.

"He needs to be protected, sugar. You can only marry one of us, and you know all about what he does. More than I even know. As a spouse, you can't be forced to testify against him if he ever gets caught."

Her eyes filled with tears, but she nodded eagerly. "Of course I will. I would be happy to."

I smiled, so much relief pouring through me that I almost lost my grip on her as my muscles threatened to just collapse from the sudden loss of tension. "Thank you, sugar." I held her close and buried my face into her neck.

"I'd be happy to, Ethan. I just wish that I'd be able to marry both of you."

I pulled back to look at her precious face. "Maybe one day." She giggled and nodded. I breathed against her lips. "I love you so, so much."

Brent finally stepped into the shower, and I stepped aside to let him under the water. "Maybe you should just fuck her. It could calm both of your nerves and let you sleep better." He was lathering up his hair with the shampoo we shared, one eye peeking open at us. Casey and I both got lost in staring at his magnificent body. All those hard muscles along his torso were bunching and flexing with his movements. We watched as bubbles slid down his neck, making a slow trail over his chest with the short golden hair that was mostly along the top of his pecs before disappearing at his belly button, where a thin golden trail led down to a cock that made me lick my lips with just the thought of having it in my mouth.

Casey let out a small whine. I tore my eyes away from Brent to glance at our girl. "What do you say, sugar? Want to take him in your mouth while I fuck your juicy cunt?" I ran a finger over her entrance from behind, then slid it slowly inside her, feeling the slickness that had nothing to do with the water of the shower.

She dropped her head back and moaned, attempting to grind her hips down on the invasion, but I had a firm hold of her with one arm across her hips and her weight propped up against the wall. It gave me all the leverage I needed to be able to play with her wet hole.

"Please!" she moaned out, getting frustrated at her lack of movement.

"What? Tell us what you want, baby." Brent moved in close, trapping her completely.

"I want to suck you," she whimpered as I rotated my finger before sliding it back out until only the tip grazed her opening.

Brent joined where my finger was swirling around the sensitive flesh. Together we sank our fingers in up to the first knuckles. The moan she let out that time came from deep inside her chest.

"Suck what, dollface. Come on, you can tell us." His tone was mocking, and she lowered her chin so she could give him a glare and spit out her words.

"Your penis. I want to suck your penis." He plunged his finger deep and withdrew quickly while I held mine still.

I cringed. "Oh, sugar. Call it a cock. Hell, call it a dick. But please don't call it a penis. That reminds me of my grandma trying to talk to me about the birds and the bees."

Brent chuckled, nipping at my chin. "After the bees had already been pollinating the flower."

Casey lifted an eyebrow but squirmed in my tight hold as Brent sank deep one more time. "You guys are weird," she began to pant.

"Yeah, but you love us."

She nodded, her eyes closed, her mouth open. "I do." The swipe of my thumb over her clit had her shuddering violently. She cracked an eye open, glaring at both of us in turn, focusing on Brent, who seemed pleased to be tormenting her. "I want to suck your cock while Ethan fucks my pussy." Her words caused my balls to tighten painfully and my cock to give a hard jerk. I lowered her to the floor of the shower as Brent sat down on the built-in bench. I bent Casey over with a hand between her shoulder blades as he guided her mouth to his hard and angry looking cock.

I placed my cock at her opening and paused. "We need to make this quick so we can all get some sleep." I probably should have kept my mouth shut because somehow I had jinxed us or something. We passed out in a heap of arms and legs and hair about an hour before the sun was due to rise. I doubted any of us would feel an ounce of regret when we finally woke for the day.

Thirty-Two

ETHAN

I WAS at my desk shuffling through another stack of papers from a report that needed finishing when someone knocked on my door. I looked up to see Miranda Holbrook standing in the doorway. I hid my grimace by picking up my fourth cup of coffee to take a swallow. The shit was foul, but not as foul as the detective who was standing in front of me. I was pretty sure she hadn't missed the look on my face if the spark of anger on hers was anything to go by. She quickly masked it with a cocky smirk, somehow raising her unattractiveness to another degree.

We had gone to school together. While I had been the jock, playing every sport I could get onto the team of, she was a cheerleader. She had been pushy as hell all through high school, not backing down from her pursuit of me. In her mind, we would have been the perfect couple. Of course, she continued to ignore the fact that Brent and I were together, not believing I would rather suck his cock than allow her to suck mine. She had never gone after him, even though I would have considered him the more handsome of the two of us. For her, he was below her and not worth her effort just because he was a foster kid.

When she followed me into the police academy, I had been worried that she would continue her campaign to convince me I wasn't gay. I never corrected her on that. If she had known I was attracted to women, too, she likely never would have stopped pursuing me. It had been several years, though, since she had shown interest. If I remember correctly, she had hooked herself a doctor, though I had no idea if she had ever gotten married since her last name hadn't changed.

I set my cup of cold coffee back down and sighed. "Detective Holbrook, to what do I owe the pleasure?"

A look of irritation flashed across her face before she schooled her features back into the smirk. I watched with a raised eyebrow as she stepped forward, attempting to roll her hips in a clearly seductive way in the few steps it took to reach my desk from the open door. It wasn't until she dropped a folder on my desk that I noticed she had been carrying anything.

I gave the folder a glance but didn't touch it. I was sure whatever case she might have been working on had nothing to do with me or one of mine. "What's this?"

"That," she gestured with a sweep of her hand, "is the file on the little drifter that wandered into our town. The one that you and your..." her pretty face twisted into a sneer, "boyfriend invited into your home."

My back went straight, and every muscle in my body got tight as I glared at her. "What did you do?"

She dropped her smirk and let me see the vindictiveness that she had been hiding. "I did what any concerned officer of the law would do when a stranger comes into town and manages to worm her way into the home of one of the town's most highly decorated detectives while also begging for a job that will pay her under the table."

"You had no right," I seethed from between my clenched teeth.

She took a step back and then straightened nonexistent wrinkles from her expensive suit.

"As I said, I was a concerned officer of the law. It's something you probably should have done." Her haughty sniff was enough to have me rising from my chair, the exhaustion from the long night and lack of sleep suddenly gone. Instead, I was livid and full of anxious energy. I needed to go see my girl to make sure she was alright.

"Get the fuck out of my office and stay away from my girl." I gritted out, my jaw aching from how hard I was grinding my molars.

She scoffed. "Your girl? You have been gay your whole life. Now suddenly, you are interested in a little nobody? It's disgusting, you know? Showing off your perversions to the whole town. Making out in public with not only a man but a woman in the very next breath." She clenched and unclenched her fists. "It's unnatural."

"What you are really saying is that I should have dumped the man I love for you years ago. The only reason you stopped pursuing me was because you thought you couldn't turn me away from being gay. Now that you see that I love a woman, too, your fragile ego can't handle it. The real issue is I never wanted *you*." I slammed my hands down on my desk, wrinkling papers and sending my pen flying to the floor. "Get the fuck out of my office *now* before I file a restraining order against you."

She backed away to the door, her face full of fury at my words. "She's nothing," she spat out. "A little nobody whose only worth is to a serial killer."

"A serial killer that you probably brought straight into this town. If he gets a hold of Casey, it won't be his hands covered in blood. It will be yours."

There was the briefest flash of regret in her eyes, but it was gone again in a blink, replaced by her usual self-assured cockiness. Without another word, she finally turned to leave. I called out to her before she took more than one step.

"Detective Holbrook?" She paused without looking back, her back going stiff as I spoke. "Casey isn't nothing. She's *everything*."

She relaxed her shoulders and walked away with a shake of her head.

I ignored the stares coming from all the officers that had stopped whatever they had been doing to watch the show and dropped heavily back into my chair. I reached for the file, already knowing what was in it but hoping I was wrong.

I flipped the cover open to see an official database search listing her full name, address, place of employment, everything. I cursed and slammed the file shut, standing up quickly, and grabbed my service weapon from my top drawer. I stuck it into the holder under my arm but paused as my eye caught on something. In the same drawer was a device that I'd used once before on someone that had been an informant on a drug case I'd worked a year ago. That case had been a big deal and resulted in the confiscation of a warehouse full of narcotics and placed several people behind bars. It had earned me a medal given by the mayor.

I scooped up the tracker and stalked out of my office, heading straight for the doors, ignoring every look from the officers as I passed, waving my hand dismissively as Jared called my name. I had only one focus at the moment—getting to Casey.

When I shoved my way through the door and out into the sweltering heat, I heard footsteps coming up from behind me. I glanced over my shoulder, not stopping on my way to the car.

"What?" I barked out.

"What do you need, detective?" Jared asked, his tone serious, ready to help in whatever way I might have needed.

I paused with my hand on the door. "I need you to keep an eye out for a man that is new to town. I don't know what he looks like. Fuck!" I paused and pinched the bridge of my nose. "There is a folder on my desk. The report inside it is the one for Casey Rivers. Check the date of the report. He would have arrived anytime within twenty-four hours of it being run." I looked at him as he stood there, sensing the seriousness of the situation. "See what you can find in the FBI database about the Castle Killer. If you have to, call the fuckers and talk to someone. They have to have more information than what the media knows."

He nodded and backed away. "Consider it done." He looked like he wanted to say more but just gave a nod and turned around to head inside. We both watched as Detective Holbrook stepped outside. As he passed her, he shook his head but didn't say a word.

I grunted and got in my car, not giving her another glance. I didn't know if she felt bad for putting Casey's life in danger over some petty jealousy that went back more than a decade, and I really didn't give a shit. The only thing that mattered at the moment was getting my eyes on my girl and making sure she was okay.

I pulled up to the diner in record time and slammed out of the car and jogged to the door of the diner flinging it open, my eyes scanning quickly. Relief settled in when I heard her familiar laugh as she stepped through the kitchen's swinging door, probably at some joke my dad had told her. My muscles lost some of their rigidness, but I couldn't completely relax. She was still in imminent danger and needed eyes on her every move until the fucker was caught. I thought back to Jared. He would be a perfect solution for the eyes.

I watched as she glided over to the table and set plates in front of the customers with a smile. She had already gotten over her nerves about being a server and was more relaxed, stepping into the role like a veteran.

"Hey, son. What brings you in at this hour?" My mom walked up to me with a smile. I had to tear my eyes away from Casey to greet Mom, giving her the usual kiss I placed on her cheek.

"Just checking on my girl." She studied me as only a mom can do and grabbed my arm, dragging me into the back with her. Once we were standing near the large griddle my dad was cooking on, she crossed her arms and glared at me. "Spill it."

Dad looked over briefly before turning his concentration back to the food. I knew he would be paying attention to every word, though.

"Casey's in danger. To make it quick, she's on the run from a serial killer. You'll find all the information if you search for Castle Killer on the internet. But just know, while she used to be safe here, someone in the police department took it upon themselves and ran an official report. The killer will now know which town she's hiding out in. I expect he's on his way, if he's not here already."

I paced away, running my hands through my hair in agitation. I spun back to face her.

"Has anyone been in that you've never seen before? A man? It doesn't matter what he looks like. Any man that is new to town." She was already shaking her head, her eyes filled with fear and glossy from tears.

Dad plated the food from the grill with a lot less finesse than he usually showed and dropped it onto the counter. "We will keep that little girl safe, son." I nodded but couldn't voice my agreement. We all knew that was an impossible promise to keep.

"Oh, that poor girl. I knew she was running from something. I just never thought..." Mom brought her hands to her lips and choked on a sob as Dad took her in his big arms.

"I need to call Brent," I muttered. He was going to go ape shit, and it was going to take everything in me to keep him calm. I turned to walk back into the dining room when the door swung open and Casey walked through. Her eyes lit up when she saw me, but the smile on her lips dropped when she took in the three of us.

"No." She shook her head and began to tremble. She looked at my mom, who was quickly wiping her face but couldn't hide the worry in her eyes. "You know?"

Mom reached out a hand. "Casey, sweetheart..."

Casey stayed where she was and looked up at me with sad resignation as she hugged herself. "He knows where I am, doesn't he?"

I strode over to her and pulled her roughly into my arms. "It doesn't matter. I will protect you. Brent will kill to protect you. We both will. I know what is running through your pretty head right now. Don't do it." I knew my voice was a plea. I wasn't above begging her to stay.

I reached into my pocket and pulled out the tracker. "I need you to keep this on you at all times. Put it somewhere it won't be easily found." I thought of the way she said he had stripped her naked and growled. "Maybe we can clip it into your hair."

She just nodded, already looking defeated. "I should go. Just being here is putting you and everyone else I've come to love at risk." She sobbed once, then drew in a breath, trying to steady herself. "I'm putting Grace at risk."

Mom stomped over and yanked Casey by the arm, pulling her into a motherly hug. "Now you listen to me, darlin'. Nothing is going to happen to me. It's not going to happen to you either, and you know why?" She palmed Casey's cheeks and gave her a look of confidence and determination. "Because my son and his man—your men —will protect you. They won't ever stop until you are safe." She brushed her hand over Casey's hair thoughtfully. "Now, let's get that tracker into your hair so everyone can relax, okay?"

Casey nodded again, letting out another sob, then collapsed into my mom's arms.

Thirty-Three

CASEY

I DIDN'T WANT to be there. I didn't want to be at the diner, but I especially didn't want to be in this town, putting the people I'd come to love at risk. The itch to run, to jump on the first bus out of town, was barely contained. The thought of anyone getting hurt... because of me. Against all my instincts to get away, I was going to trust my men. I *needed* to trust them. I just hoped I didn't regret it. I honestly couldn't see how they could protect me from a ghost.

There was now a uniformed officer sitting in the same booth I had taken on the first day I arrived in town. He was around my age and very polite, calling me ma'am like I was an old lady. He had a boyish type of appearance with light brown hair and soft brown eyes. I would bet he still went home every weekend to have dinner with his mom.

I closed my eyes briefly against the pang of pain that followed the thoughts of my mother. I needed to talk to her. I had to at least tell her I loved her and Dad. I wanted to tell her all about my men and how happy I have been. I wanted to introduce her to them and watched as the shock covered her face. It almost made me laugh to think about how my dad would react. I knew he would be shocked, maybe a little horrified, to know that his little girl was hooking up with two men at once, literally. But he loved me, and I knew that eventually, he would see how happy I was and what good men they were. He would come around and accept it because that's the kind of man he was.

The door crashed open, startling me so badly that I dropped the empty glass on the floor and shattered it into a million pieces. Grace ran over immediately.

"Don't worry about it. I'll get this cleaned up. You go calm him down before he goes on a rampage that would make Godzilla look like a puppy." I gave her a watery laugh and met Brent halfway as he stalked toward me, his eyes full of fiery rage. Before I could say a word, he crushed me to his chest, lifting me off my feet and kissing me deeply.

"Dollface." His pained groan sent shivers down my spine as I petted his arms, trying to soothe him. "I got here as soon as I could." I just nodded, knowing that there would be no arguing with him. Ethan had warned me that he would probably glue himself to me. He likely wouldn't want to let up for quite some time. All I could do was accept it and be grateful that I had someone that cared about me so fiercely.

He set me back on my feet as everyone in the diner watched on, not realizing they were getting dinner and a show. A throat cleared behind my back, and we both turned to see the police officer standing there. He held out his hand towards Brent, who reluctantly took a hand from my waist and accepted. "I'm Officer Michaels, sir. Detective Hardgrove asked me to watch over Miss Rivers. I wanted to let you know that I take my duty seriously."

Brent nodded, none of his rage dimming but accepting that another pair of eyes would be on me. "I'm grateful," he allowed with a grunt.

The officer inclined his head and pointed with his thumb. "I'll just be over there in case I'm needed." Brent grunted again before turning back to me.

My eyes left the back of the officer as he retreated and returned to Brent's. "Are you going to hang around?" I asked softly.

"Dollface, you couldn't pry me out of here with a crowbar." I led him to his favorite booth away from everyone else and waited until he reluctantly slid in.

"I'm going to go get you something to drink, okay? Is there anything else you want?"

"You already know what I want."

I smiled sadly. "Me too."

As I was getting a glass filled with ice, the door jingled, making me freeze and my heart skip a beat. I had been on the knife's edge of a panic attack ever since I'd gotten the news, and every new person that walked through the door had my nerves on fire. When I realized it was the young mother from the other day, I smiled with relief. I reached down for two packs of crayons and children's menus to take to them as soon as I dropped off Brent's drink.

I gave him a small kiss to pacify him as I slid his glass in front of him. I could hear his grunt of annoyance as I walked away. A small smile faded from my lips before it could fully form. It was cute how deeply he cared, but it broke my heart because I knew he was too scared to let me be more than an arm's reach away from him.

I slid the paper menus in front of the children and pulled the crayons out of my apron pocket. "Mrs. Banks, right? How nice to see you again. Can I get you something to drink?"

The mom smiled up at me. She looked better than she had the last time. Knowing that she was feeling the freedom of being away from her abusive husband, I understood. She was probably beginning to sleep better the longer he stayed missing. I wished there was some way to let her know that he was never coming back, but that would be opening up a can of worms that could never be closed again. It wasn't worth putting Brent in danger.

"Can I have a Coke, please? The kids would love some juice, I think." She glanced at them, and they both smiled, nodding their heads and bouncing in their seats.

"One Coke and two juices coming right up!" I smiled gratefully as Grace passed me, dropping a menu off at the table. They began talking softly, probably Grace being the sweetheart that she was and making sure the woman and her kids were doing okay.

I had just picked up the glass and two plastic kid's cups when the front door crashed open again. Fortunately stopping myself from dropping everything, even though my heart had nearly jumped out of my throat. I squeezed my eyes closed and willed myself to calm down. When I opened them again, I groaned.

"Not again."

The same older woman that had come in to harass the young mother the last time stormed in through the door, making a beeline for the table. Grace stepped in front of her, angry and determined to keep her away.

"Leave now before I call the police."

I turned my head to see the officer sitting in the back corner immediately stand up. He stopped and looked at me, clearly undecided if he should take his attention away from me. I jerked my head in their direction and mouthed, "Go!" I saw him glance at Brent first and rolled my eyes.

Before he could take more than a few steps, the woman pulled a handgun out of her purse. She pointed it right at Grace's chest, making everybody freeze, and a several of people cry out in alarm.

"Move!" she bellowed. "Get out of the way, or the first bullet is going through you." She was seething, her chest heaving. Unlike the last incident, when she had been dressed nicely but with her hair disheveled, this time she was a mess. It looked like she hadn't slept in days. Her clothing was wrinkled, and her hair was a mess, standing up in all directions as if she had been yanking on it. "She's dead, whether you're in the way or not."

Grace had her hands lifted, staring down at the gun. Her fingers were trembling, and her breaths were coming in short and fast. She was going to hyperventilate if she didn't calm down. Movement from the side had me turning my wide, frightened eyes to look, seeing Officer Michaels moving slowly toward the woman from one direction as Brent and Ethan's dad moved in from another. They were moving in slowly, likely trying to avoid spooking her while she wielded her gun.

I sat the drinks on the counter beside me and gripped the edge hard, not daring to breathe lest the older woman pulled the trigger aimed right for Grace's chest.

The low, barely audible voice sounded in my ear. Before I could even take a breath in to scream, I felt a small sting in my neck, and I knew, I just knew, he had come for me.

"Hello again."

***

My head ached and was pounding. I groaned as I tried to shift positions, wondering why the super comfortable bed I had grown accustomed to so quickly felt like rocks. For some reason, I couldn't move, and I was so cold...

Suddenly realizing what happened, I tried to jerk myself up, but all I did was choke. Through my coughing, I cursed, wondering what the fresh hell was going on. I definitely wasn't in a cage. I tried to move my arms, but it only tightened whatever was around my throat. It was rough, scratching at the skin there, and I could already tell it was chafing me raw because of the slight burning feeling. My eyes took in what I could see, but I couldn't turn my head.

All around me was wood. Wooden beams made up the ceiling, walls constructed of wood from the limited view I had from the corner of my eye. "Oh god," I whispered hoarsely. Tears immediately pricked my eyes as I fully took in the situation.

I was tied to a wooden table with some kind of rough, rustic rope. My hands were tied above my head, making my shoulders ache with the prolonged position. My legs were spread wide, probably tied to the legs of the table like my hands were, and somehow my neck was connected to my hands, preventing me from even turning my head a single inch. Trying to move my arms only resulted in the rope around my neck tightening further. Every movement caused me to strangle myself.

The hopelessness set in quickly. My heart felt like it was breaking in two, making the pain inside my chest worse than the aches from laying on the hard surface or the pain from the harsh ropes. My breathing became shallow as I began to panic.

I had never been claustrophobic. Even when I had been inside the cage, I hadn't felt this overwhelming fear of being trapped. My chest heaved as I tried to take in enough oxygen, but the fear was too strong, and I couldn't calm myself.

In a state of full-blown panic, I began to scream at the top of my lungs, gurgling and choking when I couldn't hold back my instinct to struggle free. "Help me! Someone help me! Get me out of here! Please! Help me!"

My chest hurt badly as my lungs labored for breaths that weren't enough to satisfy my body's needs, and darkness began to creep in around the edges of my vision as I stared with wide eyes at the wooden beams above me. I was inside of a nightmare that I was deathly afraid I wasn't going to wake up from.

Through my tears and screams, I could feel new pains. My throat was raw on the outside, but on the inside, it felt raw, too. My screams tapered off to whimpers as my voice left me. I couldn't have guessed how long I had laid there. My panic hadn't gone away, but my body had already become exhausted from the fight, and the bitter taste of defeat filled my mouth as the adrenaline flowed out of me in a rush.

I lay there, nothing but a pitiful, whimpering mess of tears and blood, when I heard footsteps approach from outside. It sounded like someone was coming up wooden steps. I clamped my mouth shut, biting my lips, not realizing they were bleeding from the abuse of my teeth. My entire body shook as panic receded and terror took over.

He was here.

The door creaked open, and though I couldn't see who had

entered, I could tell. He exuded an aura of pure malice and evil. It filled the room as he stepped closer and closer, overwhelming me.

I blinked as a silhouette came into view. My vision wouldn't clear enough to let me see who he was. Or maybe my mind was blocking it, protecting me. I closed my eyes and wept.

"My little bird is back in my cage." I felt his hand slide across the rope along my neck. "Her cage is a little different now, though." His voice was low, raspy, not as deep as either Brent's or Ethan's. There was a small nagging inside my brain that I may have heard his voice at one time, but I couldn't place it. It brought on a new wave of terror that I may have been face to face with a killer and never knew.

I tried to speak, but all I could do was hoarsely rasp out. "Please, why are you doing this?"

"Look at me." I clenched my jaw, not wanting to see the monster, and put a face to all my nightmares of the last few months. "Look at me!" His bellow echoed around the room. With a whimper, I cracked my eyes open. I still couldn't see properly, but his shape hovered above me. "Do you know who I am, little bird?"

My lips trembled as I tried to get the word out. A whispered "no" was all I could get through my painful throat. I blinked again as my vision began to clear. All I could make out were his eyes, the same ones that had been hidden by the mask he'd worn in the basement. I couldn't focus on anything else and truly didn't want to. I didn't want the last thing I saw before I died to be the monster.

His eyes narrowed dangerously, making more tears leak out to roll down my temples and soak into my already damp hair. "All those times I came to you, talked to you, gave you gifts, and you don't even remember me?" The malice in his tone caused the hairs on my body to stand on end as confusion flooded me.

"You little bitches are all the same." His head disappeared, and I let my tired eyes close. "I watched you. I left you flowers. But just like all the others, you couldn't even make yourself care enough to remember me." His steps were loud as he paced back and forth.

Sounds came to me as I listened to him curse and rant. Down by my feet, items were slammed down onto the tabletop.

"You know, I saw you last night. I followed you, watching. You and that man." He sounded furious. "I had no idea what you were doing. I almost went to you when you were sitting in the dark. Did you feel me watching you?" I knew the dark had seemed menacing. I thought it was just my mind running wild, playing tricks on me. Now I understood. My subconscious knew there was a monster lurking in the dark.

My trembling was so violent that even though I wasn't pulling at them, the ropes were sawing into my tender skin. My mind frantically raced as I thought back to months ago, before the nightmare began. I remembered seeing flowers show up in the bookstore. The owner had been delighted, arranging them so prettily on the counter next to the register. For a week, a new bouquet arrived every day. But there had been no note to give any indication of who they had been from. We hadn't even assumed that they would be from a secret admirer. The thought never even crossed our minds.

My mind spun as I tried to think back to that week and if there had been anyone new hanging around. I truly couldn't remember a man showing interest. If there had been, I had simply brushed it away like I usually did, uninterested in a relationship with any of the occasional men that would try to flirt with me. And now it didn't matter because whatever I had done to reject him had set his sights on revenge. I wondered if it had been the same for all the other women. I briefly wondered why the FBI hadn't connected us all with a secret admirer.

"Imagine my surprise when he brought back a person to dump in the back of that shitty truck? I followed you out into the woods. I couldn't go any further, or else you might have seen me, and it was too soon for that. But once the truck came back down that same dirt road, I pulled my car out of the trees where I had waited. Instead of following you back to town, I decided to see what you were up to."

He stopped by my side as a cold dread washed over me. "Such a surprise to find this little cabin in the woods. What were you up to last night, little bird?" Oh god. That's why everything seemed familiar. I was in the same cabin that Brent had brought me to. His kill room.

"I liked you the best." He snarled as he slowly walked around the table. "You looked more like her than any of the others. You have that same shade of gold in your hair." I flinched when he touched my hair, running his fingers over it. It was the wrong thing to do.

Even though my throat was raw and I had already screamed myself hoarse, I still managed to scream as I felt the knife sink in.

Thirty-Four

ETHAN

I WAS ALREADY PULLING up to the diner when the call came in over the radio that there was a person threatening people with a gun at the diner. Fear, rage, and adrenaline coalesced in my body, giving me an extra burst of speed as I crashed through the door of the diner.

My abrupt entrance had everyone turning to me in shock, giving Brent enough of a chance to yank the gun out of the old woman's hands. Jared immediately spun her around, slapping cuffs on her as she cried out in fury. I ignored her struggles and curses, my eyes scanning the room for Casey, not seeing her anywhere.

My heart threatened to beat out of my chest as I turned to Brent. "Where the fuck is Casey?"

His eyes grew wide, and he turned to look at the counter. "She was right there a few minutes ago."

"Fuck!" I bellowed and ran for the back of the restaurant, slamming through the swinging doors with Brent hot on my heels. "Casey!" I threw open the stockroom door, letting it bang against the wall. Not finding her there, I ran to the office next, seeing through the open door that the small room was empty.

Brent turned, ran back through the door, and turned down the hall for the restrooms. He opened the women's as I ran straight for the men's. We turned to each other, our chests heaving. As one, we turned to the backdoor, noticing right away that it was cracked, leaving a sliver of sunlight at the opening.

I shoved the door open and looked around the empty alley. Nothing but the large dumpster and a silver cat that yowled, hissed, and darted off. I ran to the dumpster, pulling myself up to the edge to peer over, seeing nothing but bags of trash.

"Casey!" Brent's frantic yell had pain filling my chest.

"Come on," I called and started running around the building. I needed to get to my laptop that was still sitting on my desk at the office.

We both jumped in the car as I threw it into gear, hitting the emergency lights. Everyone needed to get the fuck out of my way. I drove recklessly, not bothering to stop for signs or lights, only my destination mattering to me. Other cars slammed on their brakes as I weaved around them. I had to stomp on the brake letting out a vicious curse as I came to a line of cars. The Mustang fishtailed, coming to a stop inches away from the bumper of the car in front of mine.

A loud whistle sounded as the train slowly crept by. The town was notorious for having one set of railroad tracks, and the train that came through was always long and slow. I punched the steering wheel. "Goddamn it!" It had just started crossing the barriers and would likely take a good five minutes to pass. Five minutes that Casey might not have.

I ran my hands roughly over my face as I squeezed my eyes closed.

"I'm sorry." The harsh whisper that came from Brent had me opening my eyes again as I dropped my head against the back of the seat and stared up at the visor.

"What happened?" My words were much calmer than I felt, but blowing up at Brent when he was already obviously in pain wouldn't help.

"The woman came in with her fucking gun," he rasped out. "She had it pointed right at Grace's chest. I thought," he shuddered. "I thought she was safe. She was standing at the counter. I only wanted to get the gun away from that woman before she killed someone."

I looked over at him to see him staring down at his lap. He still had the gun in his hand. I reached over and gripped his free hand with mine. "You did nothing wrong. I would have done the same thing."

He shook his head. "There was already that cop in there and your dad. They didn't need me. *She* needed me." He looked over at me, his eyes red-rimmed. "I got her killed."

I leaned over, grabbed him by the back of his neck, and glared. "No, you fucking didn't. She's alive. And we will find her."

He shook his head, his watery eyes bouncing back and forth between mine. "How do you know that? How could you possibly know that?" I took our joined hands and raised them to his chest, right over his heart.

"Because we would know here if she were gone." He closed his eyes, a wave of grief washing over his features.

"I don't want to lose her."

"We won't." My tone was final. I had to believe it, or I would be drowning in pain and unable to function. She needed me at my best so I could rescue her. I leaned in and kissed him fiercely before letting go and putting my hands back on the wheel. The end of the train was in sight, and the station was only another mile down the road. I would have her location within a few minutes.

My foot itched to hit the gas as soon as the cars started moving forward. "Get out of the fucking way, assholes," I gritted out through clenched teeth. "Fuck!" It was taking too long. My lights were already flashing. The fucking drivers should have been pulling to the side already. If I could give every single one of them a ticket, I would have.

A path was slowly cleared for me, and as soon as there was a hole big enough to slide through, I finally stepped on the gas, rocketing forward as fast as I could go. It felt like hours, but was less than a minute until I screeched to a stop in front of the station, my tires screaming in protest. I threw the car into park and jumped out without bothering to remove my keys.

Together, we ran through the doors, every single person in the building halting whatever they had been doing. I slammed through the door of my office, just another door that felt my wrath, and dropped into the chair. My laptop was already open, so I moved the mouse, waking it up. I had to type my password twice my fingers were shaking so fucking bad.

As soon as it was running, I clicked on the program I needed and waited while the department issued laptop started up the tracking program. I nearly sagged in relief when it was fully loaded and began to show a little green dot on the map.

"What's that?" Brent asked from his position, leaning over my shoulder to watch.

"That," I pointed at the dot, "is our girl. I gave her a tracker to wear as soon as I found out that the background check was done on her." I clenched my jaw as I remembered what had started all this today. "I don't know where that is, though. It looks like it's in the middle of the forest."

"I do."

I turned to look at him over my shoulder to see fear in his eyes, along with a healthy dose of rage. "Where is it?" But I think I already knew. The look on his face gave it away.

"It's where I go to get rid of monsters." It was all I needed to hear. I was grateful because he would know the way there. All I cared about was saving our girl, and he had first-hand knowledge of the location.

Brent backed up as I pushed the chair back and shoved out of it. "Let's go."

We both headed straight for the door when my name was called out. I wouldn't have stopped for anyone else, but it was my Captain. I turned my head to see him striding through the room, a nervous-looking Miranda trailing behind him, wringing her hands. In the glance I threw at her before focusing on the Captain's face, I could see her worry and sorrow. But I gave zero fucks about her feelings.

"Sir?"

"I have been told about your... situation. I want you to take officers with you. Yes!" he barked out as I started to shake my head. "That's an order, Detective. You are messing with a known killer and psychopath. You aren't going alone." He glanced over at Brent but looked away quickly. I knew he could demand that Brent stay behind, he *should* stay behind since he was a civilian, and it would be dangerous. Instead, the Captain was pretending he wasn't there, for which I was grateful. There was no way I was going to leave him behind, and though I had no problem disobeying a direct order, I was glad I wouldn't have to.

"Sir, I'd rather—"

"It's done. You aren't going in alone. And, Detective? Get her back. I'd rather not have to deal with the FBI if that fucker gets away again."

I nodded, ready to head back out. "I intend to, sir."

As I began to stride toward the door again, Miranda rushed up beside me. I could see her out of the corner of my eye glancing over to Brent and back to me. "I'd like to go..." she began, but I cut her off with a sharp no.

"You've done enough, don't you think?" I snarled as I reached my running car. Sliding into the seat, the doors still wide open, waiting just long enough for Brent to get in to take off again. I ignored the determined look she had as I drove out of the parking lot and onto the street.

My phone rang, and I hit the button to accept the call, seeing that it was the Captain calling. "Sir," I gritted out with the limited amount of patience I had left.

"The location, detective?"

I glanced over at Brent before speaking. "There's a small cabin in the woods on a dirt road off Highway 51. It's still up on my computer if someone takes a look to get a better idea."

"Good enough. Try not to kill yourself on the way. I've already taken three different calls about your reckless driving today."

"Sir."

The call ended, and we drove the rest of the way in silence. Once he directed me to the dirt road, I slowed down, despite the need I felt to get to our girl quickly. The road was in shitty condition, and my car wouldn't be able to make it in one piece if I drove too fast. And I needed stealth. If I drove up too fast, making too much noise, it would alert him to our arrival, and I didn't want to think about what that would mean for Casey.

"The cabin is about a quarter mile up the road," Brent said quietly after a short drive, and I nodded, coming to a stop. We climbed out of the car. I checked my service weapon and looked up to see Brent doing the same with the gun he had taken from the old lady. I would have a lot of shit to answer for if he used it, but I was grateful to know he had a weapon.

Together, we jogged up the road until the cabin came into view. "This isn't a fucking cabin, Brent. It's barely a shack," I whispered.

He shrugged. "It holds a purpose. Nobody knows it's here, and it's expendable if anyone ever finds out." He huffed out a breath. "I guess they know now."

"You know this means he followed you last night, right?"

He nodded as we crept forward, inching closer to the shack that had a small black car sitting in front of it. "Yeah."

I was sure we were both thinking that things could have gone badly if the Castle Killer had chosen to make his move last night when Brent would have been caught unaware. Then all thoughts of possibilities vanished when a tortured scream full of pain tore through the air.

Together, we sprinted to the door, the time for stealth beyond us.

The first thing I saw as I entered the pitifully small shack was my beautiful girl laid out, tied to a wooden table. She was completely naked, and it appeared that she had put up quite a struggle. The ropes had rubbed her skin raw, and then was blood where the rough fibers were pressing tightly against her delicate flesh. Her chest was heaving, and there were sounds of distress coming from her. It wasn't until my eyes took in the man hovering above her head that I noticed the knife he was holding that was still embedded in her chest.

"Fuck! Dollface—" Brent moved as if to go for her when the asshole pulled a gun out from behind his back and pointed it at Brent.

"Stay back!" His scream had spittle flying from his mouth. His eyes were wild as he stared at us in shock.

"Brent," I warned in a low tone. "Step back." I flashed my eyes between the gun that hadn't left its target and the knife that was piercing Casey's clavicle, filling me with concern for its location. I didn't think it was close enough to her heart, but, fuck, I was trying to think back to any biology lesson I'd had to remember where all the arteries were in a human body.

I tore my eyes away from the blood that had pooled around the knife and took in the man that was the cause of so much pain and heartbreak for so many people. He was nondescript with little notable about him. Average height, average build, brown hair, brown eyes. Much like all the men that Brent meted out justice to.

"You have nowhere to go, and you can't take out both of us," I warned. "It's over."

He slid his panicked gaze over to me, and before I could react, he yanked the knife out with a hard jerk. Casey screamed out as Brent took a step forward, his hand reaching toward her. The loud sound of a gunshot had my ears ringing as anguish filled me. My heart stopped, and I watched in horror as Brent clutched at his stomach, redness already seeping to cover his t-shirt.

Through the haze of disbelief, I heard Casey's screams turn from those of pain to those of fright. "Please, please don't hurt them! Kill me instead! Kill me! Please. Please. Please don't hurt them!"

Brent dropped to one knee. One hand still covering his wound and the other bracing himself on the floor. His head was down as he breathed through the pain. I wanted desperately to go to him. Motionless, I didn't know who to go to, I needed to see to both of them, but I couldn't move. I was sure the only thing that was keeping them alive was the gun I was holding, pointed right at the Castle Killer.

I swallowed hard. "Brent? Brent, talk to me." I couldn't help the pleading in my tone.

He grunted, swaying in place and looking like he was about to fall over.

"B-Brent? Is Brent okay? Ethan!" Casey was crying hysterically, not even seeming to notice that the killer had placed his bloody knife at her throat, digging it in.

I watch the small trickle of blood sliding down her pale skin. "He's fine, sugar. It will be okay. Calm down for me, love. I don't want you to hurt yourself."

"Don't call her that!" The man screamed in outrage and turned his gun from Brent's form that was slumped over, to me.

"What? Don't call her love?" I asked without flinching. "But I do love her. Brent and I are going to marry her, and we will have a beautiful life together. She's going to be the mother of our children. And twenty years from now, no one will remember you existed."

He roared in anger, and so many things happened at once I could barely make sense of it all.

Thirty-Five

BRENT

FUCK, *that hurt.*

Fiery pain exploded through my system from the motherfucking bullet wound as I pressed hard against my abdomen and cursed under my breath. I tapped my fingers on the wooden boards that made up the shack floor, knowing that Ethan would see. It had been a long fucking time since we had played a game of football together, but I knew he hadn't forgotten. We were the goddamn dream team. There wasn't a play that we couldn't win together because we had learned how to communicate.

I moved the fingers I had braced against the floor, doing my best to make sure he would understand what I was trying to tell him. I had to pause as my vision went black for a second, and I had to breathe through the pain. I panted and then repeated the gestures again once I could continue.

Ethan tapped his foot the same as he used to when he was the quarterback and was ready for the next play to begin. I hung my head as the relief washed over me. I tensed my body in preparation, biting back the instant sharp pain that stabbed through my abdomen. And waited.

Seemingly from nowhere, a commotion sounded outside the door as several feet ran up the porch steps and through the open doorway. There was another gunshot and a scream of pain. Not taking the time to see where it came from or who had been shot, I launched myself forward, both arms extended, ready to wrap them around the asshole and tackle him to the ground.

Unable to get the full movement I had hoped for, I did manage to get a good grip around his hips and, with all the strength I could muster, pushed him backward until our bodies had nowhere else to go. Through the fog of pain that took over my senses, I heard the clatter of the knife as it fell to the floor beside my head and the heavy thud of the gun as it hit the floor. Another shot boomed out next to my ear, and then I couldn't hear anything but a sharp ringing as my vision blurred, and the pain in my stomach almost made me vomit.

I rolled onto my back, but when the pain threatened to overwhelm me, I curled into a ball. Hands began to run over me, trying to turn me back over, but I shoved them away, only to have them come back. Slowly, sounds other than ringing began to filter back in. I cracked my eyes open to see Ethan above me, his mouth moving and looking frantic.

"Brent! Can you hear me?" Brent!"

"Dollface?" was all I could rasp out. Ethan was obviously okay, but was our girl? She'd had a knife held to her neck and already had a stab wound. Did my attack make things worse? Oh god! What if I'd caused the knife to dig in deeper and slice her throat open? I needed to get up. I shoved at Ethan, needing space to get to my feet. I fought through nausea and weakness while Ethan stood next to me and grasped me by the arms, lending me his strength and helping me to stand.

I staggered to my feet and leaned heavily against the table, ignoring Ethan's muttered curses about me being a stubborn son of a bitch. I glanced back down at the floor to see the killer lying at an odd angle with his head at the base of the wall and the rest of him on the floor. There was a puddle of blood coming from his head, expanding along the floor at a steady rate. I would have spit on his body, if I could. Turning away from him to what was really important, my eyes took in Casey as she lay there silent and still, blood covering most of her chest.

"Dollface?" My words were dragged from my chest as I choked them out. "No…" I hovered my hand over the main source of all the blood, ignoring the fact that my hand was as bloody as her chest.

Movement caught my attention, and I stiffened, looking up to see one of the other detectives that worked with Ethan. I vaguely remembered her from high school as a cheerleader or something, but didn't give enough of a fuck at the minute to try to remember. I relaxed as I saw her bend down and pick up the knife that had fallen to the ground, and quickly but carefully started sawing the ropes that were binding Casey to the table.

Once her hands and neck were free, the other woman paused, setting the knife on the table, and took off her suit jacket. Before I could cuss her ass out for not finishing the job of freeing Casey, I blinked, relief and gratefulness overwhelming me as she laid her jacket over the top of my girl's body, covering her nakedness. Why that one act was enough to make my eyes water, I had no idea. Maybe I had just lost too much blood.

I sagged back against Ethan as he continued to hold me up, and we both stared down at Casey. "She'll be alright," Ethan rasped out.

"Yeah," I whispered, neither one of us daring to really believe it.

After cutting all the ropes, the woman laid the knife on the table and pointed with her thumb over her shoulder. "I'm just going to step outside and wait for the ambulance to arrive." We both nodded in thanks as she gave Casey one last long look filled with sorrow and regret.

I reached over to gently touch Casey's neck, looking closer at the knife wound there now that the rope was gone. It was bloody and would leave a vicious scar, but it wasn't as deep as I had feared. "Her neck doesn't look too bad. She's lost a lot of blood from her chest, but why is she still passed out?"

"I don't know, maybe shock?"

I lowered my head as her jagged breathing started to register. "Ethan, her breathing. Her lungs..."

He pulled back the jacket and ran his hand through the blood over her chest, but the only wound was the one in her clavicle. He started shaking his head. "I don't know why she's breathing like that. The knife wound is too high to be near her lungs."

There was a scraping sound coming from behind us. Before either of us could react, Ethan was hit in the temple with the butt of the gun the killer was holding in his hand. I watched in disbelief as Ethan's eyes rolled back into his head. As he crumpled to the ground, I lost my balance, not having enough strength left to hold me up. My hands scrambled for purchase and landed on Casey's shoulder, making her moan out loud in pain. Instinct had me jerking my hand off of her injury.

It had happened so quickly. Between seeing Ethan getting knocked out by the guy we all thought was dead, to see him standing over me with blood dripping in his left eye. The gun was held steady, pointed at my fucking chest again while I lay on the floor, barely breathing from the pain that took over the second I hit the ground.

I glanced over at Ethan, wishing that I had told him I loved him more. Then I dropped my head back and looked up at the table, and the regrets I had when it came to Casey vanished as I began to comprehend what I was seeing.

The stray bullet.

The strange breathing.

Why she was passed out when the blood loss hadn't seemed that bad...

I watched as the blood dripped from the bullet hole under the table to the puddle of blood that my hand was lying in. I raised my hand off the ground and stared at it in disbelief.

"Casey..." I croaked out her name as tears pricked my eyes. All of this for what? This asshole was going to win? He was going to kill me, my girl, and then my man? No! It couldn't end like this. He was nothing but a monster that preyed on innocents. The monsters didn't win. They weren't supposed to win.

"I told you," he said, cocking back the trigger and leveling the gun at my chest, stepping forward slowly until he was right over me, next to the table. He looked like the monster he truly was, with the blood covering half his face and dripping over his lips, into his mouth, and coating his teeth in a macabre smile. "She belongs to me."

"I belong to whoever *the fuck* I want to." The wet, raspy words were punctuated with a knife through the center of the killer's throat.

The last thing I heard was the sound of the gun falling to the floor. Another bullet being fired and embedding itself into the wooden wall about two feet above my head. I was already floating in darkness by the time the stampede of officers, along with the Detective, ran into the cabin to see the carnage. I also missed when Casey slumped to her side just as the sound of a siren wailed in the distance.

***

The beeping of the heart monitor wasn't what woke me out of my medically induced coma. It wasn't even the sound of the alarm on the infusion pump as it alerted the nurse to change my IV bag. Instead, it was the sound of a man crying while squeezing my hand.

"Did she... Did she die?" I had to choke the words out through my dry throat. I refused to open my eyes, not wanting to face the reality of a world where Casey didn't exist.

The nurse cleared her throat as she pushed a few buttons. "I need to get the doctor now that you are awake. Are you in any pain?"

I didn't answer, just shook my head. The pain in my heart was so much worse than any physical pain I could have.

"Alright, I'll be right back. Detective, please don't get him too worked up, okay?" She didn't wait for a response, just backed out of the room, shutting the door quietly behind her.

I turned my head and finally opened my eyes. He looked tired. His hair was a mess, and his five o'clock shadow looked more like a five-day shadow. He looked beautiful. "When did she die?" My heart broke as I grated the words out.

"She's not dead," he whispered. "They say she's going to make a full recovery. She had a collapsed lung from the bullet that went through the table, and she'll have to be careful, but overall, she'll be fine."

I stared at him in confusion as I finally accepted the cup of water and straw he'd been trying to shove at me since the nurse had left. After cooling my parched throat, I pushed the cup back. "Then why the hell are you crying?"

He shoved away from the bed, the slight jostling making me wince. "Because *you* almost died, you stupid son of a bitch! Because I watched the man and woman I love get loaded into the back of an ambulance with a bullet hole in his belly and one in her back! Because I have just spent the last week watching over you both, counting every breath."

I didn't know what to say. If I had been in his position, I didn't know if I could have handled it. I probably would have ended up in jail for going on a rampage through town, destroying everything in my path while lost in my grief.

"The two of you were the last thing I thought of when I was sure I was dying. As I looked at the barrel of the gun, all I could think of was everything we weren't going to have. I wanted it so much, you know? The wife, the babies, and the dog. I wanted it for us—with you and with her. I thought it was gone, and I just..." I guess I gave up. How could I say those words out loud? I fought for every good thing in my life and gave up right when I needed to hang on the most. Shame filled me.

Ethan sat back down in his chair, grabbed my hand, threading our fingers together, and brought them to his forehead. He breathed hard before taking in a big inhale, but before he could speak, the sweetest voice I'd ever heard came quietly from the doorway.

"I want that, too."

We both looked over to see Casey looking pale, dressed in a hospital gown, and sitting in a wheelchair with a fluffy pink blanket tucked in around her legs and hips. She had one arm in a sling and the other clutching the blanket. There was a woman with the same hair and eyes as our girl, with one hand resting on the handle of the chair and the other pressed to her chest. A man stood next to the women, a hand on the shoulder of his wife. His eyes took in Ethan and me. I tensed, waiting for the judgment, the condemnation for being gay. The disapproval for his daughter.

The man stepped around his wife and daughter and strode to the side of the bed, where Ethan continued to hold my hand as he stared at Casey with a soft look on his face.

I stared up at her dad, meeting his eyes with all the bravery I could muster. I'd stared into the eyes of killers, rapists, and pedophiles, but this was the first time I felt my nerves jump and my heart race. I cleared my throat and got ready to start begging.

"Sir, I—"

He dropped to his knees at the side of my bed and put one hand on Ethan's shoulder and the other on my forearm. His sobs filled the room, echoed by delicate sniffles from Casey's mother. "Thank you."

I lay there, stunned, unable to open my mouth. I glanced over to Casey as she sat in her wheelchair, holding her mother's hand over her good shoulder. She gave me a small, reassuring smile. The doctor was standing in the doorway behind them but took a step back and rested against the wall in the hallway. I looked back down as the man's shoulders shook.

Thirty-Six

CASEY

I HAD NEVER SEEN my dad as upset as I had when I'd opened my eyes a few days ago in the hospital bed. He'd raised his voice, paced, turned red, and then collapsed in the chair next to the bed and listened while holding Mom's hand. I told them everything from the time I'd climbed onto the first bus while keeping the story PG-rated, of course.

By the time I was done, my mom was crying almost inconsolably, and my dad had stalked from the room, not returning for over two hours. I didn't know where he went, but I had an idea it included a long walk and a tall coffee. He'd never been that great with showing emotions beyond the usual fatherly displays of happiness, pride, love, and anger. He never raged. He never cried. Though we knew he loved us deeply, his outward display rarely went beyond a pat on the head for me and a peck on the lips for my mom.

Ethan had been sitting by Brent's bedside once he got back from the hospital cafeteria. They both looked up when my dad strode back inside the room. He'd glanced from my position in my hospital bed and over to Ethan as he sat by Brent. Ethan was holding Brent's hand, much the same way my mom was holding mine. Ethan stood slowly from his chair and held out his hand. Dad had knocked his hand away, making me gasp in shock before I started immediately coughing, of course. A collapsed lung wasn't fun.

As soon as dad had knocked Ethan's hand away, he had embraced him in a huge hug as mom and I looked on with tears in our eyes. I couldn't remember my dad ever looking so grateful as he had pulled back and looked into Ethan's eyes. They'd had a long, quiet talk sitting next to Brent's bedside. For the last five days, both Mom and Dad had taken turns sitting with Brent as Ethan shared his time between the two of us.

Now that Brent was awake, my dad was apparently done with holding back. His control over his emotions had come undone, and though Brent looked shocked, there was also a massive amount of relief there, too.

Unfortunately, the doctor had to come in at that exact moment. He allowed them several minutes, letting my dad calm himself, before clearing his throat and knocking on the door as if he hadn't witnessed the show of emotions.

My parents went down to the cafeteria, and Ethan sat with me on my side of the curtained room during my thorough check-up. Now we had to break the news to Brent that I was being released for home—doctor's orders. I didn't want to tell him which home that was going to be, but I couldn't continue to be a coward.

Once my bag was packed with the few items I had with me, my mom kissed the top of my head and squeezed my hand. Dad gave me a nod. They had already told the guys goodbye, but I don't think either one of them had caught on that it wasn't the same as it had been the last few days. I finally looked up at Ethan and immediately noticed that his jaw was clenched tight. Maybe he had.

"You're coming back," it wasn't Ethan's voice. I turned to see Brent with his eyes narrowed and looking like he was ready to rip off all the wires and tubes and jump out of the bed. "Say it, dollface. Say it." His voice cracked on the last word, and I couldn't take it anymore. I carefully pushed myself up with my good arm, ignoring Ethan's protests.

"I have to go back to California."

I watched as he closed his eyes and turned his head. The expression that came over his face was enough to shatter my heart.

"But..." I waited several long beats before he finally opened his eyes again, all of his anguish pouring out as he looked at me. I reached out and cupped his face, blindly reaching behind me until I could grasp Ethan's hand in mine. "I *will* be back. It's only for a short time. I swear it. There are things I need to settle there." I looked down at the bed. It hurt me to leave them, too, and I felt like the worst asshole for leaving like I was, with him in the hospital. My parents had to get back, though. They needed to work for a living and wouldn't be able to pay their mortgage if they didn't get back to work soon. They promised me it would be a quick trip and that they would help me get my stuff sorted so I could get back as quickly as possible.

It was my turn to look up at him when he gently placed a finger under my chin and lifted my gaze back to his. "We will wait for you, dollface. Forever. We'll wait for you forever."

A tear slid down my cheek and onto his finger, but neither of us broke eye contact.

"I love you."

"And we love you." Their words were said together, one from the dark in front of me and one from the light behind me.

***

The flight back to California was excruciating. I couldn't get into a comfortable position where neither the gunshot wound nor the stab wound wasn't throbbing. The pills I had taken before the flight barely put a dent in the pain. But what hurt the most was my heart. I hadn't wanted to leave, but I let my parents convince me to go back with them to California to get my life wrapped up there before I moved to Texas permanently.

With every mile that passed, my regret grew. I felt like a monster for abandoning the guys. Especially Brent, who was still in a hospital bed because of me. I felt my mom squeeze my hand.

"It will be okay, Casey. You'll be back before you know it."

I gave her a forced smile before I couldn't hold it any longer and let it slip off my face. I turned to look out the small window to stare at nothingness. "I shouldn't have left."

"We would have taken care of things for you, but you know that your friends and family need to see you."

I nodded glumly because, yes, they did. Mom had brought my phone with her when she'd received the phone call that I was in the hospital. Once I'd turned it on, my notifications had gone crazy. My voicemail box had been full, and though I listened to a few of the messages, I quickly became overwhelmed and had to delete them all. I ended up copying and pasting a simple text to everyone, telling them I was fine and would talk to them soon. Then I'd promptly turned the phone back off and closed my eyes for a nap.

"We'll help you go through your things, and then it will get done faster. And we can have a BBQ at our house so everyone that wants to see you and make sure you're alright can come to you instead of you traveling all over the city."

I nodded in agreement because while those were great ideas, I still felt like shit for leaving. Unfortunately, she'd been mistaken when she'd said it wouldn't take long.

Almost a full month later, I was finally finishing up sorting through all of my belongings that had been put into storage. It had taken a while before I could do more than one box a day. The pain in my wounds would wear me out quickly, and though my parents had been a big help when they could, they also had to get back to their jobs.

I was finally sorting through the last of my things, making piles to keep and another to donate to the local second-hand store. I had liked the idea that they donated a large portion of their profits to the women's shelter in town. I shoved the last discard box to the side of the storage unit and brushed off my hands. I wasn't surprised that my keep pile was much smaller than the one I planned to donate. After living on the run for weeks, I guess I had lost the attachment I'd had for a lot of things.

I pulled my pull out of my pocket and hit FaceTime.

"Dollface," Brent's deep Texas drawl had butterflies fluttering in my stomach. I hadn't realized how thick it was until I'd landed back in California. A second, equally handsome face moved into view.

"Hey, sugar. Are you finally done?"

I beamed back a smile at the phone screen. Talking to them, and seeing them, always made me happy. I turned the screen so they could see the boxes before bringing it back to face me. "All done! There aren't nearly as many as I thought there would be." My voice lowered as I swallowed back a whine. "I just want to get back home to you guys."

"Sugar, we can have you on the next plane leaving the state if you give us half a chance."

"I can fly out to help you get the last of your things settled." I shook my head before Brent was even done speaking.

"I would love to have you here, but I know you are in the middle of a deadline to get that office building completed. Just concentrate on work. I'll be okay."

I looked back at the boxes one last time before pulling the door down over the unit. "I think I'll be ready to get on the plane in about two days..." I paused on my walk over to my car.

"Sugar, that pause better not be doubt."

I laughed softly. "No, no doubt here. I can't wait to get back to you. I just... it's bittersweet. I'm closing the chapter on this part of my life before opening the next. I'm excited, but I'm going to miss my family here."

"You know we can go back to visit any time you want, right? Texas isn't that far away."

"It's not that close, either."

"Dollface, it's not the moon. If you want to make a weekend trip, we'll make a weekend trip. Obviously, we couldn't drive it, but planes take off all day, every day."

"I'm being ridiculous, I know," sighing as I opened the door and slid behind the wheel. I hadn't lied all that time ago when I'd told the guys I didn't have a license. I didn't—not with me. Now that I could be myself again, I was able to do all the things I had previously taken for granted. I placed my phone in the dash holder and buckled my seatbelt. "I'm going to head over to my old job at the bookstore to say bye to my boss. How's Grace and the diner doing?"

I would never have thought that I'd enjoy working at the diner as much as I did. I actually missed it; how nice the customers were and how welcoming Ethan's parents had been.

"They are doing great. Mom said to tell you to get your sweet ass home before she has to drive out there and drag you back."

I snickered. "I'm sure she called my ass sweet."

"I was paraphrasing."

I pulled to a stop at a light and turned to look straight into the phone. "I love you guys. I will be home soon." After being back in California, one thing had become very clear: my home was with my men.

I pulled to a stop in front of the bookstore and looked up at the cute sign that looked hand-painted hanging above the door. When I stepped inside, the scent of books filled my lungs and reminded me why I had enjoyed working there during the last few years.

I walked up to the counter slowly, taking in the new titles that hadn't been there the last night I had worked. I swallowed back a lump in my throat and pushed back the melancholy.

"Hi, can I help you find your next favorite book?" The voice was bubbly, way more energetic than I had ever been.

"Hi, I was actually wondering if Janet is in?"

"Sure! She's in the back. Should I tell her who is asking?"

I tipped up the corner of my mouth. "Tell her Casey is here."

It wasn't thirty seconds later that I heard a high-pitched squeak come from the back office, followed by running footsteps. I was yanked into the older woman's arms and held tightly. I hadn't seen her since before I had been captured. After my ordeal, I hadn't wanted to see anyone who wasn't my parents, basically closing myself off from the world. Part of coming back to California was to apologize for shutting out the people that loved me. They hadn't deserved it, even if it had been to protect my own mental health.

After several minutes of the two of us crying and apologizing, telling each other that we had no reason to be sorry, then laughing at the ridiculousness of the whole conversation, Janet stepped back and took me in from head to toe.

"How are you really doing, love?"

I smiled, letting her see. "I'm good, Janet. Really good. I fell in love with two wonderful guys. My visit here today was to say good-bye. I'm moving to Texas permanently."

"Who are you going to choose?" The blurted question came from the bubbly shop assistant. She'd been sitting there watching us talking and crying with wide eyes the whole time, not even trying to hide the fact that she'd been staring. I almost wanted to ask if she'd like some popcorn.

"I don't have to choose."

She shook her head. "That's not how it works. Not in the long term. Eventually, guys will get jealous that you are dating someone else. It happened to my sister. She was dating two guys that had said they were okay with it. But eventually, they started getting mad when she'd spend the night with one and not the other. They made her choose, and because of hurt feelings, she ended up with neither of them."

I winced. "That's rough. But that's not the same way our relationship is. The guys were already together before they brought me in. We all fit together, and there's no jealousy."

After a long minute, she closed her mouth where her jaw had fallen open. "You are so lucky!"

Janet shook her head. "Mary, if you only knew what Casey had to go through to end up with those two guys, you wouldn't think she was lucky at all."

I nodded. "It was hard, not going to lie. But if the end result would be me with Ethan and Brent... I would do it again."

Thirty-Seven

CASEY

I WALKED into the house with the key I'd borrowed from Grace. The guys hadn't known I was going to be back in the morning instead of later in the evening like I had told them. I hoped they would enjoy the surprise. I had a feeling they would love it.

I closed the door softly behind me and put in the security code. I kicked off my slip-on shoes and stepped into the living room, taking in the subtle changes. There weren't many, but the ones that were there had tears springing to my eyes.

The house had changed into a home in my absence. Before, there had been no personal touches, no pictures. Now, there were small framed pictures along the fireplace mantle. I stepped forward, walking past the couch with the new throw blanket over the back. I leaned closer and realized that each picture was of me and the guys. There were ones of all three of us and a combination of two of us in the other pictures. It was beautiful.

I moved down the hall after taking a quick peek in the kitchen, noting that everything looked pretty much the same as it had before.

I paused in the hall and just stared at the large bed facing the open door. Just thinking about what went on in that bed had me rubbing my legs together and my heart racing with anticipation.

With slow steps, I entered the room, taking a look around. I tilted my head, searching for the changes that I could sense were there but didn't see. There was a new picture sitting on the nightstand. An inspection showed it was one of me that had to have been taken while I was asleep. I looked so peaceful and pretty. It was obvious that I was naked in the picture, a sheet draped just right to keep it from being too x-rated. I set it back down and turned around before I froze.

Where the closet doors were, there was a third door that hadn't been there before. Holding my breath, I opened the middle one and looked inside. I gasped as I realized what I was seeing. Brent must have renovated the closets, turning two large separate closets into three. They had already stocked most of it. Several dresses hung on one of the rails, alongside shirts and pants. There was a tall dresser against the back wall. When I inspected the contents of the top drawer, I sniffled. They had been busy while I was gone.

I didn't bother to look in the rest of the drawers, knowing they had already filled them with things they knew I would like. The kindness and thoughtfulness they put behind this closet was enough to have me fall deeper in love with them. They had made room for me in their lives. It looked like they had welcomed me into their relationship with open arms.

I turned to call them and beg them to come home early. I couldn't wait anymore to see them. But when I turned, I gasped, my feet moving, rushing toward the two men that were standing in the doorway to the closet with looks of love on their faces.

I flung an arm around each of their shoulders, bringing us into a single embrace. Kissing them in turn, one cheek and then the other, back and forth until Brent put a hand on my chin and held my face still. The kiss he gave me was nothing like the innocent cheek kisses. His tongue invaded my mouth and had my toes curling into the carpet. The next thing I knew, he was lifting me, bringing my thighs around his waist. I held on, clinging to him breathlessly as he devoured my mouth. But something was missing. Until it wasn't.

Ethan moved in behind me and moved my hair to the side so he could attack my neck with as much passion as Brent was kissing my mouth. I had to pull my mouth away so I could take in deep gulps of air while moaning as they both nipped and sucked the skin of my neck.

"I missed you both so much!"

"We missed you, too, baby. I hope you got everything done in California that you needed to because we aren't letting you leave us ever again." Hands were stripping my clothes off so quickly that I was naked before I could blink.

"Never!" I vowed, and then my body was moving, being laid down on the bed. I lay there with my chest heaving as my men stripped their own clothes off. I watched, entranced, as Brent pulled his t-shirt off over his head with one hand, his six-pack rippling as he moved. Turning my gaze to Ethan, his golden eyes were blazing as he stared down at me. He lost his patience with the last few buttons of his shirt and just pulled, sending the buttons flying.

They both had their pants off in record time and were on the bed, their large cocks bobbing, the steel in Brent's glinting in the light. Both of them leaked precum from their tips, making me lick my lips.

"Oh, sugar, don't you ever stop looking at us like that."

I shook my head, arching my back as he leaned down to suck on my nipple. My legs were wrenched open, and a warm tongue was probing at my entrance, licking up the copious moisture there. "Please!" I called out desperately. It had been too long, and I couldn't stand not having one of them inside me. Both of them. "I need you now. Please, I can't wait."

Brent licked up the center of me one more time before pulling away from my pussy, growling. As he sat up between my legs, his cock hard and throbbing, Ethan leaned over to lick across Brent's lips with a moan. "So good."

I watched them kiss deeply, much harder than they kissed me. It was frantic and full of passion, and hot as hell. I was going to combust just from watching them kiss. Ethan's hand went to Brent's cock without breaking their kiss, and he stroked it roughly. Then he angled it down, somehow finding my entrance with little effort, and held me there until Brent punched forward with his hips.

My whole body seemed to freeze and then shake as if I had been electrocuted, every inch of his cock entering me in one swift motion. I didn't need the added stimulation as Ethan's thumb circled my clit. I was already coming.

Brent didn't stop thrusting through my tremors and screams. Over and over, he slammed into me, seemingly unable to stop moving any more than I could stop coming. When I collapsed, my breaths ragged and my chest heaving, I opened my eyes to see Ethan and Brent both staring at me.

"That was only the beginning. We aren't stopping until morning, dollface. I hope you have been taking your vitamins." His words, punctuated by his thick cock sliding wetly in and out of me, began the buildup all over again. But I wanted something more.

I dug my fingers into Brent's and Ethan's thighs. "Wait!"

They both paused, Ethan's fingers stilling the movement he had been doing as he played with my entrance where Brent's cock was stretching me. One of his favorite things to do was to drive Brent crazy while he fucked me.

"I need both of you... together." Ethan's cock bobbed as it jerked, a line of precum dripping down to the bed. We were going to have to change the bedding by the time we were done. That was likely only the first of all the fluids that were going to find their way to the covers before we were through.

I blushed like I hadn't just been getting railed by a giant cock in front of another giant cock waiting his turn. "I have been, umm, preparing myself. There." My eyes drifted down toward where we were joined, hoping that someone would be able to read between the lines.

"Baby, are you saying you want us to both take your pussy? Because while the thought of that is hot as fuck, I don't think..."

My horrified expression and frantic head shaking must have clued him in that it wasn't the double penetration I was talking about. He looked confused. It was Ethan that chuckled.

"Sugar, have you been preparing your ass for me?" I breathed out a sigh of relief and nodded. He shoved Brent over, making him slip out of me and fall to his side. "Lay down, fucker."

Brent growled, ready to jump back up, but Ethan had already yanked me up, then turned my back to him before grabbing me by the hips and lifting me. While he was a detective and not the construction worker that Brent was, he had one hell of a six-pack himself. He may have been leaner, but he was still strong. My legs spread wide, and I straddled Brent's hips as he grabbed his cock and held it in his fist as Ethan slowly lowered me.

I sighed in pleasure as Brent's cock filled me again. It was bliss that went beyond the physical, knowing that we were connected much deeper than that. A hand at my back had me leaning over Brent, pressing my breasts to his chest. Our faces were so close we shared breaths as we stared into each other's eyes. I could see the blue and gold flecks in his mossy green eyes.

"Love you," he mouthed to me. I smiled at him, joy filling my heart. Even though he'd already given me the words, they meant as much as they had the first time. I pressed my lips against his gently. Our kiss was sweet and soft; it melted my insides and brought tears to my eyes. Then I gasped as cold liquid poured over the crack of my ass, making me shiver.

I looked over my shoulder to see the look of reverence on Ethan's face as he pressed his thumb against my flesh and rubbed gently against my asshole. "I don't think you know what this does to me," he began as he swallowed hard. "The trust that you are giving me. I know what it's like," he looked up and winked salaciously, "to have your ass taken for the first time. I wouldn't have chosen anyone else than Brent. So I'm thankful you are trusting me."

My lips trembled as I smiled at him. "I wouldn't want anyone else. Besides, Brent's dick is covered in all those piercings. I'm not sure if they would be a great idea for my first time." I giggled as Brent mock growled and punched his hips up, bucking into me and letting me feel all that metal. Ethan laughed and pressed his thumb until it popped inside, making me gasp and shiver.

"I don't know, sugar. I think you'll change your mind after the first time he gets into this tight ass." He withdrew his finger and pressed the head of his cock against my hole. "But for now, this is mine." His words ended on a groan of deep male satisfaction as the head sank in. He paused as I panted.

"So... full." Ethan ran his hand over my back, soothing me as every inch of my body suddenly felt like I was holding a livewire. No, I *was* the livewire.

I barely heard the whispered words or the praises coming from the men as Ethan pressed in until his hips were flush with my ass. In some unspoken agreement, the men began to alternate their thrusts and withdrawals, keeping me full at all times. The noises coming from me probably sounded like I was being murdered, but they weren't sounds of torment. Not unless you counted being pleasured within an inch of your life as torment.

It wasn't long before their movements lost much of the smoothness, becoming jerkier and harder.

"Fuck, man. I can feel you inside her," Ethan moaned into the back of my neck as I just shook and my pussy pulsed. Every stroke had the root of Brent's cock rubbing against my clit, and even though I had come just a few minutes ago, I was ready to explode again.

"I know," Brent gritted out before throwing his head back against the covers. "Fuck, I can't hold on anymore!" He roared out to the ceiling while thrusting deep and holding. I could feel the pulsing of his cock easily with how full I was. My scream was muffled into his chest as I flew apart, not even a second after his warmth began to fill me. Ethan wasn't far behind, pounding jerkily into my ass while gripping my hips so hard I knew I would have bruises. I couldn't wait to see them.

I gasped for air as I lay squished between their bodies, not from actually being squished, but from the intensity of the orgasm. My lips turned up as I stared down at the dark pink nipple in front of my eyes. I couldn't wait to do that again.

Thirty-Eight

CASEY

WE ALL LAY TANGLED TOGETHER in the sheets, our hands lazily roaming on whoever's skin happened to be nearest. I hadn't felt so relaxed in ages. Utterly content to be back in the arms of my men. I was also finally safe. There would be no need to look over my shoulder any longer.

One of the strangest parts of being a survivor of a monster was having sympathy for them. I was not prepared to have any compassion for the man that had terrorized me and murdered at least seven women in cold, calculating blood.

A few days after getting back to California, there had been a knock at the door. We'd had many visitors showing up to the house, everyone from distant relatives, to neighbors from a block over that we had never even waved to. So when my mom opened the door to see two well-dressed men in suits standing on the porch, we knew it was an official visit.

The two men were from the FBI, and they had come by to take my official statement. I had already given it to the police, but it was a requirement for them to close out an open case. After I repeated the story I could have recited in my sleep by that point, the agents shared what they could about the man that was known as the Castle Killer.

Paul Payne had been raised by a single mother, never knowing anything different Linda Payne was, by all accounts, a decent mother; she loved her son and provided the necessities. Having been kicked out of her religious parent's home at the young age of seventeen, Linda turned to what many other young women did to survive —prostitution.

Young Paul ended up developing an unhealthy fascination with watching his mother work. Linda had no idea that he had been watching and had created his own peepholes in the thin walls of the trailer they lived in. From the records of the psychiatrist that Paul had been sent to after his mother's death, Paul had fallen in love with her and began trying to woo his mother. He would leave her flowers, and it pleased him when she immediately knew that they were from him, even without a fancy note attached. The wildflowers he plucked from the park and neighborhood gardens weren't fancy, but his mother had loved them.

Unfortunately, she didn't understand what the flowers symbolized to her son. By accepting the flowers as any mother would, he had felt she was accepting him as a man. When he tried to get physically intimate... well, the FBI believed Linda Payne was Paul's first victim.

They were still trying to connect any unsolved murders similar to the ones Paul Payne committed, but it was pretty obvious that everyone involved was relieved to finally close the book on the Castle Killer. Even when I had called the guys to let them know, there was a collective loosening of muscles. We had watched the man die, and had known he was the one behind my kidnapping and imprisonment, but having confirmation of who he was, it was a relief. Even so, I couldn't help a small bit of sympathy for the young boy that obviously needed help at an early age.

I sighed and shifted in bed, rolling over carefully so that my bony knees wouldn't take out one of my favorite body parts on the guys.

"I need to go get cleaned up really quick." I kissed each of them on their barely there scruff, giggling as they reached for me, trying to get a real kiss. Somehow, I managed to slide out from between them and made it into the bathroom, shutting the door behind me. I was in no way ready for the guys to know that I did gross things. They were supposed to think that I was naturally sweet-smelling and perfect.

I quickly used the toilet, then hopped in the shower for a super fast wash and rinse. I couldn't resist the urge to brush my teeth quickly as well. I wanted to be as fresh as possible for as long as possible with these two. Our reunion had barely begun, and there were things that we needed to discuss. Serious things. Life-changing things. I took in several deep breaths, pulling the air in, then letting it back out nice and slow with my eyes closed and my head hanging down. I had my palms braced against the bathroom counter as I had my mini panic attack. When I opened my eyes back up, I blinked.

There were three sinks. *He added a third sink for me!* There was my favorite scented hand soap. My face cream. They put me in the middle. Tears immediately welled in my eyes. While I was in California packing up my life there, they were getting ready for me to come back home.

"Sugar," Ethan's deep voice rumbled softly from behind me. I swiped at my eyes, ready to make excuses for my tears, when I turned around. Only, he wasn't where I had expected him to be. My chin dropped until I could see his eyes, almost level with my boobs.

It took me an embarrassing amount of time for my brain to understand what I was seeing. Not only Ethan but Brent was also kneeling next to him, and together, each of them was holding out a ring. I gasped, my hands flying to my mouth. The tears I had just wiped away began again in earnest, and before they could get another word out, I was sobbing.

Ethan jumped to his feet and wrapped his arms around me,

whispering soothing words that I could barely grasp into my ear. Brent continued to kneel, looking scared, and that's what made me start to laugh. I dropped to my knees in front of him and threw my arms around his shoulders as he wrapped me in a tight hug and burrowed his nose into my neck.

Then I thought of what kind of sight we would have made, all three of us naked, kneeling on the floor, laughing and crying.

Brent pulled back and smiled at me, wiping away the remnants of my tears with his thumbs. "Dollface, we talked about marrying you before. But..." He looked up at Ethan, who knelt beside us, holding out his ring again. I could see the diamond looked almost like a teardrop but was curved. I tilted my head, trying to make sense of what I was seeing, until Brent held his up, too.

One clear diamond. One black diamond. Each curved in a way that they would nestle together to make one whole, like a yin and yang symbol. Balance. Holy shit, I was going to cry again.

"We want you to know that we love you beyond measure. You complete us in a way that we never could have guessed was possible." Ethan took my hand and slid his ring onto my finger, and Brent followed, sliding his black diamond to sit next to Ethan's. Once they came together, there was a small clicking sensation, and that's when I realized they connected with a magnet. Jesus, it was so gloriously perfect. I was going to pass out or throw up from the overwhelming feelings.

I began to take long, slow, deep breaths to steady myself while the guys watched me apprehensively. I held up my hand, the completed ring catching my eye and snapping me out of it.

"I love it! Yes, of course, I will marry you!" I leaned over to kiss Ethan fiercely as I tightened my right arm around Brent's neck, refusing to let him go. Once our kiss broke off, I turned to Brent and kissed him with just as much passion. I pulled back to take them both in, looking as happy as I felt. "I've never been happier in my life. Thank you for being there for me when I needed you the most."

"Sugar, you'll never be rid of us." Ethan winked at me and stood to his full height, holding out a hand for me. "Let's go lay down. I don't like you on this cold floor."

"Maybe I should get those floors heated like we talked about," Brent muttered as he scooped me up into his arms and carried me back into our bedroom. He gently laced me on the bed and smoothed his hands over my belly as Ethan looked on with a look of pure male satisfaction.

I glanced between the two of them and let out a deep sigh. "You already know."

They both chuckled, crawling up next to me and holding me close between them. "As soon as your shirt was off, we knew," Brent said as he drifted a fingertip over one puckered nipple. I hadn't thought they'd notice the subtle changes.

"If you don't think we know every inch of your body by now, you're a little bit delusional," Ethan teased as he gently cupped my other breast, careful not to squeeze. How they knew to be gentle with my sore breasts, I had no idea, but I was grateful for their thoughtfulness.

"You're going to be daddies. That doesn't scare you?" I asked, glancing between them as I tried not to let on how turned on I was getting for their soft caresses.

"Sugar, I think we are both scared shitless. But we are excited, too."

"Because you are giving us everything. You are everything." Brent kissed my lips with just the slightest pressure. He leaned back up and gave me an evil little smirk. "Now, why don't we celebrate properly? I think our man here would love to have his ass taken while his cock is sunk deep inside your pussy. What do you think?"

I could only nod and give a breathless "Uh huh," as Ethan rose above me.

Epilogue

EIGHT YEARS LATER

ETHAN

I WALKED INTO THE HOUSE, immediately stowing my service weapon away into the safe by the front door, double-checking to make sure the lock was secure before shrugging out of my jacket. It had been a long day, and I was exhausted, but hearing the little giggles coming from down the hallway had a smile coming to my face and lightening to my heart. Coming home always brightened my mood.

The door opened behind me as I was hanging up my jacket in the hall closet, Brent stepping through the door after me. He looked about as exhausted as I felt, but he had the same goofy grin on his face that I probably did. Home was where the heart was, and every bit of our hearts was within these walls.

Without even bothering to take off his own jacket, Brent reached for me and tugged me roughly into him. As our mouths and hard bodies collided, I breathed out before taking his kiss even deeper. Once we broke off the kiss, our foreheads pressed together for a long minute, just taking each other in. Twenty years now, we have been together, and I would never change a single minute.

It had been eight years since Casey had come into our lives, and we cherished every single day with her and the children she had given us. After toeing off his work boots and hanging up his jacket, Brent and I walked down the hall, guided by the sounds of the giggles, finding our son and two daughters watching a movie in the playroom while stacking blocks.

Casey was in the big recliner in the corner with her feet up and a box of crackers sitting on her huge belly. As I watched, the box jumped, and Casey let out a small wince. I noticed that what she was putting in her mouth didn't look anything like the crackers the box claimed to be in there. I hid a grin as I stepped into the room.

"Daddies!" All three kids jumped up to greet us. Our son waiting patiently for his younger sisters to run forward, throwing themselves against our legs, and then immediately pulling back so they could trade places. Our youngest, Madeline, lifted her little three-year-old arms and demanded up. Of course, I dutifully bent down and picked up my angel, snuffling into her neck and making her giggle. The sound was a burst of warmth filling my heart.

I set her back down and ruffled Gage's hair when he stepped forward for his turn after his sisters ran back to the blocks to continue building whatever it was they had been working on.

"How was school today, son?" I knelt down so we were eye to eye and listened as he told me about his day. Brent stood next to us with his hand on his son's shoulder. We never had any kind of testing done; our children were all of ours, regardless of DNA. The fact that Gage had Brent's eyes and his stubborn chin didn't make him any less mine.

After the quick hug, the only thing a seven-year-old boy would allow his dads at that age, he went back to play with his sisters as the movie continued to play quietly in the background. We both started moving toward our girl, watching with amusement as she popped another cookie in her mouth and closed the lid on the box.

I raised an eyebrow. "That's kind of genius."

"She's a little sneak," Brent laughed.

"What? I had a craving!" Casey mumbled through a mouthful. I placed a kiss on her closed mouth and then dropped to my knees in front of the chair. As she struggled to right herself, Brent moved quickly, dropping the footrest to the ground with a growl.

"You're supposed to ask for help."

She just rolled her eyes as he kissed her lips next. "I'm pregnant, not dying."

"Still, sugar, you shouldn't strain yourself." I ran my hands over her belly, feeling our twin boys roll in what little space they still had inside their mother. "Two days left," I murmured, still in awe of what our girl was capable of. She was our miracle, and every day she gave more and more to our lives. In two days, she would be giving us two more children to love and cherish. We already knew that they would be our last. It was bittersweet, but right for us.

"Two days," she whispered.

Brent was quiet as he swept his eyes over Casey and then back over to where our children were playing. I saw Gage watching us with a thoughtful look on his face. He was always so serious, and I knew he was absorbing what he was seeing. He was learning from our actions. One day he would grow up to be the kind of man I would be proud of because every day, he showed that he had a big heart and a strong mind.

Brent gently pulled Casey to her feet. "Why don't you go take a nap while I get dinner ready and Ethan tends to the children?"

Casey stifled a yawn. "I'm fine, really."

We both chuckled, cutting off the sound as Casey gave us a death glare. Without another word, Brent scooped her up and carried her from the room, intent on seeing her rest. As he nuzzled her throat, making her giggle, I toed off my shoes and walked over to kneel on the floor with the kids. "How tall do you think we can make the tower, son?"

"Before Madeline knocks it over?" His little boy laugh had me grinning.

I pointed at our six-year-old daughter, Elizabeth. "I don't know. I think it will be the Lizzy monster that frees the princess this time." They all started bouncing in their places, ready to start the game.

SIX MONTHS AFTER THAT…

BRENT

Casey moaned as I bit the side of her neck. I was holding her against the side of the shower, my long, hard cock steadily sliding in and out of her wet heat. Ethan was putting the kids to bed, and the twins would be down for at least three hours. It was finally time for us.

Having five children was amazing. There was always laughter, though there was a lot of crying, too. But with the crying came a sort of peace, knowing that the tears would dry, the arguments between the children would end in hugs and forgiveness, and that the twins would be fed or changed. There was no soul-deep pain, no hurt that couldn't be forgiven. As a child, it was a normal I hadn't known existed. I thanked whoever, whatever, was listening in my quiet moments alone for allowing me to have this life.

I also never stopped grieving for my sister. I wished with every part of me that I could have saved her. I wished that she could have known her beautiful nieces and nephews, known the little girl we had named after her. The only way I knew to avenge her was to continue ridding the world of the scum like our father. As long as I could continue to do so safely, without putting my family in danger, I would. Gladly.

The door to the shower opened, and Ethan stepped inside, his thick cock already hard and glistening. I licked my lips, thinking of how good it felt to have him in my mouth, but there was another purpose for his cock at the moment. It had been too many days since we had taken our girl at the same time.

I turned around so my back was to the wall and held Casey under her thighs, using my hands to spread her ass cheeks. She leaned her head into my chest, snuggling in, and she vibrated with excitement.

"Come here," I beckoned with a quiet, husky tone. "Our girl needs both of us."

She let out a whimper and a full body shiver as Ethan popped the lid to the bottle of body wash. "Fuck yeah, she does." The bottle dropped to the floor as he blindly attempted to put it back on the shelf, not taking his eyes off of where my cock was stretching her wide. None of us paid any attention to the sound as he stepped forward.

She let out another shiver and a long moan as he fingered her ass, then briefly stiffened as I felt pressure against my cock as he slowly, carefully slid into her back entrance. Feeling his cock sliding against mine, even though it was through a thin layer of flesh and not skin-to-skin, still made me hot as fuck. I loved his cock as much as I loved her pussy, but feeling them at the same fucking time? Mother fucking heaven on Earth.

TEN YEARS AFTER THAT…

CASEY

I wasn't going to make it.

I watched from the stands as my son stood in front of the entire graduating class and gave his salutatorian speech with both of my husbands sitting on either side of me. I had my head resting on Ethan's shoulder and was grasping Brent's hand so hard with mine I was likely leaving nail marks on his skin.

My kids were the light of my life, and I loved them all equally, but there is just something about your firstborn child. He was the first to take his place in my heart, reserved only for my children.

Gage was still so serious. He was also loyal, almost to a fault. There had been more than one instance of me trying to convince Gage he didn't have to beat up every kid that talked shit about one of his siblings. I was almost grateful that he was joining the military this summer because I could tell that the thought of Lizzy beginning to date was already getting to him. My boy would probably end up in jail for beating the shit out of some guy that he'd decided wasn't treating his sister right if he didn't move away and join the military.

But I was still going to miss the hell out of him.

As far as I knew, Gage had never had a girlfriend or a boyfriend. I did know that his dads had taken him out one afternoon a couple of years ago for some fishing and man-talk. Whatever had been discussed had only seemed to increase the seriousness that he carried around him like a cloak. My boy was always watchful, and I often caught him watching the interactions of his fathers and even how they were with me. I had a feeling he was learning a lot from those study times.

When his speech was over, I was probably the first one on my feet, screaming his name and clapping my hands until they stung.

His green eyes met mine over the crowd, and he smiled while mouthing the words "love you". All I could do was hold my hands to my chest and allow Ethan to draw me into his side as I sent a watery smile back to my son.

THE END

Acknowledgments

Thank you for reading! I hope you enjoyed Casey and her guys, I know I enjoyed writing them. If you are interested in a signed copy, you can find one in my Etsy store. And, just saying, I have some very NSFW character art that comes with it.

I want to say thank you so much to my Alpha/Beta girls!

Shonnah, Lucy, Brittany, you all are life saviors and keep me sane. Thank you for being there when I am questioning everything, and for giving me that extra push I need to believe in myself. I love you all more than you could ever know. Mel

Nicole, you are absolutely the best thing since sliced bread. I love you and am so glad to have found you. Truly, I don't know what I would do with out you.

About the Author

R. Sullins is a USA Today bestselling author, an International Bestseller, and a KDP All Star.

Family is number one in her life, followed by her menagerie of pets. Be patient with her, she's not very good at peopling.

She is a lover of fairies, tattoos, and coffee cups, has a vast collection of them all, and receives a glare from her teenager every time she brings home a new cup to squeeze into the cabinet.

When she's not writing, you will probably be able to find her reading a book. But, no matter what genre you find her immersed in, there is always one thing that her favorite stories have in common... you will never, ever find her reading any book with cheating. So rest assured! She will never write one, either.

A bit of drama, a dash of spice, a little bit of innocence, and a large dab of alpha is what makes up the recipe for her stories. Find more of her here: www.rsullins.com

Also by R Sullins